Die
Another
Dane

Books by Laurien Berenson

Published by Kensington Publishing Corp.

Die
Another
Dane

Laurien Berenson

Kensington Publishing Corp.
kensingtonbooks.com

KENSINGTON BOOKS are published by

Kensington Publishing Corp.
900 Third Avenue
New York, NY 10022

All Kensington titles, imprints and distributed lines are available at special quantity discounts for bulk purchases for sales promotion, premiums, fundraising, educational or institutional use. Special book excerpts or customized printings can also be created to fit specific needs. For details, write or phone the office of the Kensington Special Sales Manager: Kensington Publishing Corp., 900 Third Ave., New York, NY, 10022. Attn. Special Sales Department. Phone: 1-800-221-2647.

KENSINGTON and the KENSINGTON COZIES teapot logo Reg. US Pat. & TM Off.

Library of Congress Control Number: 2025938121

ISBN: 978-1-4967-4665-8

First Kensington Hardcover Edition: November 2025

ISBN: 978-1-4967-4667-2 (ebook)

10 9 8 7 6 5 4 3 2 1

Printed in the United States of America

The authorized representative in the EU for product safety and compliance is eucomply OU, Parnu mnt 139b-14, Apt 123
Tallinn, Berlin 11317, hello@eucompliancepartner.com

This book is dedicated to my editor, John Scognamiglio.
The decades I've worked with you have been enriched
by wisdom, humor, and always sage advice.
I will always be grateful for the opportunities you
gave me.

Die
Another
Dane

Chapter 1

"I want a dog," my son Kevin announced.

He was six years old; a blond, blue-eyed, sneaker-wearing dynamo. Someday his full-lipped pout would make teenage girls swoon. Today it was aimed in my direction. Kevin could be utterly charming when he wanted to be.

Even so, in a household that already consisted of four people and six dogs, this request was going to be a hard sell.

It was the first day of summer vacation. So far, my family of four had done nothing more than enjoy the opportunity to sleep late, followed by a leisurely breakfast. But with so much free time now stretching out ahead of us, it suddenly looked as though I needed a plan to keep both my boys busy enough to prevent ideas like this one from taking root.

"You already have a dog," I pointed out.

The dog in question was Bud, a small, spotted dog of indeterminate lineage. Kevin and I were in our living room of our Connecticut home, and Bud was in his favorite spot beneath a nearby couch. Also in the room with us were five black Standard Poodles. All the Poodles were related to each other. All but one were homebred champions. Unlike Bud, their pedigrees had been documented for generations.

"I need a bigger dog," Kevin said firmly.

The Poodles pricked their ears. Compared to Bud, they *were* bigger dogs. Standards are the largest variety the breed comes in. And being Poodles, they were always happy to join in a conversation. Ten-month-old Plum, the newest addition to our canine crew, walked over and nudged the back of Kevin's neck with her nose. He giggled and dodged away.

"You'd better not let Bud hear you say that." I glanced toward the couch. The little dog's stubby tail was the only part of him that was visible. Even so, I was sure he was listening.

"Bud understands," Kevin said firmly.

"Bud understands what?" My older son, Davey, came strolling into the room.

He and Kevin were half-siblings. My first marriage had ended more than a decade earlier, but I saw reminders of my ex-husband in Davey's tawny-brown hair, lean build, and confident demeanor. Though nine years apart in age, Davey and Kevin were best friends. Most of the time, anyway.

One thing they always agreed on was the benefit to be gained by ganging up on their parents. I figured that would probably be their next move.

"Bud understands that he's little," Kevin replied. "And it made sense for him to be my dog when I was little, too. But now I'm not anymore."

Davey squinted downward. Kev barely came up to his waist. "Says who?"

"Says me! I've grown two inches."

He was right about that. It was a good thing it was June and he could wear shorts because over the winter, he'd outgrown all his long pants.

"But you love Bud," I pointed out.

"I could love a big dog too," Kev said practically. Like this was something we were actually going to consider. Which it most definitely was not.

"What kind of big dog do you want?" Davey asked, throwing gas on the fire under the guise of being helpful.

"A Great Dane."

"A Great Dane," I echoed faintly.

Kevin crossed his arms over his small chest. "Yes. A big one."

As if there was any other kind.

"I saw one at a dog show. It was the size of a pony."

Davey grinned. "I had a pony when I was just about your age. A palomino with a long white tail."

"No." Kev's eyes widened. "Really?"

"Really. I got to ride her for the whole summer."

Kevin turned back to me. "Now I want a pony," he said.

This conversation was definitely heading in the wrong direction. Barely midmorning, my day had already gone totally off the rails. I heard a laugh from down the hall. It came from the room that served as my husband's office. Sam could clearly hear what was going on.

"I could use a little help out here," I called.

"It sounds like you're doing just fine," Sam replied.

When the pony incident had taken place, his and my relationship had hit a rough patch. So he'd managed to circumvent most of that debacle. Maybe Sam needed a recap because I wasn't doing "just fine." The boys had me outnumbered, and they knew it.

"No pony," I said to Kevin.

He pushed out his lower lip. "How come Davey got to have a pony and I don't?"

"It's a long story."

The pony had been a surprise present from ex-husband,

Bob. And yet, a few months later when Davey lost interest, it had fallen to me to find her a new home. I wasn't about to take on that kind of responsibility again.

I heard footsteps; then Sam appeared around the corner. Taller than me by half a foot, he moved with the easy grace of the athlete he'd been in college two decades earlier. He had broad shoulders, shaggy blond hair, and the same deep blue eyes as Kevin. Right now, they were twinkling with suppressed mirth.

I had hoped Sam was coming to lend me support. Instead, it looked like he was trying not to laugh.

"Compared to the alternative, I'm guessing the idea of a Great Dane is sounding pretty good right about now," he mentioned.

"Yay!" Kevin cried.

"Not so fast," I said. "No yay. No Great Dane. No pony."

"And no fun either." Davey made a sad face for his brother's benefit.

I looked around at my family, wondering which one I should try to smack some sense into first. Why was I the one who always had to be the voice of reason?

"I'm not the bad guy here," I said. "We already have six dogs. We definitely don't need another one."

"We have a big yard—" Davey began.

I quelled him with a look, then turned to Kevin. "How about this? Aunt Peg knows everyone in the dog show world. I'm sure she must have a friend who breeds Great Danes. I'll give her a call and see if she can arrange for you to meet some Danes close up."

"Good idea," Sam said.

"You mean good save." Davey chortled. "But you won't have to call Aunt Peg, because you're going to be dropping me off at her house shortly."

"I am?" That was news to me.

"Sure," Davey replied. "It's summer."

"I'm going to need more information than that."

"School's out," he added unhelpfully.

"Keep going."

"So I needed a job."

Right. Two summers ago, Davey had spent his vacation doing odd jobs around the neighborhood. The previous year, he'd been a counselor at a local camp. This year, I hadn't heard about any plans for summer employment. But with Davey starting his junior year of high school in the fall, he was already under pressure to keep his grades up and prepare for the not-too-distant college application process. I hadn't wanted to add to his worries.

"A job." The words seemed to stick in my throat. "With Aunt Peg."

Davey smiled. Then nodded. Poor kid. He had no idea what he was getting into.

"Doing what?"

"Whatever she needs," he said brightly. "Aunt Peg's pretty old, you know. I'm sure she could use some help around her house."

Aunt Peg might be in her seventies, but she possessed the energy and mental acuity of a person half her age. For decades, she'd bred a family of Standard Poodles that ranked among the best in the country. Now she traveled the globe as a much-in-demand judge. A legend in the dog show world, Aunt Peg was a woman of great intelligence and forceful opinions. Standing six feet tall, with a commanding presence, she tended to run roughshod over anyone who didn't see things her way.

Clearly Davey was going to need an attitude adjustment before he reported to work. I was about to offer one, but Sam was quicker.

"Just so you know," he said, "calling Peg 'old' is going to get you fired on your first day."

"I wasn't going to say it out loud—"

"Don't even think it."

Davey smirked. "Come on. I know everyone thinks

Aunt Peg has some kind of special powers, but it's not like she's telepathic."

"Are you sure?" Kevin piped up. "Because she talks to her Poodles all the time, and she says they answer back."

"That's not special," I said. "We all do that. Even you."

Kevin frowned. He looked confused.

"Think about it. Don't you usually know what Bud is thinking?"

"Bud's easy." Davey laughed. "He only ever thinks about one thing. Food! Food! Food!"

The little dog heard us talking about him. Plus, he'd heard the word *food*. He began to inch his football-shaped body out from under the couch. He was probably hoping we'd offer him a second breakfast.

Davey's pronouncement had also attracted the Poodles' attention. All five dogs jumped up from their perches around the room. The oldest of the group was Faith. She and I had been together ten years, and we shared a special bond that was both intimate and deeply meaningful. When Faith pressed her body against my leg, I slid my fingers under her chin and gave her a gentle scratch.

The other female Poodles were Faith's daughter, Eve, and Sam's puppy, Plum. Sam and I had whelped a litter for Aunt Peg the previous summer, and he and Peg had both kept puppies to show this year. Our male Poodles were Sam's former specials dog, Tar, and Davey's dog, Augie. That duo was a boisterous pair whose antics kept us on our toes.

The four older Poodles each had a short blanket of dense curls covering their bodies, their faces and feet clipped, and a pompon on the end of their tails. Plum, the puppy, was "in hair." Her show coat needed to be bathed and brushed frequently, while also being guarded against tangles or tears.

Tar lifted his head and looked around. He knew something was about to happen, but he had no idea what. Tar was endearingly sweet and gorgeous to look at, but unfortunately, he was also the only dumb Poodle I'd ever met. All three bitches, even the puppy, could think rings around him.

Kevin giggled. "Tar wants a biscuit."

He'd said the magic word. Six heads swiveled around; six pairs of dark eyes fastened on my younger son. Tails began to wag.

"See?" I said. "You do understand what they're thinking."

Kevin smiled in sudden recognition.

"Now you've done it," Davey warned him. "They won't be happy until we get them a biscuit."

"Now you said it." Kevin laughed again as they all left the room, heading for the kitchen. Bud led the way and the Poodles followed close behind.

I watched them leave, then turned back to Sam. "How come I didn't know about Davey's plans for the summer?"

He shrugged.

There was no way I was going to accept that non-answer. I stood there and waited him out.

"It was Peg's idea," Sam said finally.

Of course it was. I should have expected that.

"Why?"

"You and she usually do lots of things together. I guess she thought you might feel slighted if you knew she had a plan to spend much of the summer with Davey instead."

"Things," I repeated slowly. "You mean like solving mysteries? That's hardly my fault. You know how nosy Aunt Peg is."

Sam smiled down at me. "I also know the trait runs in the family."

Yes, well. I could hardly dispute that.

"I was bound to find out where Davey was going every day," I pointed out. "Especially since he thinks I'm going to be driving him."

"Maybe Peg didn't think that far ahead."

Neither one of us believed that for a minute. Aunt Peg *always* thought that far ahead. Even when nobody else did.

"What do you suppose she's up to now?" I mused.

"You could try asking her," Sam said.

Right. Like that would help. Aunt Peg would let me know what was going on when she was good and ready. And not a single minute before.

Chapter 2

Sam went back to his home office. I loaded Davey and Kevin in the car for the trip to Aunt Peg's. Faith sat in the back seat of the Volvo with Kevin. Davey was up front next to me.

We live in Stamford, a thriving city on the Connecticut coastline, but our house is well north of the bustling downtown area. In our quiet neighborhood, houses are set back from the road, kids can play outside all day, and no one cares that we have six dogs contained behind the tall cedar fence enclosing our large backyard. It's a great place for children to grow up.

Davey would be turning sixteen in September, and he'd been looking forward to getting his learner's permit for months. We had picked up the state driver's manual, and I knew he'd already memorized most of it. Now he scrutinized my every move as I rolled the car slowly down the driveway. Aware that I was being observed, I paused at the end, even though the road was empty.

"Don't forget to look both ways," Davey said. "And you should probably put on your turn signal."

"My signal?" I glanced his way. "Doesn't that seem like overkill?"

"You're changing direction. It's in the manual."

Heaven forbid I set a poor example, but *seriously?*

"Surely that only counts when I'm already on a road," I said.

"But you're merging into traffic."

I made a show of looking both ways. The road was still empty. "What traffic?"

Davey sat up straight and stuck a hand out in front of him—like maybe he was preparing to brace for impact. As far as I could tell, the only thing in the vicinity I could possibly hit was the low curb.

"Better safe than sorry," he said earnestly.

Kevin bounced up and down in his car seat. "Sorry, not sorry," he chortled.

I wondered where he'd learned that dismissive phrase, but at the moment I had a bigger problem to attend to. Faith stood up and peered over my shoulder. She was wondering why we weren't moving. Frankly, so was I.

"Are you going to critique my driving all the way to Greenwich?" I asked Davey.

"Maybe."

I stared at him across the front of the car.

"Only when you do things wrong," he qualified.

"How about never?" I said.

"Yes, but—"

"Or we can go back inside and you can ask Sam to drive you."

"He's busy," Davey pointed out.

"I'm aware of that."

Sam worked for himself, designing interactive software. I was a special needs tutor at a private school in Greenwich. When the boys were on summer vacation, in theory so was I. Now it was beginning to look as though Davey thought that meant I would be at his beck and call.

"Or," I said reasonably, "you can call Aunt Peg and tell her you can't make it today."

"That's not fair." Davey echoed the tried-and-true teenage anthem.

"Why not?"

"Yeah," Kevin said from the back seat. "Why not?"

My objection hadn't accomplished anything. Kevin's, for some reason, carried weight.

"Okay." Davey sat back. "You guys win."

"I don't want to win," I told him. "I just want to drive the car." Note that we still hadn't moved from the end of the driveway.

"Not me," Kev said. "I want to win. What do I get for winning?"

I turned around to face him. "How about a ride to Greenwich?"

He considered that. "Will Aunt Peg give me cake?"

Even though we'd eaten breakfast not too long before, sadly, she probably would. I nodded.

"Yay!" Kev pumped a fist in the air. "Let's go."

Kids were so much easier at that age.

When we were finally on the road, the trip down the Merritt Parkway to Aunt Peg's house took less than twenty minutes. She lived in Greenwich's bucolic backcountry. Her home was a decades-old former farmhouse, set on five acres of rolling land that bordered a tract of woods filled with riding trails.

A kennel building behind the house had burned down several years earlier, and Aunt Peg hadn't bothered to rebuild it. Because she spent so much time traveling, she now lived with just three Standard Poodles. Her older bitch, Hope, was Faith's litter sister. The young dog, Joker, was Plum's brother. The third was Coral, a lovely bitch whom Davey had handled to her championship the previous summer.

I barely had time to park the Volvo before Aunt Peg opened her front door and the three black Poodles came spilling down the steps into the yard. In a flash, Kevin had his harness unfastened and was out of the car. He quickly disappeared into the swirling melee of dogs. Since he'd left the car door open behind him, Faith jumped out to join them.

"No hair pulling, you lot!" Aunt Peg called out as she came down the stairs. "Joker has a show next week."

Casually dressed in sneakers, lightweight jeans, and a T-shirt with the name of a local kennel club on the front, Aunt Peg still made an imposing figure. Her gaze was direct and her posture excellent. She wore her shoulder-length gray hair pulled back in its customary bun. Despite her age, Aunt Peg glowed with vitality. If, in the course of him doing his job, she and Davey were ever to disagree, I suspected she could probably arm wrestle him into submission.

Aunt Peg satisfied herself that the Poodles were behaving, then stopped at the foot of the steps and waited for us to come to her. Davey quickly obliged. I paused briefly to check on Kevin, before following.

"Good morning," I said. "Davey tells me you have a summer job for him."

"Indeed." Aunt Peg nodded. "I have every intention of keeping him busy."

"Doing what?"

"This and that," she replied blithely. "I thought we might start by setting up an agility course in the backyard."

"Agility?" I was surprised. "When did you start doing that?"

"I haven't yet. That's why we need to build the course."

Agility was one of the most popular and fastest growing canine sports. To compete, handlers directed their dogs over a course of varied obstacles—jumps, tunnels, and weave poles among them. Entrants were scored on their accuracy and speed in completing the course. The sport was wonderful exercise for both dogs and their humans. Poodles, athletic and outgoing, often excelled in the competitions.

Even so, I still couldn't help but be skeptical. Aunt Peg

was not only an older woman, she also had a schedule that was already jam-packed with activities. This seemed like an unlikely time for her to take up a new dog sport, much less one that vigorous.

"Agility," I said again, in case Aunt Peg wanted to revise her earlier statement.

She didn't. Instead, she doubled down. "That's right. I'm going to need all kinds of obstacles. Davey and I will be building them."

I looked at Davey, who had yet to say a word. "I guess you're going to have a busy summer."

"So I've heard." Now he grinned. "This is going to be fun."

The Poodles had finally stopped racing around the front yard. Their tongues were hanging out the sides of their mouths, but they all looked pleased with themselves. Kevin picked himself up off the ground. I could see the grass stains on his shorts, but he was smiling too.

"Is there cake?" he asked.

Aunt Peg snorted under her breath. "What do you think?"

"I think there's always cake at your house," Davey said.

"You might be right about that. Let's go inside and see what we can find."

Though the exterior of Aunt Peg's house was rustic, the interior was totally up-to-date. Her kitchen was a large airy space. Its high ceiling held a big fan that was turning in lazy circles. A wide picture window in the front wall let in plenty of light. Davey and Kevin took seats at the butcher-block table in the middle of the room. The Poodles ran to the two water bowls near the back door.

I waited until all four dogs had taken a drink, then I picked up the bowls and refilled them. The Poodles found cool spots to stretch out on the floor. Aunt Peg had gone straight to the refrigerator. The door was open, and she had her head stuck inside.

"I see plenty of fresh fruit," she said. "Also a dozen eggs and a gallon of milk. Will that do?"

Kevin looked dismayed. But also determined. "Cake!" he cried.

"Excuse me." I was making myself at home with the coffeemaker on the counter, but I took a moment to turn and look at him. "Is that any way to make a request?"

"Please?" Kev added. I continued to look at him until he tried again. "Pretty please?"

"You're getting closer," I said.

"Please, Aunt Peg, may I have a piece of cake?"

I started to smile, then Davey spoke up.

"Me too," he said with a smirk.

My gaze shifted his way. "Perhaps you should take a moment to think about how many more teenage years you're going to spend with your parents before you leave for college. And about how long your parents can make those years feel."

Davey quickly got the point. "Please, Aunt Peg, may I have a piece of cake too?"

"I should hope so," she said, straightening as she emerged from the fridge with a large white box in her hands. "This chocolate fudge cake is too big for me to finish by myself. You boys had better help out."

Davey and Kevin were more than happy to comply. I served the drinks—milk for the boys, coffee for me, and a cup of Earl Grey tea for Aunt Peg—while she sectioned off four wide slices of cake. Then we all dug in with gusto.

Kevin sighed happily. "We should have cake every morning."

I noticed that Joker had gotten up and sidled over to position himself beside Kevin's chair. Aunt Peg would never allow begging at the table. But even without a nudge from the puppy, Kevin still might slip him something when he thought no one was looking.

I caught my son's eye. "You know chocolate is bad for dogs, right? You wouldn't want to make Joker sick."

Kev's head swiveled my way. He did his best to look innocent. "I wasn't doing anything."

"Of course you weren't," I agreed. "I'm just making conversation."

Aunt Peg nodded. She'd noticed the same thing, but I'd beaten her to the punch. "After you boys finish your cake, why don't you go down to the garage and check out the supplies I've bought for the course?"

"Sounds good." Davey was already pushing back his chair. Kevin quickly followed suit. They put their empty plates in the sink and left.

When they'd gone, I turned to her and said, "You know you can buy all the agility equipment you might need. There's no need to build it yourself."

"Of course I can," Aunt Peg replied, "but where's the fun in that?"

She reached into the middle of the table and cut each of us another sliver of cake. I'd long since given up on counting calories when we were together. Instead, I simply slid my plate over, making it easier for her to dish out seconds.

"So . . . agility. *Really?*"

Aunt Peg blinked. "Why not?"

"Do I need to point out the obvious answer?"

She swallowed a bite of cake, then frowned. "You're saying I'm too old."

Sam had warned Davey about this very thing. And yet, here I was. "No," I replied carefully. "But you're not young."

"Some people would say I'm in the prime of my life."

"Some people would be wrong." The comment was bad enough on its own. The fact that I laughed made it even worse. I pressed on regardless. "Besides, your age is a moot point. You don't have *time* to take up a new sport. So instead of us discussing something that isn't going to happen, why don't you tell me what's really going on. Why did you offer Davey a job?"

Aunt Peg put down her fork. "Can't I do something nice for someone without you asking a lot of questions?"

Nice? I didn't think so. Aunt Peg was shrewd, and practical, and often smarter than anyone in the room. But nice? Not so much. The woman had more ulterior motives than Machiavelli.

"Try again," I said.

"All right, I will. Davey needed a summer job. Apparently his mother"—she stared at me across the table—"was remiss in encouraging him to plan ahead. By the time he began to look around, all the good jobs were already gone."

Oh. That reason hit home. In my defense, I'd had a crazy busy spring. Not that it was any excuse.

"So this is my fault," I said.

Aunt Peg shrugged. "You're a mother. That means everything is your fault. I would think you'd have learned that by now."

"Then thank you."

"You're welcome." She gestured to the plate in front of me. "Now eat your cake."

I sectioned off a piece with plenty of icing and slid it into my mouth. "Are you really going to build an agility course?"

"That remains to be seen. Maybe Davey and I will find something else to keep us busy. I suppose the living room could use another coat of paint."

Not really, but I wasn't about to argue the point.

"Davey's a pro at painting. He also has plenty of experience bathing and blow-drying Poodles," I said instead.

"That's useful too." At the rate Aunt Peg was hoovering her way through her second slice of cake, she'd soon be ready for a third.

I paused to take another bite myself, then said, "I need a favor."

"Another one?" She lifted a brow, letting the implication sink in.

"This one will be easy. Do you know anyone who breeds Great Danes?"

Aunt Peg choked slightly. "Is that a serious question?"

She had a point. "Okay, how about someone who breeds Great Danes and likes small children?"

"Like Kevin?"

"Precisely. He saw one at a dog show and fell in love."

"Of course he did," Aunt Peg said. "Great Danes are splendid animals."

"Now he wants one."

She nodded. "The boy has good taste. You can't fault him for that."

"We're not getting a Great Dane," I said firmly.

"Pity, that." She finished her second slice and pushed the plate away. I guessed that meant we weren't having thirds.

"I was hoping he and I could visit a breeder so he can see some Danes up close. Once he realizes how big they are, maybe he'll understand why we can't add one to our household."

"Good luck with that." Aunt Peg didn't look convinced. "So what you're asking me to do is to set up a play date for Kevin?"

I huffed out a laugh. "I wouldn't have phrased it that way, but yes. If you can."

"Of course I can. Just let me think for a moment. . . ."

I finished my cake, then took our plates over to the sink. I rinsed everything off and was filling up the dishwasher when she spoke again.

"Audrey Kane is who you need. She has lovely Great Danes. Her kennel name is Kane's Danes. Fortuitous, isn't it? I've always wondered if the rhyme was the real reason she chose to get involved with the breed."

"Surely not." I laughed again. "Great Danes aren't just any dog. They're a huge commitment."

"Never fear, Audrey is well up to the challenge. Her kennel is in Ridgefield. I seem to recall she was married at one point," Aunt Peg mused. "But now, she's on her own, living in a house that's been in her family for generations. I'm sure Audrey would be delighted to make Kevin's acquaintance."

"Will you call her and ask?"

Aunt Peg didn't believe in wasting time. Before I'd even made the request, she already had her phone out. Five minutes later, everything was settled.

Kevin and I had a date in Ridgefield in half an hour.

Chapter 3

Aunt Peg invited Faith to stay behind with her Poodles while Kevin and I went to Ridgefield. I immediately agreed with that plan. In mid-June it was too warm for Faith to wait in the car while Kev and I visited Audrey's kennel. Not only that, but I knew she would enjoy the opportunity to romp with her canine relatives while Aunt Peg and Davey got down to business.

When we reached the outskirts of Ridgefield, I was surprised to discover that Audrey Kane's street address was a busy four-lane road. Her property was only a few hundred yards away from a small strip mall with an attached gas station. Though the entrance to her driveway was marked by a wooden sign in the shape of a Great Dane, I still double-checked the street number on the fence before turning in. Considering the breed's size, I'd assumed they'd require plenty of space. I hadn't expected to find Audrey's kennel residing this close to a commercial district.

"Great Dane, Great Dane, Great Dane," Kevin was chanting softly under his breath. He looked from side to side as we navigated a gravel driveway that was at least a quarter mile long. With a thick belt of trees on either side of us, there wasn't much to see.

"We're only going to meet some Great Danes at Mrs.

Kane's house," I reminded him. "We're not going to bring one home with us."

"I know." Kevin sighed loudly. "And I have to ask before I touch."

"That's right."

"And I can't complain if one slobbers on me."

"Also right."

"Or knocks me down."

I glanced back at him. "Let's hope that doesn't happen."

We drove for more than a minute before the trees began to thin. The noise from the highway had fallen away. Now all was silent as a lovely vista opened up in front of us.

The driveway became a circular turnaround in front of a large colonial home constructed of weathered bricks. A spacious lawn, dotted with mature trees, surrounded the house and a matching three-car garage. To our left was a long, low kennel building, with wire-mesh runs extending outward along one side.

Several big dogs were snoozing outside in the sun. As I parked the Volvo and got out, a harlequin Dane in the run nearest to us lifted his head. Then he slowly got to his feet. I expected the dog to bark at us, but instead he made a rumbling sound deep in his throat.

Kevin quickly unfastened his harness. He opened his door and came scrambling out of the car. The black-and-white dog was ten yards away from us, and he was contained behind a fence. Even so, his sheer size made him look intimidating. Kevin reached up and slid his small hand inside mine.

"I don't think the one at the dog show was that big," he said.

"Maybe the one you saw was a female," a woman spoke up behind us. "They tend to be smaller and a bit daintier."

Dainty? A Great Dane? I didn't think so.

Kevin and I turned around together. The door to the

house was open, and a woman had stepped outside. She was at least a decade older than me, probably in her early fifties. Her white-blond hair was teased into a high bouffant and partially covered by a colorful scarf. Her nails were painted candy red. She was wearing white cropped slacks with a silk Pucci top. In my shorts and polo shirt, I suddenly felt underdressed.

"Hi, I'm Melanie Travis and this is my son, Kevin," I said. "You must be Audrey."

"Indeed I am." She came down the steps, crossed the driveway, and extended her hand, shaking first with me, then with Kevin. "I'm pleased to meet you, sir," she said, dropping down to his level. "I understand that you're a Great Dane aficionado. Peg told me we're going to be great friends."

Kevin looked at me helplessly. I knew where he'd gotten lost.

" 'Aficionado' means you're a fan," I told him. "We're here because you like Great Danes, right?"

My son nodded, suddenly shy. Then he cast another glance at the big harlequin dog, who was still standing there, watching us.

"Don't mind Rufus," Audrey said with a laugh. "He may look fierce, but underneath he's a real creampuff. Would you like to go over and say hello?"

Kev hesitated briefly before answering. "Yes, please."

"If you like, I can open the gate and bring him out," Audrey said. "Just be careful he doesn't lick your face. Unless you want him to, of course. But be forewarned, Rufus has a very large tongue."

Kevin giggled as I was sure he was meant to. When Audrey set out toward the kennel, he hurried to catch up, then fell in beside her. I was left to bring up the rear.

There was a gate at the end of each run. Once freed, a Poodle would have come bounding out to join us. Not

Rufus. That dog was a thinker. He walked over to the opening and stood there, half in and half out, regarding us calmly as if he was weighing his options.

"Come on, Rufie, out you go." Audrey gave the big dog a gentle nudge, then turned to us and shrugged. "He retired from the show ring years ago, so he rarely sees children anymore. I think he's not sure what to do." She maneuvered the Dane out onto the grass. "Come on now, don't act like a big baby. Kevin doesn't bite. You don't, do you?"

"No." Kevin thought that was funny. "Can I pat him?"

"Of course." Audrey beckoned. "Come over here and we'll do it together. Do you know how to greet a dog you haven't met before?"

Kevin thought for a moment. He was accustomed to Poodles' eager exuberance. No one had to worry about how to greet them. They were already in your lap before you even had a chance to say hello.

"I hold out my hand and let him approach me." Kev looked up at me. "Right?"

I nodded, and he and I stepped forward together. "We have Standard Poodles," I said to Audrey. "We're not used to dogs who know how to stand on their dignity."

"Of course you have Poodles." She chuckled. "Peg told me you were related. I doubt she'd allow you to have anything else."

When Kevin stood in front of Rufus, the two of them were nearly eye to eye. The Dane's mouth was partly open, his long pink tongue was visible. Rufus eyed Kevin curiously, then sniffed his outstretched fingers.

"That tickles." Kevin laughed.

"Now step around his side with me." Audrey deftly moved Kevin into place, just as she'd done earlier with the big dog. "Reach up and give him a pat on his shoulder." She waited until Kevin had complied. "What do you think?"

"Rufus's skin is smooth," he said. "And his teeth are *very* big."

"Everything about him is big." I reached out and ran a hand over Rufus's skull, then down the back of his neck. "Are all Great Danes this calm?"

"Not necessarily." Audrey ruffled the dog's ears. "People expect them to be dignified, as you mentioned earlier. I guess because of their size. But they can be silly and playful too. It just depends on their mood. Danes are also quite smart, and they're very affectionate with their owners."

"Gentle giants," I said.

"Exactly."

"Rufus is eight now, which makes him a senior Dane. He used to be more lively, but now he's mellowed with age. That's why I brought him out first. I didn't want Kevin to feel overwhelmed."

I'd missed it at first because of the dog's black-and-white coloring, but now that Audrey mentioned it, I could see the graying on Rufus's muzzle. "Great Danes don't have a very long lifespan, do they?"

"Unfortunately, no," she replied. "It's the worst thing about the breed. Like all dog owners, we wish our dogs would live forever."

Kevin was running his hand down Rufus's back. The dog's long tail swung around and slapped him gently. "I think he likes me," Kevin said happily.

"He does," Audrey agreed. "Rufus is a sweetheart. He likes just about everyone. What do you say, Kevin? Should I open some of the other pens and bring out more dogs?"

While we'd been speaking, several additional Great Danes had come outside to their runs. Now nearly all the pens were occupied. I saw three fawn dogs, a brindle, a black, and another harlequin like Rufus. A big dog at the other end of the row lifted his head and began to bark.

After a moment, two other dogs chimed in. The sound rumbled over us like thunder.

"No, thank you," Kevin said quickly, and I was relieved by his response. One Great Dane was magnificent. But from where we stood, several at once looked like a lot to handle.

Audrey just smiled. She probably knew what Kev and I were thinking.

"I have another idea," she said. "How about if we go inside and sit down? There's something I'd like to talk to your mother about."

"Can Rufus come with us?" Kev asked.

"I'm afraid not. He needs to go back in his run." Audrey unlatched the gate. The Great Dane knew what that meant. He turned around and strolled home. "But you can meet Betty. She lives in the house with me, and she's very friendly."

Once Rufus was secure, Audrey led the way to her house. I was pleased to have a chance to get to know her better, and grateful that she'd let us visit. But I couldn't help but wonder what Aunt Peg had told her about me. Since Audrey and I had just met, what could she possibly want to talk to me about?

Audrey's living room was decorated in warm colors and filled with comfortable furniture. The mantelpiece over the fireplace displayed an array of silver dog show trophies, most of them in need of polishing. Other surfaces were cluttered with a profusion of collectible items: crystal vases, Chinese porcelain bowls, an antique clock with gold trim. Looking around, I wondered if that was what happened when a home stayed with one family for generations. Maybe things piled up over the years.

Then my gaze went to the room's far wall, which held more than a dozen framed photographs. All of them were win pictures, each one featuring Audrey and one of her

Great Danes. She was shown winning Groups and Bests in Show at some of the top events in the country.

"I'm impressed," I said, stepping closer for a better look.

"You're supposed to be," Audrey said with a chuckle. "I call that my 'brag wall' for a reason. Ahh, here's Betty now. I knew she'd show up when she heard us come in."

The Great Dane paused in the doorway before coming in to join us. She was lovely brindle bitch. The muted gold of Betty's base color was nearly obscured by vertical black stripes that covered her body, neck, and legs. There was a black mask on her face, and her ears, hanging down on either side of her head, looked like velvet.

Though she was smaller than Rufus, Betty was still a substantial dog. When she walked across the room to Audrey, I could see she was accustomed to maneuvering carefully around the furniture in order not to bump into anything.

Audrey introduced Kevin and me to Betty. Then she and I sat down on chairs opposite each other. Betty stepped up onto the couch and carefully turned her body several times before lying down on the cushion. Kevin quickly took a seat beside her. They were already on their way to becoming friends.

"There was something you wanted to tell me?" I said.

"Actually, it's more of a question." Audrey leaned forward in her chair, closing the distance between us. "If you don't mind my saying so, your reputation as a detective precedes you." She paused to cast a sidelong glance at Kevin. Thankfully, my son was too busy talking to Betty to pay any attention to our conversation. "I'm hoping you might be willing to help me with something."

"Of course," I replied automatically, then quickly reconsidered. My tendency to leap first and ask questions later had gotten me into trouble before. "But if it has to do with dogs, Aunt Peg is the person you should talk to."

"No, it doesn't. This is a personal matter. I'd like you to locate and retrieve something for me."

The request came as a surprise. In the past, I'd been involved in solving several murders, but this was something different. I wasn't at all sure I was the right person for the job.

"What's the item?" I asked.

"A platinum brooch in the shape of a harlequin Great Dane. Diamonds and black onyx form the colors, and there's a sapphire for the eye. The brooch has been in my family for decades. Recently it disappeared. I'd like to get it back."

"Disappeared? Like you mean it was stolen?"

"Yes."

I couldn't help but glance around. Every surface in the room was crowded with small, potentially valuable, items. "Are you saying you were robbed?"

"Not exactly. The brooch is the only thing that's missing."

This conversation was growing more curious by the moment.

"I'm going to assume there's more to this story than you're telling me," I said. "But before we go any further, I should tell you that retrieving lost items isn't something I do."

"Stolen," she corrected me firmly. "Not lost."

"Have you reported the theft to the police?"

"It isn't a police matter. That's why I was hoping you'd be willing to step in. I want things resolved quickly and quietly."

"Because . . . ?" Getting information from Audrey was like prying a bone away from a pit bull. Neither was going to give anything away easily.

She heaved a sigh. "I suspect I know where my brooch went."

"Maybe you should have started with that."

"Maybe I'm wrong," she said with a shrug.

When I growled impatiently under my breath, Kevin

glanced my way. With Audrey's disclosures coming at a snail's pace, I was just as happy to be distracted.

"Are you having a good time with Betty?" I asked him.

Kev nodded. He'd found a braided rope behind one of the couch cushions, and he and Betty were playing tug-of-war. It was a testimony to the Dane's good temperament that she wasn't winning the game by a mile.

When I turned back to Audrey, she was waiting for me to give her my full attention. I hoped that meant she was finally ready to tell me what was going on.

"I have a stepsister, Lara," she said. "Our parents married when we were children. I was ten and she was eight, so for the most part we grew up together. Throughout our childhood, Lara was always jealous of me. She thought I was the favorite."

"Were you?" I asked mildly.

"Probably, but that's not the point. The brooch is an heirloom that was passed down to me by my mother. It's an item that has great sentimental value. That part meant nothing to Lara. When we were kids, she only admired the brooch because it was sparkly. And because she knew that diamonds were worth money."

I couldn't help but notice that there was a rather large gap in the middle of her story. "The two of you were children a long time ago," I said. "How do you get along now?"

Audrey's answer was blunt. "Not well."

"And you think your sister—"

"My *stepsister*."

I began again. "You think your *stepsister* has your brooch?"

"I know it was here two weeks ago. Then Lara came by for a visit. A day or two later, I realized the brooch was gone."

"That hardly seems like conclusive evidence that she's to blame."

"I don't need conclusive evidence," Audrey said. "All I

want is my brooch back. And I know in my gut that Lara has it."

"Did you ask her about it?"

She stopped just short of rolling her eyes. "Of course I did. Lara said she had no idea what I was talking about. She said she hadn't seen the brooch in years. Which is totally ridiculous. That's why I want you to use your detecting skills to determine if she's telling the truth."

If Audrey hadn't looked so serious, I might have laughed. "I think you're way overestimating my abilities."

"No, I'm not," she insisted. "I know you solve murders. Compared to that, this should be a piece of cake."

The turn of phrase reminded me of Aunt Peg, which then made me wonder if she'd known about Audrey's dilemma all along. Maybe that was the real reason she'd sent me here. It was just the kind of thing Aunt Peg would do. Then abruptly I remembered that visiting a Great Dane breeder had been my idea. *My bad.*

"Just talk to Lara," Audrey said. "That's all I'm asking. Be an impartial observer. See if you think she's credible. Or more likely, if she's guilty as sin. If we're lucky, you can catch her in a lie and convince her to return the brooch."

"Just talk, that's all?" Considering that Audrey had devoted an afternoon to entertaining Kevin and me, having a conversation with her stepsister would be easy enough to do in return.

"That's all I'm asking," she confirmed. "Are you going to the Farmington Valley show this Saturday?"

I nodded. Both Plum and Joker were entered. Our whole family would be there.

"That should work out perfectly then. Lara will be there with her Great Dane. She likes to hang out in the grooming tent and gossip with her friends. I'm sure you'll find her there."

Standard Poodles require a great deal of on-site grooming before they're ready to step in the show ring. Sam and

Aunt Peg would be busy working on their dogs for several hours while I'd be mostly superfluous. It wouldn't be a problem for me to duck out for a quick chat with Audrey's stepsister.

"How will I recognize Lara?" I asked.

"Her last name is Minchin," Audrey said. "Lara Minchin. She'll be in the catalog." Then she added with a sly smile, "Or maybe you should just look for a woman wearing a diamond brooch."

Of course she was kidding. She had to be.

But somehow, neither one of us was laughing.

Chapter 4

The Farmington Valley dog show was held in a public park west of Hartford. The location was hardly more than an hour's trip from Stamford. Compared to the much longer distances we often traveled to compete, this drive felt easy.

Standard Poodles weren't scheduled to be judged until noon, but it was Plum's first show in more than a month, so we were all excited to get going. Dog shows persevere in good weather or bad, but this time we'd gotten lucky. The temperature was mild for June, humidity was low, and a light breeze ruffled the leaves in the trees. It was going to be a great day to spend outdoors.

At the showground, more than a dozen show rings, and just as many concession stands, had been set up in the center of a large grassy field. The handlers' tent, where exhibitors did their last-minute grooming before taking their dogs in the ring, was on the side of the field near the parking lot. The back of Sam's SUV was filled with our equipment—Plum's crate, her grooming table, a tack box and cooler, plus a dolly to help us transport everything—so he drove directly to the tent's unloading area.

Before I even had a chance to open my door, someone rapped sharply on the window. I turned to look and saw

Terry Denunzio standing just outside the SUV. He waggled his perfectly manicured fingers at me.

"Perfect timing," he said. "Can I be of assistance?"

Terry was husband and assistant to professional handler Crawford Langley. He was also one of my best friends. Always the life of the party, Terry had gotten me into—and out of—more scrapes than I could remember. I would have trusted him with my life. He was gorgeous, sarcastic, perceptive, and often hilarious. He'd once volunteered to cut my hair, and I hadn't let anyone else touch it since.

"My offer has a time limit, so don't just sit there," Terry said through the glass. "Crawford thinks I'm checking on the Papillon ring. If I don't return soon, he's going to think I was eaten by bears."

"Bears!" Kevin giggled with delight. He opened his door and jumped out. "There are no bears around here."

Sam and Davey were already at the rear of the SUV. They were busy unloading our equipment and stacking it on the dolly. Plum was loose in the back seat. I was supposed to be putting on her slip lead and hopping her out of the vehicle. Except that I was still in the front seat, the leash was still in my hand, and Kevin had left his back door open when he got out.

For a rambunctious Poodle puppy, that unexpected series of events was too much temptation to ignore. Before I could reach around and grab her, Plum took a flying leap over Kevin's car seat. Terry and Kevin were standing beside the SUV, Terry illustrating the veracity of his comment about bears by pointing out a Leonberger, when Plum came hurtling out and all but knocked the two of them over.

Luckily, Terry was quick on the uptake. He managed to catch the Poodle puppy before her feet even touched the ground. Then he turned and smirked at me. "Did someone lose a dog?"

"Very funny." I got out and slipped the leash over Plum's head, being careful not to crimp any of her meticulously blown-dry hair.

The big puppy was more than an armful, but Terry held her easily and she looked comfortable in his grasp. He smiled down at her. "Hello, my pretty Plum. Are you going to beat us in the ring today?"

"That remains to be seen," Sam said, coming around the side of the SUV, pulling the loaded dolly behind him. "Who does Crawford have entered in bitches?"

On any show day, that was a key question. Crawford was a talented handler who'd been at the top of the game for decades, and his specialty was Poodles. With his services in high demand, he was able to be very particular about the quality of the dogs he presented. No one ever walked into a show ring to compete against Crawford thinking they might pick up an easy win.

Since Terry would have spent the previous day bathing and blowing dry Crawford's Poodle entry, I knew he had to be well aware of our chances. We all waited to hear what he had to say.

"We don't have any Standard bitches today. Just a class dog, and Crawford's special."

"That's good." Davey came around to join us. "At least for us. Bad for Aunt Peg though."

"Peg has Joker in the Bred-by-Exhibitor Class," Terry said. He'd already seen a catalog. "Crawford has a puppy and an open dog."

"The blue dog?" Sam asked. "That's a handsome Poodle. I'm surprised he isn't finished already."

Exhibitors often competed against the same dogs repeatedly, as each one compiled the fifteen points that were needed to complete a championship. Over time, handlers got to know their competitors' dogs almost as well as their own.

"Me too," Terry agreed. "I thought he was a sure thing

two weeks ago. But it turned out the judge had a bias against off-color Poodles."

Sam frowned. "You mean anything that isn't black or white?"

"Yup. When he handed Crawford the ribbon for Reserve Winners, he advised him to give serious consideration to dying the dog black."

"I can't imagine that went over well," I said.

Terry shrugged. Another handler might have snapped back a retort, but Crawford was the consummate professional. He would handle things differently. "It just means we won't show to that judge again for a while. Long enough to make our point."

Though I'd finally put the lead on Plum, Terry was still holding the puppy in his arms. The two of them looked quite content with that arrangement. When he turned and headed into the grooming tent, I had to either drop the leash or go with him. I chose the latter option. Sam fell in line behind me with the dolly. The boys followed behind.

"Right this way," Terry said over his shoulder. "We'll make room for you to set up next to us."

"Is there enough space for Aunt Peg too?" I asked. "She should be here shortly."

"Don't worry," he replied. "We'll figure out a way to fit her in."

It only took a few minutes to arrange our setup. The rubber-topped grooming table went in the middle. Plum's wooden crate was on one side, with the tack box and the cooler stacked on top of it. Terry deposited the puppy on the tabletop, then returned to his setup next door. Crawford was nowhere to be seen. Presumably he'd given up waiting for Terry to return, and had gone to the Papillon ring with their entry.

We had plenty of time before Standard Poodles were due in the ring, but I knew Sam would want to get started working on Plum right away. "I'll go park the SUV," I told him. "And if you're good here, there's someone I'd like to stop and talk to on my way back."

We both glanced down to check on Kevin. He was already unpacking his toy cars. They could keep him entertained for hours. After that, Davey was in charge of babysitting. When he'd handled Aunt Peg's Coral to her championship, Sam and I had done everything we could to support him. Now it was Davey's turn to smooth the way for Sam to get Plum into the show ring.

"Go," Sam told me. He was lining up a pin brush, a slicker brush, and a greyhound comb along the edge of the table. "We'll be fine. If you see Peg, send her this way."

"Will do." When I reached the SUV, Aunt Peg was just pulling her minivan up to the tent.

"You're late," I said, as she opened the door and got out. She wasn't really, but I couldn't resist teasing her. "We've already been here an hour."

"You have not," Aunt Peg huffed. She was wearing a chambray dress with buttons down the front and flat-soled shoes that were easy to run in. Joker had a big stride; she would have to hustle to keep up with him. "It's not even ten o'clock. I have plenty of time to get Joker ready for the ring. Where are you off to?"

"First, the parking lot. Then to find Lara Minchin. The Great Dane judging is this morning, and I saw a couple of Danes at the other end of the grooming tent. So I'll probably start there."

Aunt Peg and I had discussed my conversation with Audrey Kane the other day when I'd returned to her house to pick up Faith and Davey.

"Why you?" she wanted to know when I finished telling her about Audrey's missing brooch.

"Apparently I have a reputation."

"Maybe," Aunt Peg allowed. "But it's not as though you

solved all those mysteries on your own. Indeed, I would go as far as to say that I've been an indispensable member of the team."

I almost laughed. "I have a team?"

"Of course you do. And I'm it. If Audrey needed help, she should have asked me."

"It's just a piece of jewelry," I told her. "Audrey probably thought that such a small job was beneath your talents."

I thought we'd put the subject to rest, but later she texted me a picture from a dog magazine. It showed a middle-aged woman with frizzy gray hair, prominent eyebrows, and a stern expression on her face.

Lara Minchin, she wrote underneath. **In case she's not wearing the brooch.** The words were followed by a string of laughing emojis. It appeared the team was back in action.

I parked the SUV in the lot, then cut back across the field toward the other end of the handlers' tent. Unlike Poodles, Great Danes required only minimal pre-ring preparation on show day. But with less than an hour until their scheduled judging time, I was sure the big dogs would already be on the grounds.

Even in a sea of canines of all shapes, sizes, and colors, it wasn't hard to figure out where the Great Dane exhibitors were congregating. Mostly because their dogs were bigger than just about everyone else's.

As I approached their joint setup, the sound of a lively conversation carried across the tent. The group had placed folding chairs in a circle in the midst of their crates. Instead of the constant activity that characterized Poodle prep, here, three women and two men were simply sitting down to await their turn in the ring. I couldn't help but feel a jealous twinge.

Several heads turned as I drew near. Seated on the far

side of the circle, Lara Minchin was easy to recognize. It occurred to me that Aunt Peg must have found a particularly poor picture to share, because in person Lara looked both younger and more cheerful.

Probably because my gaze had gone to her first, Lara was the one who spoke up. "Can we help you with something?"

"Yes, my name is Melanie Travis. I was hoping I could have a word with you?"

"Sure. I guess." Lara glanced at the other members of the group as if maybe she was hoping for a consensus on the matter. "But if you're looking for information about Great Danes, you should probably just talk to all of us. Or maybe Ralph." She gestured toward a stocky older man who was mostly bald. "He's the acknowledged expert on the breed."

Ralph nodded, accepting his due.

"Actually, it's about another matter." When Lara glanced at her watch, I added, "I know Danes are due in the ring soon. I won't take up too much of your time."

"I suppose I can spare ten minutes." Lara stood up and smoothed her hands down the length of her pink cotton skirt. Like Aunt Peg, she was wearing flats. A wide hairband held her hair back off her face. "Melanie, you said? Why don't we step outside the tent where it will be quieter."

"That would be great." I followed as she threaded her way through several setups and out the other side of the tent. We skirted around a row of generators, then walked between some exercise pens, before ending up behind a truck that was selling tacos.

"Hungry?" Lara asked. The air around us smelled delicious.

"No, I—"

"Somehow this all feels very mysterious. I hope my ex-husband didn't send you."

"No, definitely not." I swallowed a laugh. "Your step-sister is the one who asked me to talk to you."

"Audrey?"

I nodded.

"Oh, good Lord." Her lips pursed in annoyance. "What does that woman want now?"

"She's lost a family heirloom—"

"Don't tell me." Lara sighed. "It's a brooch, right?"

"Yes."

"A diamond Great Dane?"

"Yes."

"And she suspects I have it?"

"She thinks it's a possibility," I said. "She asked me to check with you about it."

"This is so like Audrey." Lara crossed her arms over her chest. "She's always making a big deal out of nothing. Why didn't she just pick up the phone and ask me herself?"

"She said she did."

Lara stared at me long enough to make me wonder whether Audrey was the one whose veracity I should have been concerned about. But before I had a chance to follow that thought, Lara was already moving on.

"What would I even want with her stupid brooch?" she snapped.

"Audrey told me that the two of you don't get along—"

"That's an understatement. As you can probably tell from this wild-goose chase she's sent you on. How did you end up in the middle of this? Are you some kind of law enforcement person?"

"No—"

"A friend of Audrey's then."

"Not exactly."

"And yet for some reason you followed me to a dog show to accuse me of stealing something I have no interest in owning," Lara said incredulously. "That's rich."

"I didn't follow you here," I told her. "I was coming anyway. We're showing a puppy."

"Really?" Lara looked like she didn't believe me. "What's your breed?"

"Standard Poodles."

Her eyes narrowed. "Nope. Not buying it. If you were showing a Standard Poodle, you'd be much too busy to be over here bothering me."

"My husband's getting Plum ready. He does a much better job than I do. Also, my Aunt Peg has Plum's littermate entered."

There was a long moment of silence as Lara simply stared at me. It was almost as if I could see the wheels turning in her brain.

"Peg?" she said. "Standard Poodles? Are you talking about Peg Turnbull?"

I nodded.

"She's your aunt?"

"Yes."

Lara sighed again. "I guess that probably means you're not as crazy as I thought."

"Honestly," I told her, "there are days when it feels like the jury's still out."

Lara glanced back at the tent. Her friends were beginning to stand up and move around. My time was just about up.

"Okay," she said. "Your connection to Peg Turnbull bought you ten more minutes. And maybe an explanation. But not now. After Danes are finished in the ring."

That seemed fair. By my estimation, there should be time enough time between the Great Dane and the Standard Poodle judging for me to be able to stop back again. "That sounds good," I agreed.

"Meet me by the hot dog stand in an hour. If you don't show up, I'm not waiting for you."

"I'll show up," I said. Lara was already walking away. "Good luck today!"

"I'll need it," she replied, without turning around.

Well, that could have gone better. But at least I'd be getting another opportunity to talk to Lara soon. With luck, I'd be able to learn more about Audrey's missing brooch then.

Chapter 5

"You've been gone long enough," Aunt Peg said when I got back to our setup. As promised, Terry had managed to squeeze her crate and grooming table into the limited space next to us. Joker was lying on his side on Aunt Peg's tabletop. Fingers flying, she was line-brushing through his hair. "I hope you at least found out something interesting."

"I did my best," I said, then turned to greet Crawford. While I was away, he'd returned to the setup next door. He and Terry had more than a dozen Poodles to show that day, and both of them were hard at work.

"Good morning, Crawford," I said.

Occupied with putting in a topknot on an apricot Mini, the handler glanced my way as he parted the long hair with a knitting needle. "Melanie. Nice to see you."

My relationship with Crawford has its ups and downs. Often for reasons beyond my control. Closer to Aunt Peg's age than mine, he had silver hair, piercing brown eyes, and an air of confidence that was well deserved. Crawford had seen it all, and done most of it. Even so, he tended to take a dim view of the kind of trouble I was known to get myself into.

"How are you today?" I asked.

"Fine," he grunted. "Busy. Better after the judging."

Sam was a applying a slicker brush to Plum's plush leg hair. "Quit bothering Crawford, Melanie. Come over here and make yourself useful."

"Happy to," I said. "What do you need? And where are the boys?"

"They went to get ice cream," Aunt Peg answered for him. "And from the looks of Plum, Sam doesn't need a thing. I, on the other hand, need someone to talk to while I whip this puppy's coat into shape. I believe I asked you a question and I'm still waiting for an answer."

"Oh. Right." I sidled her way. "I found Lara."

"Of course you did." She wasn't impressed. "The show isn't huge. Her dog is entered and due in the ring shortly. She has to be here somewhere."

"The other end of the tent, actually."

Aunt Peg lifted her gaze. "I'm less interested in the woman's location than what she had to say for herself."

"She doesn't have Audrey's brooch."

"That's it? You were gone for at least twenty minutes. Surely there's more."

Sadly, not a whole lot. Especially when I edited out the parts where Lara had questioned my sanity. Hopefully a little flattery would appease Aunt Peg's insatiable curiosity.

"Lara knows who you are."

She stepped back from her table and drew herself up to her full height. Aunt Peg towered over me. "That's hardly noteworthy. *Everybody* knows who I am."

"Clearly the most humble person on the showground," Terry muttered under his breath.

Of course Aunt Peg heard him. She had ears like a fox. "Or perhaps the most honest," she shot back. "When you've been around as long as I have—"

"I'll be as old as Crawford," Terry said with a laugh.

I was tempted to laugh too, but I didn't dare. Crawford had his back to us, but I knew he was listening.

Without turning around, the handler extended an arm and used his knitting needle to point to a Standard Poodle whose ear hair was still in wraps. "Fix that," he said to Terry.

"Yes, sir."

When Terry hurried to comply, Aunt Peg stared at me. "You must have more to tell me than that."

"Not yet," I admitted. "But I hope to shortly. Lara had to get her dog to the ring, but she told me to meet her at the hot dog stand after the Great Dane judging is over."

"Lara's dog is a special, you know," Aunt Peg mentioned.

Actually, I hadn't known that. And now that I thought about it, I realized it had been rude of me not to ask about her Dane. That was what dog people did, after all. They talked about their dogs. Sometimes endlessly.

Not only that, but having a specials dog was a nice accomplishment. It meant that Lara's Dane was already a finished champion. She'd brought him to the show to compete against other Great Dane champions, hoping he would win Best of Breed, then go on to compete in the Working Group.

"Milo already has several group placements on his résumé." Aunt Peg was still talking.

"Milo is Lara's dog?"

"Really, Melanie, do try to keep up. Of course he's Lara's dog. His full name is Champion Kane's A Mile in My Shoes."

That came as a surprise. "Kane's is Audrey's kennel name."

Aunt Peg nodded. "It's interesting, isn't it? Perhaps you have more questions to ask than you initially thought."

So far, coming up with questions hadn't been my problem. It was answers I was noticeably short on. "When I wished Lara good luck earlier, she told me she'd need it. Why would she bring a special to the show if she thought he was going to be beaten?"

"Maybe she's superstitious about accepting good wishes," Aunt Peg said. "Or perhaps she's hoping the better Dane won't show up. It's a dog show, which means that all sorts of unexpected things can happen. No win is ever a sure thing."

That reminded me of Terry's story about Crawford's blue dog. I was about to relate it when something caught Aunt Peg's eye. She gazed toward the wide strip of grass between the show rings and the grooming tent. Several Great Danes and their handlers appeared to be returning to their setups.

"The Dane judging must be just about finished. Don't you have somewhere else you need to be?" she asked pointedly.

"I do." I glanced at Sam. "As long as you have everything under control here?"

My husband chuckled in reply. "I doubt there's a parent anywhere who's brave enough to answer that question in the affirmative." Especially since both our children seemed to be missing from the setup. I assumed Sam had that under control too.

"Actually, I was referring to Plum," I said.

"Yes, she and I are in good shape. Go do your thing, then meet us at the ring. I'm guessing Kevin's gotten side-tracked somewhere, but Davey knows what time the Poodles go in. I'd imagine the boys will meet us there too."

There was only one food stand selling hot dogs on the showground. It was located all the way at the other end of the field. On the way there, I passed a long row of concession booths offering everything from grooming supplies and dog books to canine-themed jewelry. I would have been tempted to stop and browse, but I wanted to be sure not to miss Lara.

I'd expected there to be a line at the food stand. Instead, here at the outer edge of the showground, the place was pretty much deserted. There was just a single man, wearing a somewhat grubby apron, standing behind a large grill. The hot dogs spat and sizzled as they cooked, filling the air with smoke.

"Help you, miss?" the man asked as I drew near. He gave a couple of hot dogs a half-hearted shove with his cooking fork.

"Not yet, thank you." I scanned the area. Lara was nowhere to be seen. "I'm meeting someone."

"Man or woman?" Considering the lack of customers, he probably had nothing better to do than make conversation.

"A woman."

"She have kids with her?"

"Not that I know of." I didn't bother to mention the possibility of a Great Dane.

"Then I ain't seen her. Mostly it's kids who want hot dogs, you know?"

I nodded, then turned around to look back the way I'd come. From where I was standing, some of the rings and most of the open area between them and the grooming tent were visible. If Lara had been on her way from either direction, I should have been able to see her.

"So . . ." the man said from behind me. "Want a hamburger while you wait? I can cook one up fresh."

"No, thank you. You're sure you haven't seen a gray-haired woman wearing a pink skirt?"

"Nope." He shrugged. "Sorry."

Could I have missed Lara? I knew I'd gotten to our meeting spot in plenty of time. Maybe she was running late. If that was the case, the next logical place to look for her would be the grooming tent. Depending on whether Milo had won or lost, Lara would be either settling the Great Dane in his crate to await the group judging or packing up her things and preparing to leave. Except that we were supposed to talk again before either of those things happened.

I checked my watch and saw that I still had twenty minutes before the Standard Poodles went in the ring. The only thing I could think to do now was retrace my steps and hope I could locate Lara elsewhere. She'd been very specific about meeting me at the hot dog stand, however, and I was sure she wouldn't have forgotten. Which meant she was probably avoiding me on purpose. Dammit.

When I got back to the tent, I saw that the cluster of Great Dane setups was mostly empty. The folding chairs had been put away and a couple of the big dogs were relaxing in their crates. Socializing with fellow competitors was always easier before the judge picked the day's winners and losers. Afterward, exhibitors tended to disperse.

Only one of the people I'd seen earlier was still around. Ralph was perusing a catalog that lay open on top of a crate. He looked up as I approached.

"Hey, you're back. Melanie Travis, right?"

"Right." I smiled. "You have a good memory."

"Well, you know . . . I *am* the acknowledged expert." His eyes twinkled. Ralph was probably around sixty and not much taller than I was. He had pleasant features and a hairline that had receded out of existence.

"That sounds like an important job," I said.

"No worries." He laughed. "I'm a pretty sharp guy, I can handle it. Are you still looking for Lara?"

I nodded.

"Thought you might be. From what she said earlier, I

got the impression you two were supposed to meet up after the judging."

"Yes, there was something she wanted to tell me."

"Then I'm sorry to be the bearer of bad news, but that's not going to happen. Lara came straight back from the ring, packed up all her stuff, grabbed Milo, and lit out of here like her tail was on fire."

"I guess that means Milo didn't win the breed," I said.

"Best of Opposite Sex to a bitch he's beaten several times before." Ralph grimaced. "I'm sure that didn't improve her mood any. Still, that's no excuse to leave you hanging. Is there anything I can do to help?"

"No, I don't think so. But thank you."

I wasn't just disappointed, I also felt like an idiot. I never should have been gullible enough to let Lara slip through my fingers. But I certainly hadn't expected her to bolt just because I'd asked a few questions. If Lara was intent on proving her innocence, she was going about it the wrong way.

"Don't thank me," Ralph said. "I haven't done anything useful yet. But if you need some info in the future, I'm your man. As we know, I'm a font of knowledge when it comes to Great Danes."

He took a business card out of his tack box and handed it over. RAL-DEN GREAT DANES was written across the top. Beneath that it said RALPH DENBY, OWNER AND BREEDER, along with a phone number and email address.

Aunt Peg had chided me for an earlier omission that I now realized I was guilty of making once again. At least this time I could rectify my mistake. "I'm sorry, I should have asked. How did your dog do today?"

A black Great Dane was resting on his side in the wire crate next to Ralph. He looked down at the dog fondly. "Winners Dog for two points." He dug in his pocket and pulled two ribbons, one blue and one purple, and laid them side by side on top of the crate.

"Congratulations, that's wonderful," I said.

Ralph nodded. "Not the biggest prize I've ever won, but on the day, I'll take it and count myself lucky."

It was nice to know there was at least one person whose day was going according to plan.

Chapter 6

I ran all the way to the Standard Poodle ring.

"You almost missed the whole thing," Kevin chortled as I slipped in beside him and Davey at ringside. There was a smear of chocolate ice cream down the front of Kev's T-shirt, but at least his face and hands were clean.

"No, I didn't," I said.

The Mini Poodle Best of Variety judging was wrapping up. Standard Poodles would show next. By my estimation, I had a full minute to spare.

"That's a matter of opinion." Aunt Peg was unamused by my tardy arrival. "I hope you made good use of your free time."

She was standing nearby with Joker, who would be the first of our two Poodles to compete. Aunt Peg didn't appear nervous. Then again, she was an old hand at this dog show biz. It took more than tough competition to rattle her nerves.

At her side, Joker looked calm and ready to go too. The puppy exuded breed type and had a wonderful outgoing personality. But even those sterling attributes might not be enough to beat Crawford with his more mature, and very handsome, blue dog.

"Not as good as I might have wished," I told her, then turned to Sam. "Do you need anything?"

"It's a little late to be asking that, isn't it?" A smile softened his words.

"Maybe it's the thought that counts?"

Davey snorted out a laugh. "Good one, Mom. Can I use that excuse the next time I don't hand in my homework on time?"

Terry appeared beside me. He and Crawford had just arrived at ringside. Apparently I wasn't the only one who was cutting things close. Terry had his hand cupped around the muzzle of Crawford's white specials dog, who would most likely win the Variety. Crawford was nearby with his Open dog. He was using his comb to smooth down the dog's copious ear hair.

"I see you're in trouble again," Terry said. "What did you do this time?"

"None of your business."

"Oh, honey, you know that excuse won't fly." He waggled his eyebrows at me. "Surely you've learned by now that everything that goes on around here is my business."

"Everyone has learned that," Crawford broke in. "Now stop gabbing and look sharp. The Minis are finished and the Standard puppy dogs are going in. Peg is up next."

Davey had picked up the numbered armbands our pair would need from the ring steward. The first class was Puppy Dogs, and there was only a single entry. Though Joker was also a puppy, Aunt Peg had elected to show him in Bred-by-Exhibitor, showcasing him as a homebred. She would also be the only one in her class.

In no time at all, the puppy's handler had been given a blue ribbon, and Joker was called into the ring. As Aunt Peg set up her Poodle in the shaded area beneath the tent, she studiously avoided making eye contact with the judge. Of course she knew him. And he knew her. But both of them maintained the polite fiction that no previous acquaintance would have any bearing on the day's judging.

Joker got a somewhat longer look from the judge than

the previous puppy had. Nevertheless, with no competition, her class was also over within minutes. Aunt Peg stuffed the blue ribbon in her pocket and came to join us outside the ring. At ten months of age, Joker had plenty of hair. Davey took out a comb and made minor repairs to the puppy's topknot. Sam, Aunt Peg, and I stood beside the low, slatted barrier and watched the next class.

Four Standard Poodle dogs entered the ring for Open. Crawford walked in first, which put his dog at the head of the line. Judging by the handler's confident demeanor, it was a position he had no intention of relinquishing. With good reason, as it turned out. His blue dog was clearly superior to the three other entrants in the class, and it quickly became clear to everyone at ringside that the judge agreed with us.

"Oh, well." Aunt Peg sighed. "At least I'll have the consolation of knowing that I was beaten by a good one."

"It's not over yet," I told her.

"It might as well be." She looked down her nose at me. "Let me put it this way. If I was judging today and had to make the same decision this judge will, *I* would put up the blue dog."

"But Joker's a handsome Standard Poodle. He was your pick of the litter."

"That's right," Aunt Peg agreed. "And maybe six months from now, he'll be ready to give Crawford's dog a run for his money. But not today."

As usual, Aunt Peg's prediction was proven correct. Crawford's Poodle won the Open Class handily. Then Joker and the winner of the Puppy Class went back into the ring. The three dogs were judged against each other for the Winners Dog award and the coveted points that came with it.

The judge took only enough time to send the three Poodles gaiting around the ring together, before motioning Crawford and his blue dog over to the winner's marker. As he wrote the result his judge's book, the Poodle who'd been second in the Open Class returned to the ring. Then the new trio was sent around again.

This time the judge pointed to Aunt Peg. Joker was Reserve Winners, an honorary award, as it gained the recipient nothing other than a purple-and-white ribbon.

"Nice!" Kevin held out his hand as Aunt Peg exited the ring. "I like the striped ones best." The intricacies of dog show judging still eluded Kev, but he was proud of his ever-growing ribbon collection.

Aunt Peg handed over the dubious prize, then we all turned our attention back to the ring. Sam and Plum were in the next class, Puppy Bitches. Unlike the small entry in dogs, this time there were two other puppies for Plum to compete against.

A professional handler beat Sam into the ring, so Sam held back slightly and took Plum to the rear of the line. Most handlers wanted to lead—and make a stellar first impression. Sam took the opposite tack. Plum was a lovely Standard Poodle puppy, with correct angles, a melting expression, and movement to die for. It wouldn't hurt if she was the last thing the judge saw before he began his individual examinations.

All three puppies in the class were black, yet they couldn't have been more different from each other. The puppy in the middle of the trio looked and acted like a baby. When her handler gaited her, she bounced up and down, trying to grab the leash in her mouth. By contrast, the puppy bitch at the head of the line knew exactly what was expected of her. She had more hair than Plum, and she'd been trained to execute the routine perfectly. Though she never put a foot wrong, there wasn't much joy in her performance.

Unlike me, Sam had plenty of experience in the show ring. He knew just how to stand back at the end of the lead and let Plum show herself. The puppy was well up to the task, and she was having a wonderful time. Plum caught the judge's eye with a flirty tip of her head, then wagged her tail when he looked at her and smiled.

None of us were surprised when Plum won her Puppy Class. Sam exited the ring with a blue ribbon and a Poodle who was very pleased with herself.

"Well done. That's half the battle behind you," Aunt Peg said to Sam. She shoved Joker's balled-up lead into my hand so I could hold the dog out of the way while she made repairs to Plum's coat. In the ring, the five-strong Open Bitch Class was being judged. "I suspect the judge won't find anything in there that he likes better than this pretty girl."

"How does she do that?" Davey asked me. "Aunt Peg isn't even looking at the ring. How does she know what's in there?"

"She has a sixth sense about these things," I told him. It seemed like as good an answer as any.

"Don't be silly," Terry chided me. He was holding Crawford's Winners Dog, while Crawford had his special. Both dogs would be needed in the ring to compete for Best of Variety when the bitches were finished. "Peg has eyes on the back of her head. Like Medusa."

"Medusa?" I frowned. "I thought that was snakes."

Davey looked confused. "Someone has snakes on the back of their head? That seems unlikely."

"Ewww." Kevin shuddered. "That sounds gross."

"Excuse me." Sam was holding Plum's muzzle cupped in his palm while Aunt Peg added some hairspray to the puppy's topknot. "Maybe we could focus here?"

"Speak for yourself," Aunt Peg said. "I'm very focused." She braced a hand on Sam's arm and levered herself to her feet. In the ring, the judge was pinning his class. "Plum looks stellar, if I do say so myself. Now the rest is up to you."

I'd have quaked under that kind of pressure. Sam just

smiled as if he knew exactly what he was doing. Once again, he showcased Plum's superior movement and she easily bested the Open Bitch for Winners, earning two points in the process.

Aunt Peg, the boys, and I then stood beside the ring to watch the Best of Variety judging. To no one's surprise, Crawford's special won the award, and his Winners Dog was Best of Winners. Plum was named Best of Opposite Sex. The judge then took a quick break so that the show photographer could take pictures. After that, we all trooped back to the grooming tent in a merry mood.

"I'm hungry," Kevin announced, veering away from the group as we passed the taco truck. "That smells good."

"I have snacks and drinks in the cooler," I told him.

"Who wants snacks when we can have tacos?" Davey asked reasonably enough.

"Not me!" Kev cried.

Sam glanced at me. Parental shorthand for "Yes or no? Your choice." It looked as though he was tempted too. While I'd been out gallivanting around the showground, he'd been working for much of the day. Now it was my turn to give him a break.

I reached over and took Plum's lead out of Sam's hand. "Go get something to eat," I told the three of them. "Aunt Peg and I will take care of the puppies."

"Are you sure?" Sam asked hopefully.

"Absolutely. I'll grab something out of the cooler when we're done. Just don't let Kevin order anything too spicy."

Davey and Kevin didn't wait to be told twice. Sam had to hurry to catch up with them. The trio had already joined the end of the long line waiting beside the food truck by the time Aunt Peg and I entered the tent.

Joker's and Plum's grooming tables were next to each other in the setup. Both puppies knew what was coming. When we lifted them up onto the tables, they lay down and got comfortable. It would take some time to break down their topknots, gently brush the hairspray out of their coats, and rewrap their ears.

I'd just finished lining up my grooming supplies on the tabletop when Aunt Peg spoke. "So, Lara Minchin. Surely your second attempt was more productive. What did she say this time?"

"Nothing," I muttered.

"I assume you mean nothing useful." She snipped through a row of tiny colored rubber bands, and Joker's topknot hair sprang free.

"No, I mean really nothing. I went to the hot dog stand where we were supposed to meet, but Lara never showed up."

"At that point, you must have come back here and looked for her under the tent," Aunt Peg prompted.

"I did," I replied. "But Lara wasn't here either. Neither was Milo, nor any of her things. According to another Great Dane breeder, she'd come straight back from the ring, packed up, and left for the day."

"That was fast." Aunt Peg glanced over to check on my progress. I was feathering a pin brush through the hair over Plum's shoulders, knocking out some of the sticky spray. "I take it Milo must have lost?"

"Best Opposite."

"So she lost." Aunt Peg frowned. "No reason to stick around after that."

"Except to talk to me," I said. "She was the one who chose our meeting place. The least she could have done was show up."

"The hot dog concession is all the way on the other side of the showground," Aunt Peg pointed out.

"It is," I agreed. "So?"

"So it sounds as though Lara sent you on a wild-goose chase that was intended to take you as far away from the grooming tent as possible. If I had to guess, I'd say she was giving herself enough time to make an escape while she knew you'd be held up elsewhere."

I pondered the idea for a moment. "Possibly. Although that assumes she knew ahead of time that Milo was going to lose in the breed."

"No," Aunt Peg said firmly. "That assumes Lara knew ahead of time that she had no intention of speaking with you further. For all you know, she might have left the showground regardless."

My hand stilled. I put down my brush and looked at her. "But why? What would be the point? Doesn't this seem like a lot of bother to go to over a missing brooch? Especially one that Lara claimed to know nothing about?"

"Maybe she was lying to you."

I snorted a small laugh. "Considering the way things turned out, that seems like a given. But once again, why?"

Aunt Peg shrugged. "If you want to know the answer to that, I guess you're just going to have to track Lara down again and find out."

Chapter 7

Monday morning, Davey and I were in the car on the way to Aunt Peg's house when my phone buzzed, indicating that I had a text. I reached over to the console and picked it up.

It was from Aunt Peg: **I have news!!**

Knowing Aunt Peg, her bulletin probably had something to do with results from the weekend dog shows. Though the use of two exclamation points seemed a bit excessive.

Davey frowned at me across the front of the car. "No texting and driving allowed."

"I'm not texting," I told him. "I'm reading."

"That's not allowed either."

"Hey," I said. "Who makes the rules around here?"

"You do. Which is why it's backwards that I'm the one who has to enforce them."

Davey had a point. Besides, we would be at Aunt Peg's soon enough. I could hear her news then. When I put the phone back on the console, Davey glanced over and read the message.

"What's that about?" he asked.

Eyes on the road, I said primly, "I would tell you if I knew."

"Aren't you curious?"

"Of course I am. But you just told me to put the phone down."

"Sure." Davey grinned. "But I didn't think you'd do it." He picked up the device. "Should I reply?"

I hesitated. But not for long.

"Yes, but tell Aunt Peg you're the one who's texting back, not me."

He looked up. "Why?"

"In case the news is something private that Aunt Peg wouldn't want you to know."

"Nah. Aunt Peg tells me everything."

I sincerely doubted that. "Do it anyway," I said, and Davey did.

Ten seconds later, the phone rang. Of course it was Aunt Peg.

"She's calling me. Right?" Davey said hopefully.

"No." I held out my hand and beckoned with my fingers. "It's my phone. It's for me."

"Yes, but you're busy driving."

The phone continued to ring.

"Adults can talk and drive at the same time." I was still waiting.

"That's not what the Connecticut driver's manual says. 'Handheld cell phones may not be used while operating a vehicle on any public highway,'" he quoted.

"Really?" I had no idea. "Not at all?"

"Nope. It's a law."

Abruptly the phone stopped ringing. We both stared at the now-silent device as if we were waiting for it to change its mind. It didn't.

"Now look what you've done," Davey said, as if the missed call was my fault. He put the phone down. "Maybe Aunt Peg will leave a message."

I felt a sudden bond of solidarity with all the other

mothers of teenagers who were—at that very moment— trying not to tear out their hair.

"She *did* leave a message," I told him. "The text was it."

"That's not a message. That's a teaser."

There seemed to be little point in continuing a conversation that was going around in circles. "We'll be at Aunt Peg's house in five minutes. Whatever her news is, we can hear about it then."

Thanks to her canine early-warning system, Aunt Peg was always alerted the moment visitors arrived. She usually had her door open before anyone had a chance to knock. Now, as I parked the Volvo in her driveway and Davey and I got out, the home's front door remained closed. No trio of Poodles came racing down the steps to greet us.

"That's different," Davey said.

Indeed. "Maybe we should have called her back."

Davey went skipping up the stairs. "She knew we were on our way. She told me to be here by ten."

I followed close behind. When we reached the top, I heard a chorus of canine voices coming from inside the house. Aunt Peg might not have realized we were here, but her Poodles certainly had.

Seconds later, the door opened. Aunt Peg had one hand on the doorknob; the other was pressing her phone to her ear. She held up a finger, indicating she'd be right with us.

Davey and I corralled the Poodles who were milling around the porch, then took the liberty of letting ourselves inside. By the time I'd shut the door, Aunt Peg was already striding away again, heading down the hallway toward the kitchen. We all fell in behind her.

"I understand the magnitude of the problem," she was saying, "and I'm happy to help out any way I can. Given the dire nature of the situation, I'd imagine we'll be able to rally other support as well."

Davey and I shared a look. It sounded as though we definitely should have tried harder to hear Aunt Peg's news.

The conversation lasted another minute. Finally she ended the call and turned to face us. "Don't get comfortable," she announced. "We're about to leave."

"Where are we going?" Davey asked.

Aunt Peg was striding around the kitchen. First she refilled the Poodles' water bowls, then she retrieved a handful of dog biscuits from the pantry. "Ridgefield," she said.

I had just been to Ridgefield recently. My mind leapt to make the obvious connection. "Does this have something to do with Audrey Kane?"

Aunt Peg finished passing out biscuits. Then she stopped and stared at us. "When you didn't answer the phone, I assumed you'd already heard."

"Heard what?"

"Brace yourselves, because I'm afraid I have some bad news. Over the weekend, there was an accident at Audrey's house. I'm sorry to say she's deceased."

I stifled a gasp. Though I'd just met Audrey, her warm personality and unmistakable love for her dogs had made a wonderful first impression. I'd hoped to have a chance to get to know her better.

Beside me, Davey didn't say a word. I reached over and squeezed his hand. Even though he didn't know Audrey, I was sure that hearing this had to be upsetting.

"Don't worry about me," he said under his breath. "I'm okay."

I turned back to Aunt Peg. "What happened?"

In the moment my attention had been elsewhere, Aunt Peg had started moving again. Now it looked as though she was on the way to her garage. If we wanted to hear the rest of the story, Davey and I had no choice but to follow.

"I'm not sure," she said over her shoulder. "I heard the news from one of her neighbors. He said her dogs had been barking all night, which was very unusual. Audrey had a zoning variance for her kennel, so she always took care to ensure that the Danes' presence wouldn't bother anyone."

Audrey's dogs were big in size and had a loud bark. I wondered how close the neighboring property was. I hadn't seen any other houses when I was there, though it was possible they were in the woods that surrounded Audrey's estate.

Ahead of us and still moving quickly, Aunt Peg had almost reached the door that led to the garage. "Do you want me to drive?" I asked. "My car's right outside."

"No, that won't work." Aunt Peg opened the door, then reached around to push a button. The outer garage door opened. "We're going to need the minivan. I'll explain on the way."

"Wait a minute," Davey said. "Am I coming, too?"

Already in the garage, Aunt Peg and I paused. We both looked at him.

"It's up to you," I told him. "Do you want to come with us?"

Davey considered, then nodded. "I want to know what happened."

"A child after my own heart," Aunt Peg said briskly. "Both of you, climb in."

I gave Aunt Peg a chance to drive out to the main road before I started pressing for more details. "So Audrey's neighbor showed up at her place to complain about the barking Danes. How did that lead to him calling you? Do you know him?"

"I've never met the man," she told me. "His name is Bill Godfrey, and he didn't go to Audrey's house to complain. He said he was afraid something might be wrong. Bill knew where she kept her spare key for emergencies. So when he'd rung the doorbell several times and Audrey didn't answer, he let himself in. He's the one who found her."

"That must have been quite a shock," I said.

"I gather it was." Aunt Peg took her eyes off the road

and glanced my way. "Audrey was lying on the floor in her office. At first Bill thought she was merely unconscious. Then he realized the situation was worse than that and called nine-one-one."

"And you," I added.

"Yes, although that came about later. According to Bill, once the police had arrived and taken over, he began to wonder what would happen to Audrey's Great Danes. He knew how important the dogs were to her, and he was concerned that Animal Control might just shove them in a van and take them away."

A *van*, I mused, as one small detail suddenly made sense. We were driving to Ridgefield in Aunt Peg's minivan. A vehicle that might, in a pinch, have just enough room for a Great Dane or two.

"Bill told me there was a note with my name and phone number on Audrey's desk. She must have jotted it down when I called last week about your visit." Aunt Peg continued her story. "When the police told him to go and wait outside, he took the note with him, then called to ask if I was one of Audrey's dog show friends."

"Good call," I said. Both literally and figuratively.

Aunt Peg nodded. "When I said yes, Bill explained what had happened. He was still very shaken up. At first, I could hardly make sense of what he was trying to tell me."

"But when you did, you decided to race to the rescue," Davey said from the back seat.

"Actually the first thing I did was text, and then call, your mother. Who, I might add, didn't bother to respond to either summons."

"That was Davey's fault," I said.

Aunt Peg didn't care. "When I got tired of waiting for her to pick up the phone, I called the president of the local Great Dane Club and apprised him of the situation. That's who I was talking to when you arrived. I told Ralph there might be as many as a dozen Danes in need of immediate relocation. He agreed to call around and see if he could mobilize some of the other members to come and help out."

"Is that Ralph Denby?" I asked.

"Yes. Do you know him?"

"Only a little. We just met at the dog show."

"Ralph's a useful person," she said. "I'm glad I was able to reach him right away."

Coming from Aunt Peg, that was high praise. Useful people were her favorite kind.

"Did Bill tell you how Audrey died?" I asked.

"He mumbled something about a head injury, but I wouldn't take that as definitive. He also heard one of the responding officers speculate about whether one of Audrey's Danes might have knocked her down."

"Not Betty!" Until that moment, I'd forgotten all about the brindle bitch who'd played so nicely with Kevin.

"Who's Betty?" Aunt Peg shot me a look.

"The Dane who was Audrey's companion. Kev and I met her when we were there last week. All the other dogs were outside in a kennel, but Betty lives in the house. She was a real sweetheart. I can't imagine her injuring anyone. Even accidentally."

"That's interesting. I wonder where Betty was when Audrey died," Aunt Peg mused. She'd also immediately discounted the death-by-Dane scenario. "The poor girl must be terribly upset. I hope the authorities have someone there who's capable of dealing with a large unhappy dog."

As she spoke, Aunt Peg's foot pressed down on the accelerator. The minivan shot forward. Now we were going twenty miles over the speed limit. I saw Davey grip the armrest next to him, but he didn't utter a word of protest.

"Maybe Ralph's already there," I said. "He'll know how to handle Betty."

"One can only hope," Aunt Peg replied.

"It's going to be a big job to relocate all those Great

Danes temporarily," Davey spoke up again. "But it'll be an even bigger one to find new permanent homes for them."

"I'd be surprised if the Danes aren't taken care of in Audrey's will," Aunt Peg replied. "I know I have my Poodles thoroughly covered."

"Ours are too," I told him. "Sam and I have seen to that. Maybe Lara Minchin can take Audrey's Danes. I wonder if she counts as next of kin, even though she and Audrey are only related by marriage."

"Audrey and Lara are stepsisters? I didn't know that," Aunt Peg said with interest. "I believe there's also an ex-husband somewhere."

"Children?" I asked.

"Not that I'm aware of. Then again, there's no reason I should be. I suppose all these details will be made clear in time. But for now, our first priority will be making sure that Audrey's Danes are well placed and cared for."

"I hope the police don't decide to hassle us about releasing them," I said.

"Why would they?" Aunt Peg sounded slightly outraged. "We're doing them a favor."

"Yes, but they might not see it that way."

"Then we shall just have to convince them. Besides, I'm sure they'll be too busy figuring out what happened to poor Audrey to give us another thought."

Aunt Peg was almost always right about things. I hoped this time wasn't going to be an exception.

Chapter 8

"This is a lovely property," Aunt Peg said as we neared the end of Audrey's long driveway. The stately brick home and the manicured lawn around it had just become visible up ahead.

"Yes, it is," I agreed, as Davey leaned forward to take a look. For a moment, it was as if we'd all forgotten why we were there.

Then the woods that lined both sides of the driveway fell away and the entire view opened up in front of us. Immediately, the appearance of the scene changed. Two police cars and the coroner's van were parked in front of the detached garage. Opposite them, near Audrey's kennel, were even more vehicles: two vans and a midsize truck.

Aunt Peg pulled in behind the second van. The kennel's outdoor runs were empty, but the side door to the building was standing open. Ralph poked his head out and waved a greeting.

"More reinforcements," he said to someone behind him as we got out of the minivan.

A moment later, another man and two women joined Ralph in the doorway. As the four of them came outside, I saw that Lara wasn't part of the group. I wondered if anyone had spoken to her.

"Thanks for the heads-up, Peg." Ralph came over and shook Aunt Peg's hand. "And for coming to help. This is a terrible situation. It's bad enough what happened to Audrey, but she'd have been horrified by the thought of her dogs being dispersed willy-nilly. The club and I will make sure they're well cared for until her heirs decide what they want to do."

"I appreciate that, Ralph, and thank you for your quick response." Aunt Peg motioned me forward. "I believe you've met my niece, Melanie, and this is her son, Davey."

"Nice to meet you, Davey." Ralph looked thoughtful. "Melanie, I didn't realize you and Peg were related. Small world, I guess."

The second man stepped over to Aunt Peg. Dressed in khaki pants and a button-down shirt, he was in his sixties and had an athletic build. His gray hair matched the wire-rim frames of his glasses. Under the circumstances, his smile looked slightly forced.

"I'm Bill Godfrey, we spoke earlier," he said. "Thank you for stepping in on a moment's notice. I have to say that I'm gutted about what happened in there." He nodded toward Audrey's house. "At least now, with you people here, there's one less thing for me to worry about."

The older woman of the two was Miranda Falk. She was nearly as tall as Aunt Peg, but as skinny as a reed. She wore a peasant top over a pair of faded jeans, and there was a row of bangle bracelets on her arm. Miranda knew who Aunt Peg was, although they hadn't previously met. After they'd shaken hands, she sketched a wave in Davey's and my direction.

"And you are?" Aunt Peg walked over to the remaining woman, who had hung back from the rest of the group. She was much younger than everyone else, probably not yet thirty. There was a spray of freckles across her nose, and two long braids hung halfway down her back. Her T-shirt and shorts looked like they'd been slept in.

"Tasha," she replied, without quite meeting Peg's gaze. "Tasha Gilbert."

"Tasha is Audrey's dogsitter," Bill said. "When Audrey goes out of town for dog shows, Tasha takes care of everything around here. Don't you?"

Tasha nodded, but didn't speak. She appeared to be overwhelmed by the situation. I could hardly blame her.

"Tasha and I have each other's numbers as emergency contacts," Bill added. "Before I got in touch with you, Peg, I called to see if she could come and help. Nobody knows these dogs better. Well, except for Audrey."

Bill swallowed heavily. Like the rest of us, he was having trouble processing the tragic news. "If anyone can facilitate handing these big dogs over to their new caretakers, it's Tasha. She was kind enough to drop everything and come right over."

"That was good thinking," Aunt Peg agreed. She looked around at the four of them. "Has anyone made a plan for how this rescue operation is going to work? Do we know how many Danes are on the property, including the ones in the kennel and in the house?"

I was struck by a sudden thought. "Speaking of the house, where's Betty?"

For the first time, Tasha looked up. She even managed a small smile. "Don't worry about her. I went in and brought her outside as soon as I got here. The officers weren't happy about it. They had the nerve to tell me Betty might be evidence."

Tasha grimaced. "I wasn't about to let them stop me. I was doing exactly what Audrey would have wanted me to do. Especially since they'd locked Betty in the pantry to keep her out of the way. She was going crazy in there, barking up a storm. They were probably relieved to see her go."

I considered what Tasha had said, then turned to Bill. "If Betty was loose in the house when the police arrived, what was she doing when you went inside earlier and found Audrey?"

Bill looked surprised. "I have no idea. To tell the truth, she never crossed my mind. I know I didn't see her in there. Maybe she was already locked away."

I frowned, still trying to make sense of the timeline. "Except the only reason for the police to wonder if Audrey had been knocked down by a dog would be if they'd seen a loose Dane in the house."

Aunt Peg also looked confused. "If Betty was put away when Bill got here, who did it? Certainly not Audrey. I know she has a couple of crates in the house. She would never have locked Betty in a pantry."

So far, Davey had remained silent. Now he spoke up. Six pairs of eyes turned to look at him, and he squirmed slightly. "For all the things you're saying to be true, there must have been someone inside the house in the time between when Bill went in and the police arrived."

Miranda gasped out loud. "That's a ghastly thought."

"I certainly didn't see anyone else," Bill said quickly.

Aunt Peg's reply was ominous. "Perhaps whoever it was didn't want you to see them."

"Especially if it was the person responsible for Audrey's death," I added. Then suddenly everyone was looking at me. "Surely I'm not the only one who's considered the possibility."

Ralph and Miranda shook their heads. Bill briefly closed his eyes. Tasha just looked pained. And then there was Aunt Peg. I was pretty sure she was every bit as curious about this odd sequence of events as I was.

"Wait just a minute," Bill said abruptly. "Let's not jump to any conclusions. I'm not even sure we should be speculating about what happened to Audrey."

"Why not?" Davey asked.

Bill whipped around. "Who are you again?"

I looped my arm around Davey's shoulders and pulled him closer to my side. "Davey's my son. He came with Aunt Peg and me today to see if he could help."

"Speaking of which," Ralph broke in, "us standing around here jabbering isn't solving our problem. The police are doing their job, and we need to do ours. We have to get these dogs off the property and into homes where they can be taken care of."

"Here, here," Miranda agreed. "Peg was right a minute ago, we need to make a plan. Including Betty, who's now in the kennel, there are ten dogs on the property. Eight bitches, including two older girls who are spayed, and two dogs, neither of whom are neutered. Thankfully none of the bitches are in whelp."

"Are we sure about that?" Aunt Peg asked.

"Yes," Tasha replied. "I keep very good notes on all my clients, and my information is up-to-date."

"Good to know," Aunt Peg said. "Because that brings me to my next question. Rather than dispersing the Danes in several different directions, why don't we—Bill, Miranda, Ralph, Melanie, and I—chip in and hire Tasha to look after them right here until we find out what Audrey's will says. Wouldn't that be a simpler solution?"

Tasha quickly spoke up. "I'm sorry but that won't work for me. I can't take on a job of this magnitude with no advance notice. Summer is my busiest season, and I already have other bookings."

"Fair enough." Aunt Peg nodded. "Then we'll move on to Plan B. It appears we'll be dividing up the dogs and taking them home with us."

It was no surprise to me that Aunt Peg was taking charge. Nevertheless, I held up a hand before she could continue. "I understand the need for what you want to do, but is anyone else worried that we don't actually have permission to remove Audrey's dogs from her property?"

"Not me," Ralph said firmly.

"Me either," Miranda agreed.

"Permission from whom?" Aunt Peg wanted to know. "I don't see anyone around here to ask."

"I'm just thinking it could be a problem if the police decide the dogs have been stolen."

"They won't." Tasha sounded very sure of herself. "Those guys inside didn't want anything to do with Betty. If we load the Danes up and move them out, I bet they won't even notice."

"Excellent. Then we're all in agreement," Aunt Peg said.

It appeared that my vote didn't count. I glanced at Davey. After being snapped at by Bill, he'd chosen to remain silent. I understood why. Playing devil's advocate wasn't getting me anywhere either.

"I have room to take two of Audrey's bitches," Miranda offered. "Preferably two that get along with each other."

"I can probably manage Betty," Audrey's neighbor, Bill, announced. "She's smaller than some of those big guys in there. And not nearly as scary looking."

Ralph glanced at the truck that was parked nearby. "There are a couple of other club members who couldn't make it here this morning but are willing to lend a hand. I'll take one of the dogs and three of the bitches. I can put all of them in my kennel for now, then pass them around later when I get a chance."

I could see why Aunt Peg had called Ralph a useful person. He'd be taking nearly half the Great Danes home with him.

"That's a big help," Aunt Peg said. The rest of us looked appropriately grateful.

"Rufus can come home with me," Tasha decided. "He does better when he's with people he knows."

I was totaling the numbers in my head when I realized that once again, everyone was looking at me. "What?"

"How many Danes do you have room for?" Ralph asked.

Me? I was just along for the ride. Wasn't I?

"Umm . . ." I waffled.

"One," Davey said. "Mom and I will take one."

"Wait—" I began.

"Thank you for your offer, Davey." Ralph overrode my objection. "That's much appreciated. Unless your mother doesn't think you're mature enough to make a decision like that. What do you say, Melanie? Will you vouch for your son?"

"Of course I will," I sputtered. "But that doesn't mean—"

"Too late." Miranda laughed. "You're committed now. We'll give you someone easy. Why don't you and Davey take one of the older bitches?"

"Daisy," Tasha said. "She'd be perfect."

Since the young woman knew nothing about us or our living situation, there was no way that assessment could be based on anything other than wishful thinking. On the other hand, managing an older Dane sounded easier than keeping up with a young one. I hated to think what Sam was going to say when Davey and I arrived home with a giant dog. Whatever it was, I probably deserved to hear it.

"That leaves me with the one remaining bitch." Aunt Peg moved on before I could change my mind. "Now that all the Danes are spoken for, let's load up and move along before someone comes out of the house and tries to insist that we do things differently."

Ralph and Miranda had both brought extra leashes. All of Audrey's Great Danes were former show dogs. They were accustomed to traveling in vehicles and being handled by unfamiliar people. Tasha offered the dogs reassurance that they were doing the right thing. One by one, the indoor runs were emptied. The Danes seemed to be curious about what was happening, but they followed our instructions without complaint.

Daisy was a fawn bitch with a chiseled head and dark

eyes. When Davey opened the door to her pen, she regarded him with equanimity, then gave her tail a friendly wag.

"My what big teeth you have, grandma," Davey said as he slipped the leash over her head. When Daisy replied with a doggy grin, her long pink tongue slipped out the side of her mouth.

Davey had passed me in height the year before. Even so, he looked small standing beside the Dane's large head, strong neck, and muscular body. I was willing to bet that Daisy outweighed him, too. Nevertheless, she was happy to accompany us out to Aunt Peg's minivan.

Once there, we saw that Aunt Peg had rearranged the seats in the back of the van to make more room. She'd also loaded the black bitch she'd be taking home with her. "Meet Ebony," she said to Davey and me.

The Dane was standing near the open side door, and I reached up to give her a pat. Ebony and Daisy hadn't been in adjoining runs in the kennel. They touched noses briefly to renew their acquaintance.

"Up you go." When Davey patted the floor of the van, Daisy knew what was expected of her and quickly obliged.

"That was easier than I thought it would be," I said. Davey climbed in after the Dane, and Aunt Peg slid the door shut.

"Some people find Great Danes intimidating, but they can actually be quite gentle," she said. "They're very aware of their size, and most would never try to take advantage. They adapt to all sorts of living situations, even ones that aren't ideal for such big dogs."

I figured I'd be putting that attribute to the test later myself.

Aunt Peg and I got in and fastened our seat belts. The other vehicles were already pulling out around us. She waited her turn, then joined the end of the queue.

I took a last look back. The police cars and coroner's

van were still parked on the other side of the driveway. In the twenty minutes we'd been on the property, it appeared that none of the authorities had even noticed our presence, much less come out and talked to us

The kennel was empty, and Tasha had locked the door behind us. The place looked forlorn as we drove away. When I'd come to visit Audrey less than a week earlier, it had never occurred to me that I would be back so soon and under such a somber circumstance.

"Great Danes aren't one of the breeds you judge," Davey said. Daisy was lying on the floor beside him, and he was resting his hand on her back. "How come you know so much about them?"

"They're not one of the breeds I judge *yet*," Aunt Peg clarified. She had been approved to judge the Non-Sporting and Toy Groups for several years, and she'd recently added the Herding Group to her resume. "But it's hard not to be aware of them, don't you think? Great Danes are such splendid animals."

Aunt Peg had glanced back over her shoulder to check on the two Danes, so I was the first to notice what was happening ahead of us. I leaned forward in my seat for a better look. "What's going on up there?"

Ralph's truck was at the head of our line of vehicles. He had almost reached the main road when he suddenly braked. There appeared to be an incoming car blocking the end of the driveway.

"I haven't a clue." Aunt Peg stopped too. "I hope it's not more police, showing up now when we've almost succeeded in making our getaway."

We watched as a man got out of the dark sedan, then went striding over to the truck and knocked on the driver's side window. Ralph opened the window and leaned out. We were too far away to hear what was being said, but it looked as though the two men were exchanging angry words.

"That's not good," I said. "What do you suppose it's about?"

Aunt Peg frowned. "I have no more idea now than I did a moment ago, when you asked virtually the same question."

"He's not in uniform," Davey pointed out as we sat and watched. "And that doesn't look like a police car. Maybe that's a good sign."

"Finally," Aunt Peg said after another minute passed. The stranger had stopped speaking. He stepped away from Ralph's truck. "Things seem to have gotten themselves resolved."

I wasn't so sure. It was clear the man was still angry. He went stalking back to his car, gunned the engine, then yanked the sedan partway off the driveway onto the verge.

Slowly, the line began to move again. We could barely fit our larger vehicles around him, but each driver managed to make it work. One by one, we inched past.

Meanwhile the man sat in his car with a ferocious scowl on his face. His gaze never wavered. As we drove by, he made sure to glare at each and every one of us.

Chapter 9

"That was interesting," I said once we were underway. "That was creepy," Davey corrected me from the back seat. Now Daisy was sitting up with her head in his lap. The Dane had her eyes closed, and he was scratching behind her ears.

"I agree with Davey," Aunt Peg said. "That was very strange." She took out her phone. "Let's find out what it was about, shall we?"

"Who are you calling?" I asked.

"Ralph, of course. He's the one who just got yelled at. That makes him the most likely person to know why."

"You're not allowed to drive and talk on the phone at the same time," Davey said.

"Really?" Aunt Peg had the steering wheel in one hand and her phone in the other. "I thought that was texting."

"It's both," Davey informed her.

"Sadly, he's right," I told her. "He and I had the same conversation on the way to your house earlier. Davey has become an expert on the Connecticut driver's manual."

Aunt Peg slanted him a look over her shoulder. "You don't need to worry about me. I'm an old hand at driving. I've been doing it since before that manual was even written."

"I don't think that's a point in your favor," Davey said, and I choked down a laugh.

Aunt Peg, still juggling steering wheel and phone, pretended not to hear him. "As long as there aren't any police around to see me—"

"Wrong answer." I reached over and took the device out of her hand. "You're supposed to be setting a good example. How about if I put the phone on speaker, and hold it for you? That way you can talk and drive at the same time."

"Does Davey approve of that?" Aunt Peg arched a brow.

"I'm keeping my opinion to myself," he said. "While you two lawbreakers carry on with what you're doing, Daisy and I will be back here getting to know one another."

"Don't forget about Ebony," Aunt Peg reminded him. "She needs attention too."

Ralph Denby's number was near the top of Aunt Peg's recent call list. I hit redial, and we only had to wait a few seconds before he picked up.

"Don't ask," Ralph said.

"As if that would be enough to dissuade me. Who was that odious man and what did he want with you?"

"Not me, us. *All* of us. He wanted to know who'd given us permission to remove valuable possessions from Audrey's property. He called us a bunch of scavengers. And"—Ralph paused to blow out a breath before continuing—"grave robbers."

"How positively vulgar." Aunt Peg winced. "Who was he, and what made him think he was entitled to an opinion?"

"His name is Carter Ridley. Apparently he's Audrey's ex-husband."

Aunt Peg and I shared a look.

"If today was an example of his usual behavior, I can understand why she divorced him," she said. "Did Mr. Ridley happen to mention what he was doing there?"

"Audrey must have still had him down as a contact somewhere. He said the police called and told him what had happened. He was on his way to consult with them."

"Consult? What does that mean?" Aunt Peg frowned. "No amount of *consulting* is going to bring Audrey back. Besides, whether or not his name is on a piece of paper, he's still her ex. It was my impression, the very few times she mentioned him, that Audrey wanted nothing to do with him."

"Unfortunately, she isn't here to make that point," Ralph muttered. "Maybe Carter Ridley is looking to do a little scavenging himself."

"You might be right. If Ridley does have larcenous tendencies, let's hope the fact that the authorities are still on the premises will keep him in check. I assume his hurry to get to the scene had nothing to do with wanting to check that Audrey's dogs were all right?"

"Not as far as I could tell. Ridley didn't pay the slightest bit of attention to the Danes I've got in here with me. At least not until Bear—that's Audrey's big male—leaned his head over the front seat to see what was going on." Ralph chuckled. "That's what sent the guy scurrying back to his car. If it wasn't for Bear, we might all still be sitting in Audrey's driveway."

Ralph disconnected the call.

"He called Audrey's dogs 'possessions,'" Davey said with distaste.

"Actually, he referred to them as *valuable* possessions," I mused. "Maybe Mr. Ridley is low on funds. That could explain why he went rushing over to Audrey's house as soon as he heard the news."

"All I know is there was no love lost between Audrey and her ex-husband," Aunt Peg said. "If the circumstances were reversed, I might suspect she showed up just to be sure that Carter Ridley was actually dead."

My original plan for the day had been to drop Davey off at Aunt Peg's house in the morning, then return home in a timely manner to take charge of Kevin so that Sam could get to work. By now, that agenda had flown out the window.

On the way to Ridgefield, I'd texted Sam to let him know I was going to be a little late. My estimate wasn't even close. Instead, more than two hours passed before I got back. Not only that, but I'd gained possession of a Great Dane along the way. In the immortal words of Ricky Ricardo, I was going to have some 'splaining to do.

Daisy had fit easily into Aunt Peg's minivan, but she took up the Volvo's entire back seat. Despite her size, she was an amiable dog. She'd climbed in the car, glanced around to check out her options, then wedged her large body into the available space and promptly gone to sleep.

She didn't wake up again until I'd pulled into the shaded area beside my garage, parked the car, then opened all the car windows for ventilation. A Poodle might have been tempted to jump out. Daisy didn't even rise from her reclining position.

"Good girl." I reached over the seat to stroke the Dane's large head. "I'll be right back. I just have to break the news to Sam, then you can get out."

I was on my way to the front door when it drew open. Kevin was standing in the doorway. His T-shirt had a new tear along the seam, and one of his sneakers was untied.

"You're in trouble," Kev announced. He didn't seem displeased by the prospect.

He doesn't know the half of it, I thought.

Seconds later, we heard the clatter of running feet. Tar, Augie, and Bud came skidding into the hallway, then spilled out over the threshold. Rather than checking out Kev's attire, I should have been anticipating the stampede. Too late, it occurred to me that if the three dogs ran around the side of the house and discovered Daisy, all hell was going to break loose.

"Hey guys, come back!" I clapped my hands loudly. "Let's go inside and have a biscuit."

Bud stopped in his tracks and whipped around. Augie's ears pricked. When the first two dogs came running to me, Tar decided to follow them.

"Why are you handing out biscuits?" Sam appeared in the doorway. There was a shadow of stubble along his jaw, and his hair was standing up in tufts as if he'd been raking his fingers through it.

"Desperation," I said without thinking. "I need to get the dogs in the house *now*. We have an unexpected guest."

"We do?" Sam stepped outside and glanced around. "Where?"

"She's in my car," I said. "But first I have to explain."

Sam looked perplexed. *Welcome to my life,* I thought. So far today, nothing had gone the way I expected.

Sam and I herded the Poodles and Bud back in the house, then shut the door. I hoped the dogs didn't mind a short delay on the treats.

One thing accomplished, I turned around and took a deep breath. Now to address the next problem. Then abruptly I realized someone was missing.

"Where's Kevin?" I asked.

A shriek that came from around the side of the house answered my question. Kev had either fallen and injured himself or found Daisy. Either way, the next few minutes weren't going to be easy.

And there went my chance to break the news to Sam gently.

Kevin came racing back to where we were standing. There was an expression of awe on his face. "Mom got me a Great Dane!" he cried.

"No, she didn't." Sam laughed at the idea.

Nonplussed, I couldn't think of a thing to say. It hadn't occurred to me that Kevin might think Daisy was here for him. Of course, I also hadn't expected him to see the Dane before I had a chance to explain.

I was uncomfortably aware that Sam was staring at me. "Tell me you didn't get Kevin a Great Dane."

"I didn't," I said quickly. That part was easy. "But, um . . . there is a Great Dane in my car. Her name is Daisy."

"Daisy." Kevin giggled. "Daisy Dane."

"Why?" Sam's tone was pleasant. His expression was pained.

"It's a long story. But it's not my fault."

"Somehow it never is." He sighed. "Peg's responsible for this, isn't she?"

"Yes," I said, then felt compelled to add, "And also no. There were extenuating circumstances. Lots of them. And mostly beyond our control."

Together, Sam and I walked around to the driveway. Daisy was sitting up on the back seat of the Volvo. Her head was out the open window and she was checking out her new surroundings. The sight of two adults and one excited child, all of us hurrying in her direction, didn't even make her blink.

"There she is!" Kevin cried, as if anyone could possibly miss seeing the big Dane. "Can she come out?"

"Yes, but slowly," I told him. "She's old. So let me help her hop down."

"How old?" Sam asked.

Despite his initial aversion to the idea, he was the first one to reach Daisy. He held out his hand, his fingers rubbing along the side of her face. The bitch's mask, once black, was now threaded with gray hairs. Her dark eyes were slightly rheumy. Daisy leaned into the caress with a delighted quiver.

"I don't know her exact age," I said.

"Maybe that's something you should have asked?"

"Yes." My voice dropped. "But unfortunately, her owner is d-e-a-d."

Kevin's spelling skills were still rudimentary. He'd begun to learn to read in kindergarten, but luckily a string of letters in adult conversation would go right over his head.

"Time to get Daisy out," I said. "She's been in transit for a while. I know she'd like to stretch her legs."

When I opened the back door to the car, Sam stood ready to support the Dane on one side. I took the other. Daisy didn't seem to require much help, however. As soon as the path was clear, she stepped carefully down onto the driveway. Once there, she gave her body a massive shake that started with her head, and ended at the tip of her tail.

"Daisy's amazing!" Kevin cried excitedly. He slipped his arms around the large dog's neck and gave her a hug. "She's going to love living here."

"Not so fast," I told him. "Daisy's only going to be staying with us for a little while. It won't be forever."

"Thank God for that," Sam muttered.

"Be glad we only ended up with one Dane," I said. "There were ten to find homes for, and not a lot of time in which to do it."

I watched him put the pieces together. "Who?"

"Audrey Kane," I whispered, but Kevin heard me anyway.

"I know her." He looked up at us. "She's a nice lady. We went to her house last week to meet Rufus and Betty. Did she decide she didn't want Daisy anymore?"

"Not exactly," I waffled. There was no reason Kev needed to know that someone he'd recently met was also now recently deceased. "Let's take Daisy to the backyard and let her walk around a bit."

"She probably needs to pee," Kevin said practically. Children in our family learned responsible canine care at an early age.

"You're right. And after she's comfortable, we'll start bringing the Poodles out one at a time so they can start getting acquainted. We don't want her to be overwhelmed by everyone at once."

"Don't forget about Bud!"

"Nobody ever forgets Bud." Sam laughed at the thought.

"She'll like him the best," Kevin said with a nod.

"Why do you think that?" I asked.

"Because Bud's my first dog," Kev replied happily. "And now Daisy is my second. So the two of them will be best friends."

"Now look what you've done," Sam said to me. It was a good thing he was smiling.

Chapter 10

Fortunately, the backyard introductions went off without a hitch. It helped that the Poodles loved everyone, even unexpected canine interlopers. Daisy also did her part to be agreeable. She stood in the middle of the yard and greeted our dogs with all the dignity of a queen bestowing an audience on her subjects.

Despite Kevin's prediction, Bud was mostly irrelevant to the proceedings. When he barked at Daisy and ran circles around her, she benevolently ignored him. When he tried to whip the Poodles into a frenzy to match his own, they ignored him too. By the time I finally got around to handing out the peanut butter biscuits, the dogs had settled into a companionable pack.

"That was easier than I thought it would be," I said, relieved.

Sam smirked. "Meaning you didn't stop to think things through before you volunteered to foster a dog the size of a small sofa?"

"Actually, I didn't volunteer. That was Davey's doing."

Sam and I had taken seats in the wicker chairs on the back deck. Kevin was out in the yard with the dogs. He was throwing a ball for Daisy to retrieve. He didn't seem to mind that Bud was the one who kept bringing it back.

"Now that we have a moment of privacy, tell me what

happened this morning," Sam said. "I'm assuming Audrey Kane's demise was unexpected?"

"Yes, Aunt Peg had just heard the news from one of Audrey's neighbors, and she was on her way out the door when we arrived. The neighbor knew how important Audrey's dogs were to her, and he was worried about what might happen to them."

Sam was a breeder, too. He understood the dedication and hard work it took to create and nurture a family of top quality dogs.

"I didn't know Audrey personally," he said. "But I was aware of Kane's Danes. Audrey bred some wonderful dogs, the kind that make an impact beyond the local show scene. It's a good thing her neighbor was able to step in."

"He wasn't the only one. Aunt Peg contacted the local Great Dane club, and a couple of their members showed up too." I slanted him a look. "That's how you ended up with just one Dane rather than a handful."

"Lucky me," Sam said drily. "Did Peg have any details about Audrey's cause of death?"

"She heard something about a possible head injury—also the speculation that one of Audrey's Danes might have knocked her down."

Sam turned to look at me. "That seems unlikely. Sure, Danes are big and strong—and I wouldn't be surprised if the responding officers were intimidated by their size. But Audrey lived with those dogs for decades. She had to have known how to navigate around them safely."

"Maybe all those decades were her downfall," I pointed out. "Audrey had gotten older, and maybe she wasn't as careful as she used to be. Besides, accidents can happen to anyone. I've even been knocked over by a Poodle occasionally." I paused, then added, "Usually Tar."

Sam nodded. If one of our Poodles was doing something he wasn't supposed to, we both knew which one was the most likely culprit.

"That's all I know so far. I wouldn't be surprised if Aunt Peg has an update this afternoon when I go to pick up Davey."

"Just as long as you don't come back with any more Great Danes," Sam said. "We already have a full house."

Together, we gazed out across the yard. Augie, Tar, and Bud were toward the rear of the expanse, chasing a squirrel that was racing along the top of the cedar fence, well beyond their reach. Daisy and the Poodle bitches were lying in the shade beneath the huge oak tree that was home to the boys' treehouse.

Kevin was in the grass beside the Dane. He was leaning against her side with one slender arm draped over her shoulders. Daisy supported his weight easily. Panting lightly, she almost looked as though she might be smiling. I slid my phone out of my pocket and took a picture.

Sam noted the movement. "We can't let him get too attached to her. Daisy isn't our dog."

"I know," I sighed. "I'm just not sure how we can keep it from happening."

To my surprise, Aunt Peg didn't have any additional news for me that afternoon. She insisted that she and Davey had been much too busy to chase down further updates, though they both declined to specify exactly what it was they'd been doing.

Another time, I might have called her on that obvious piece of fiction, but Davey looked so pleased with himself that I decided to let things lie, at least for now. It wasn't as if I didn't have bigger things to worry about. Like a one-hundred-and-forty-pound Great Dane gently burrowing her way into my younger son's heart.

The next morning, over breakfast, Sam volunteered to drop Davey off at Aunt Peg's house. Our first meal of the day was often a free-for-all. Everyone ate whatever they wanted—within reason. Both boys had bowls of banana-topped Cheerios in front of them. Sam had scrambled some eggs for himself, and I was munching on half a bagel.

The Poodles and Daisy were camped out in various spots on the cool kitchen floor. Bud had parked himself beneath Kevin's chair. So far, I hadn't seen any cereal or fruit land on the floor, but the little dog was ever hopeful.

"That sounds good to me." I peered at Sam suspiciously. "Unless you're going to Aunt Peg's to try and convince her to take Daisy."

He shook his head. "No, I'm going out anyway since I need to stop at the hardware store."

At the mention of the Dane, Kevin had looked up in dismay. Now he relaxed back in his seat. "The hardware store is amazing. Can I come with you?"

"Sure," Sam agreed. "We'll drop Davey off on the way there."

"Yay!" Kev pushed away his mostly empty bowl. He was ready to leave right then.

For some reason, the hardware store was a place of endless fascination for the men in my family. I'd never understood how they could stand and stare endlessly at a wall display of tools or electrical gadgets. It was if they were fantasizing about all the things they could potentially build, enhance, or repair—even though we all knew it would never happen. I could have asked Sam what he needed to buy, but honestly, it didn't make the slightest bit of difference to me.

"What's your plan for the morning?" Sam asked.

Until that moment, I hadn't known I needed one. Now, unexpectedly, it appeared that I was going to be on my own for a couple of hours. I could read a book. I could climb the ladder and sit in the treehouse. Or, I could vacuum the downstairs and mop the kitchen floor. Nope, that last one definitely wasn't happening.

"I think I'll take the dogs for a walk," I said.

"All of them?" Davey looked up from shoveling Cheerios in his mouth.

"Sure. Why not?"

"Maybe because you don't want to die?" he said.

Walking six dogs at once, even in our quiet neighborhood, was a bit of an undertaking. The Poodles would listen and behave. Travelling as a pack, they tended to keep each other in line. They also knew not to go near the road, chase bikes, or run across people's lawns. Bud was the problem. He knew the rules, too. He just wasn't sure they applied to him. More often than not, he ended up on a leash.

"You're taking Daisy too?" Kevin asked.

"Of course. A little exercise will be good for her."

"Until she sees something she wants to chase and drags you down the road," Sam said. "Daisy must outweigh you by twenty pounds."

More like ten, I thought, but I wasn't about to correct him.

Instead I gestured toward the elderly dog who was sacked out on the floor, snoring in her sleep. "I'm pretty sure Daisy's chasing days are behind her. She and I will take it slow and steady. If she gets tired, we'll turn around and come back."

"Good luck with that," Davey said with a grin. "Maybe we should stay and watch."

"Not me." Sam pushed back his chair and stood. "I have places to go and widgets to see. Anyone who wants a ride better be ready to leave in ten minutes. That includes you." He pointed at Kevin who was slipping Bud a slice of banana.

"Coming." Kev slid down out of his chair. He had dressed for the day before coming downstairs. Now all he had to do was find his sneakers and put them on. He ran out of the room, with Davey close behind. Sam followed after them.

"Don't forget to put your cereal bowls in the sink," I said to the empty doorway through which they'd all disappeared. "I swear, sometimes it's like I'm living with a bunch of heathens."

Faith was lying next to my chair. She lifted her head and looked at me inquiringly. "Not you," I told her. "You're perfect."

Her pomponned tail flapped up and down on the floor. She knew that. I reached down and stroked the top of her head.

"What do you think?" I asked her. "Can I control seven dogs at once, including one who's the size of a small pony?"

Poodles are highly intelligent. So it was no surprise that Faith looked skeptical. I took her opinion under advisement and decided to take my chances anyway.

Getting the Poodle pack and Bud ready to go was easy. All I had to do was ask if they wanted a walk. All six dogs went racing to the front door and waited there for me to catch up. Daisy was another matter. When the rest of the dogs ran from the room, she slowly sat up, then gazed at me with polite interest, as if to say, "What?"

"Walk," I repeated. There was still no response. Not so much as a cocked ear. I had thought the word was part of the universal canine vocabulary, but apparently not.

Several leashes were hanging by the back door. I took two down and slipped one over Daisy's head. That, the Dane understood. She lumbered to her feet and got ready to move out.

The dogs and I spent an enjoyable half hour strolling through the neighborhood. Bud was so intrigued by Daisy's presence among us that he rarely left her side, which made things much easier. I'd thought the older Dane might slow us down. Instead, she moved along at a brisk pace, her long stride covering more ground than I was accustomed to. Daisy was eager to see and experience everything. She looked like she was having a blast.

The Poodles spent most of the outing running big, looping circles around us. They were worn out when we finally turned for home. Daisy was ready to go back too. Bud was still dancing on his toes. When we cut across the lawn in front of our house, he was the first to notice the unfamiliar car in our driveway.

Bud immediately went racing toward the silver hatchback, his shrill bark sounding the alarm. I dropped Daisy's leash and went running after him. Luckily, I managed to scoop him up before he could throw himself at the vehicle. Despite his size—or perhaps because of it—Bud's guard dog instincts were always on high alert.

Lara Minchin was sitting in the car, with the side window rolled down. Her gray hair had been partially tamed by a short ponytail, and there were three small silver hoops in the helix of her ear. She was looking down at her phone when Bud and I came flying into view.

"Goodness!" Lara lifted her startled gaze to Bud. Since he was in my arms, the two of them were now at eye level. "I hadn't expected that."

"Sorry about the noise." I took a tighter hold of the little dog who was now squirming in my arms. "He thinks he's a watchdog."

"I wouldn't call that a delusion on his part." Lara stared past us at the five black Standard Poodles, and Daisy, who'd just caught up. "That's a lot of Poodles."

"It is," I agreed. I wondered what she was doing here.

Lara's hand reached for the door handle, then she paused. "Is it all right if I get out?"

"If you're asking if you'll be safe with all these dogs, then yes. If you're asking if you're welcome, maybe you should start by explaining why you stood me up at the dog show, and I'll decide whether or not I feel like talking to you."

"Last weekend, Audrey was alive," Lara said.

"If this is about her brooch—"

"It's not about the stupid brooch," she broke in. "It's about Audrey's murder."

Chapter 11

"I was under the impression the police thought Audrey's death was an accident," I said five minutes later.

In the meantime, the dogs had been watered, and the leashes returned to their hooks. Then I'd led Lara to the living room where she'd taken a seat in an upholstered chair. I sat down on the couch opposite her. Bud scooted underneath the low coffee table between us, then Faith and Eve hopped up to flank me on the couch. The remaining dogs settled around us on the floor.

"That was their first idea," Lara said. "Then the coroner found bruising around her neck and on her hands. Audrey didn't fall and hit her head on the corner of the desk. She was pushed."

I drew in a sharp breath. "That's terrible. I'm very sorry for your loss."

Lara waved away my condolences. "I didn't come here for platitudes." Her gaze shifted to Daisy who was snoozing on the carpet near her feet. "That's one of Audrey's Danes, isn't it?"

"Yes."

"Daisy?" The bitch opened one eye, confirming her guess. "What's she doing here?"

"Being well cared for," I said. "I hope you don't have a problem with that."

"Perhaps I should, since I heard Peg Turnbull was the person responsible for emptying out Audrey's kennel."

"You're only partly right. Aunt Peg is just one of the people who were there. She was contacted by Audrey's neighbor, Bill Godfrey—"

"Bill?" Lara looked surprised. "What does he have to do with this?"

"He was concerned about who was going to care for the dogs. You know Bill is the one who found her and called the police, don't you?"

"Yes. Of course." She frowned. "It's what happened after that doesn't make sense to me. You had no right to abscond with my sister's dogs."

Lara and I were on the same side of that argument. Not that my objections had accomplished anything at the time.

"You could have shown up yesterday morning and said something," I pointed out. "Or volunteered to take some of the Danes yourself. If you're really determined to get Audrey's dogs back, I'd be happy to make some calls right now."

Lara's eyes narrowed. She stared at me in stony silence.

"Of course, that assumes you're the beneficiary of Audrey's will," I added. "If not, you have no more right to them than the rest of us do."

"Audrey's will is not your business," Lara snapped.

"I agree, it's not. None of this should be my concern. Except for Daisy." The Dane groaned softly and flopped over on her side. "And yet, here you are, sitting in my house, and making it my business. Why is that?"

Lara straightened in her seat. "I want to know what else was taken."

"Excuse me?"

"You heard me. You *people*"—her tone implied that we were a bunch of degenerates—"helped yourselves to the contents of Audrey's kennel. Did you do the same for her house?"

She had to be kidding, I thought. Her expression said different.

"Let me be clear," I stated. "We *people* included members of your Great Dane club, people who are presumably your friends. Also, the police and the coroner were in Audrey's house the whole time we were there. As far as I know, none of us went inside."

"As far as you know," she repeated. "What does that mean?"

"Aunt Peg and I were the last to arrive. I have no idea what went on before we got there. But since the authorities were in the house at the time, I think I can safely assure you that no looting took place."

Lara didn't look convinced. But since she'd finally stopped firing questions at me, I figured it was my turn.

"Why weren't you at Audrey's house yesterday morning? Ralph said he made a bunch of calls. He must have asked for your help."

"He did not."

That was interesting. "Why not?"

"Audrey's and my relationship was . . . difficult. He knew I wouldn't have come."

Both Audrey and Lara had alluded to their fractured relationship earlier. Neither of them had mentioned what caused it, however.

"You wouldn't have come—even if she needed help?"

Lara shrugged. "As I understand it, Audrey was beyond help at that point."

Man, that was cold. She didn't even have the grace to look distressed.

My thoughts must have shown on my face because she added, "You know we weren't real sisters, right?"

"Audrey mentioned there was a step relationship."

"Yeah. My father married her mother." Lara grimaced.

"Marjorie. That woman was the life of every party. Everyone loved being around her. My father was a widower when they met. He told me he felt lucky that Marjorie had chosen him. He devoted the rest of his life to making her happy."

It wasn't hard to read between those lines. "Where did that leave you?"

"On the outside looking in, and pretty damn annoyed about it. But somehow that didn't stop Audrey and me from becoming friends. Our parents were so wrapped up in each other, they didn't have much time left over for either one of us."

"That must have been a difficult way to grow up." Faith was leaning her body along the length of my leg. I tugged her up into my lap.

"It was," Lara agreed. "But you don't need to patronize me."

"I wasn't—"

"Pity isn't welcome either."

The woman had a hide like a rhinoceros. At least she looked like she'd relaxed somewhat. I tried another question.

"So you and Audrey were friends, and then you weren't. What happened?"

"We got older," Lara said. "And we went our separate ways."

"There has to be more to it than that."

"My, you're a curious person. Do you ask everyone this many questions?"

"Quite often, yes." Bud had begun nibbling on the tip of my shoe. I nudged him away. "But I'm also a good listener. Keep talking."

Honestly, I was half-surprised when she complied.

"Hormones kicked in when Audrey and I became teenagers. We squabbled over everything: boys, clothes, you name it. I hated that she was two years older than me and got to do things I didn't."

I nodded. I could see that.

"Then, when I was seventeen, my father died." Lara nailed me with a hard stare. "And don't even bother telling me you're sorry."

"I wouldn't dream of it," I lied. The impulse to do so had definitely been there.

"You can probably guess what happened next. My father left everything to Marjorie. I wasn't even mentioned in his will, except for some throwaway line about how he knew my stepmother would care for me like I was her own child."

"Ouch," I said with feeling. Eve lifted her head to check in, and I gave her a reassuring pat.

"It was my senior year of high school. Audrey was at some pricey college in Vermont, when Marjorie broke the news to me that there wasn't enough money for both of us to go away to school." Lara winced at the memory. "I knew she was lying, but there was nothing I could do about it. Marjorie had all the control. She started talking about community college and student loans. Then she told me maybe I should just think about getting a job to support myself when I graduated."

This time I was the one who winced. If Lara appeared heartless, I knew who her role model had been.

"I was about to turn eighteen, and it felt like my whole life—everything I'd envisioned for myself—was blowing up in my face. I tried to enlist Audrey's support, but she wasn't about to argue with her mother." Lara laughed bitterly. "Not when it would have meant taking money out of her own pocket."

Lara clearly didn't want my sympathy. Still, it was hard not to feel compassion for the child who'd lost her father, and then felt abandoned by the rest of her family. Much as she annoyed me, her prickly personality was beginning to make sense. Especially when it came to interactions with her stepsister.

When the silence lasted a beat longer than was comfortable, I decided we needed a break. Faith and Eve were both draped across my legs. I moved both of them aside, then stood up.

"I don't know about you, but I could use a drink," I said.

"Alcohol?" Lara asked hopefully. It was barely eleven o'clock in the morning.

"I was thinking more along the lines of iced tea or a soda. But alcohol works too." At this point, I was willing to go along with anything that would make her comfortable enough to keep talking.

"Do you have vodka? And limes?" Lara hopped to her feet.

"Yes, and yes. And maybe some tonic water."

"No water for me. I like my liquor straight."

The vodka was in a corner cabinet in the dining room. The limes were in the kitchen, along with the tumblers. I poured a generous shot of vodka for Lara, and a portion half that size for myself, while she cut up the limes. I topped off my glass with a splash of cold water.

The Poodles had followed us into the kitchen. When Lara and I sat down at the table, they once again spread out across the floor.

"Do they always do that?" she asked.

"What?"

"Follow you around the house."

"Sure. I guess so." I'd never really thought about it. It seemed normal to me that wherever I was, the Poodles would be there too.

"How many dogs do you have?" I asked.

Lara swallowed a large sip of her drink. "Just the one, Milo. I'm really more of a cat person."

She'd caught me by surprise. "That's unusual."

"Why?"

"In my experience, cat people don't end up at dog shows. Or with Great Danes, for that matter."

"Yeah, well. That wasn't my idea."

Suddenly I remembered something I'd wondered about earlier. "Milo has Audrey's kennel name. Considering the estrangement between the two of you, how did you end up with one of her dogs?"

"Funny story," Lara said. Her drink was already half gone.

"I'll bet." I got up and brought the vodka bottle over to the table. "Tell me about it."

"A couple of years ago, Audrey decided it was time for us to let bygones be bygones. She got the idea that she was going to make amends for the things her mother had done by giving me a dog."

I snorted under my breath. "Did you even want a Great Dane?"

"Hell, no." Lara chuckled as I refilled her glass. "But since Audrey was just about the only family I had left, I was open to the idea of a reconciliation. When she made the first move, I went along with it."

I took my first sip. The vodka, even watered down, went straight to my head. Apparently I wasn't good at day drinking.

"Milo was just a puppy when she gave him to me. I thought he seemed kind of small, but what did I know about Great Danes? Later I found out that he'd been sick, but of course Audrey hadn't mentioned that. All she said at the time was that she and I could work together to finish his championship. It was supposed to be the beginning of a new connection between us."

It would also add another champion to the Kane's Danes record, I thought cynically. With Audrey needing to do only half the work.

"How did that go?" I asked.

"Not the way either of us imagined, that's for sure. After his sickly beginning, Milo grew up to be a much better Dane than Audrey had anticipated. He went on to finish his championship easily."

"So it was a success."

"You would think so. But no." Lara held up her glass. When her hand stopped swaying, I refilled it.

"What went wrong?"

"At that point, Audrey decided I should give Milo back to her so she could special him. And maybe breed to him. I refused." Lara peered at me across the table. "As you may have noticed, Audrey gets mad when someone says no to her."

"I only met her for the first time last week," I said. "So the situation never came up."

"You were lucky," she muttered.

"But Audrey must have been pleased when you decided to special Milo yourself."

"You're kidding, right?"

Actually, no. "She wasn't pleased?"

Lara tipped back her head and drained most of her second glass. "Not even close. To be honest, I only did it to spite her. This dog show stuff doesn't really interest me, and I'm not particularly good at it. Audrey hated seeing me and Milo in the group ring. She called my handling skills an embarrassment both to her and the dog."

"That's pretty rude."

"Tell me about it." She braced her elbows on the tabletop and leaned closer. "Audrey and I were estranged for decades, reconciled for a year and a half, and then suddenly we were on the outs again. My life story sounds like a soap opera, and most of it is Audrey's fault."

It seemed to me that Lara's father and stepmother were due an equal share of the blame, but I didn't feel the need to point that out. Instead, I finished my drink and set my glass down on the table.

"Pour yourself another." Lara was happily tipsy and eager for me to join her in that delightful state.

"No thank you. One's my limit."

"Hey!" she cried suddenly. "Did you ever find Audrey's missing brooch?"

"No, I'm afraid not." Only a few days had passed since we'd spoken about it. Plus, I hadn't actually been looking.

"Do you want to hear something ironic?"

"Sure."

"Back when we were still talking to each other, Audrey told me she'd changed her will. She decided to leave me some of her things, including her jewelry. Which is bonkers, when you think about it. Because if I did have her brooch—which I don't—it would belong to me now anyway."

"You're right," I agreed. "That is ironic. What else do you know about Audrey's will? Who will inherit her Great Danes?"

"She didn't tell me that." Lara shrugged. "It can be something for you to find out."

"Me? Why?"

"Because I asked about you before I came over here today." She looked pleased with herself, as if she thought she'd discovered a great secret. "People told me you solve mysteries."

"Sometimes," I allowed.

"Is that why Audrey asked you to find her brooch?"

"Yes."

"I thought so. And now you can solve the mystery of her murder."

"I didn't do very well with the missing brooch," I pointed out.

"Water under the bridge." Lara waved a hand in the air. When she stood up, I was happy to see she was steady on her feet. "Just make sure you do a better job this time."

Chapter 12

Sam and Kevin returned from the hardware store soon after Lara left, and we ate lunch together. Then the two of them devoted the afternoon to repairing Sam's zero turn mower. Judging by the number of parts that lay scattered around the garage floor when I went to check on them, it was a big job. Later that afternoon when Faith and I were ready to pick up Davey, it still hadn't been a successful one.

"I'm thinking we should have something easy for dinner tonight," I said, trying not to grimace as I surveyed the mess. "Like pizza."

"Yay, pizza!" Kevin popped up from the other side the mower. His hands were filthy and there was some kind of oily substance in his hair. At least Sam had made sure both he and Kev were wearing their oldest clothes before beginning the project. "I want mine with pepperoni on it."

Sam stood up and wiped his hands on a rag that was draped over the mover's hood. He looked only marginally better than his son. "Are you saying that because you want pizza, or because you think I haven't got a hope in hell of finishing this job by this evening?"

"A little of both," I admitted.

"Daddy said hell!" Kev was clearly hoping his father would get into trouble.

"Grown-ups are allowed to do that when they're frustrated," I told him. "If it wasn't for your help, I'm sure Dad would have finished working on the mower an hour ago."

Sam dipped his head in a small nod. Thankfully, Kevin misunderstood.

"That's because I'm a big help," he said proudly.

"The biggest," Sam agreed, then turned to me. "Whatever you want for dinner is fine with me. Depending on how long you're at Peg's, you might as well just pick up something on the way home."

"Pizza," Kevin said again in case I hadn't gotten the point. "With pepperoni."

"Really? Because I was thinking I could stop at the new salad place—"

"Pizza!" Kevin yelped, loud enough to make Faith flatten her ears.

"Pizza it is," I said.

My Volvo was parked outside in the driveway. I hopped Faith into the back seat. She looked just as happy to be out of the smelly garage as I was.

"You know he could have hired someone to do that, and the job would have been finished this morning," I told her.

Faith woofed softly. She agrees with almost everything I say. I also agree with everything she says. Between ourselves, we're a pair of sparkling conversationalists.

When Faith and I arrived at Aunt Peg's house, she and Davey were at the front of the fenced field, near the spot where her kennel had once stood. In the years since the building burned down, nothing had grown there but grass. Now Davey was using a shovel to turn over a rectangular patch of soil.

Aunt Peg stood nearby, supervising. Joker, Coral, and Hope were lying down in the shade of the house. Ebony was sacked out a few feet away. When Faith and I got out of the car, all four dogs jumped up and ran to the gate to greet us.

"What are you doing?" I asked, as Faith and I entered the yard.

"Planting a garden." Davey paused his work. He stuck the shovel upright in the ground, then crossed his arms on top of the handle. "What does it look like I'm doing?"

"With Aunt Peg, you never know." He and I were both aware of that. "Maybe digging a shallow grave?"

"That's not funny," Aunt Peg said. "And besides, I only bury bodies on weekends when there are fewer people around to act as potential witnesses."

"I wish I thought you were joking." Faith had run off with the other Poodles. I stepped in for a closer look. "Aren't you a little late to be starting a garden?"

"It depends on what you want to plant," Davey told me. He must have been reading up on the subject.

"And what are you planting?"

"Beets, carrots, and kale," Aunt Peg said.

Those wouldn't have been my first three choices. "How very health conscious of you."

"Indeed. I can't live on cake alone, you know."

"Since when?" I asked. No one replied. It was too bad Faith wasn't around to take up the slack. Instead, I had to soldier on by myself. "I thought I might find the two of you out here working on your agility course."

"That's for another day," Aunt Peg said blithely. "In this lovely weather, Davey and I decided we would rather garden."

My son wanted to dig up soil and plant seeds? I thought not. He'd never shown any interest in gardening before. It was a stretch to believe that he would suddenly do so now. Something fishy was definitely going on. I wished I knew what it was.

"Enough about us." Aunt Peg shut down that dubious topic in a hurry. "What have you been up to today?"

"I started the morning by taking the dogs for a walk, then the next thing I knew I was day drinking with Lara Minchin."

"Now that's a sentence that requires further elucidation," Aunt Peg said with relish. "Let's go inside for a chat. Davey, may we leave you to continue digging on your own?"

"Yup. I'm good." He didn't even bother to look up.

I would have corrected his manners, but Aunt Peg had already left the scene. She was marching toward her house like a woman on a mission. I left Davey to his job and hurried to catch up.

"Which part did you like best?" I asked Aunt Peg. "The day drinking or Lara Minchin?"

"Either one would have piqued my interest." She paused on the back porch to look out over the spacious meadow that served as her rear yard. The Poodles and the Dane were amusing themselves by chasing each other around the fence line. That activity must have been agreeable to Aunt Peg, because she opened the door and ushered me into the kitchen. "Taken together, they sound perfectly irresistible. I'm looking forward to a full report. Don't leave out a single detail."

I took a seat at the butcher block table. "Okay, but first I have a question."

Aunt Peg took a pitcher of iced tea out of the refrigerator and poured us each a drink. It appeared my earlier comments meant I was no longer entitled to cake. That was too bad. The next time the topic arose, I would keep my mouth shut.

"Go ahead," she said, sitting down opposite me.

"Why did Lara Minchin show up at my house this morning rather than yours?"

"Why would she come here? I barely know the woman."

"I could say the same," I pointed out. "Also, she was aware you were the one who spearheaded Operation Move-the-Danes."

"I'm sure I have no idea what Lara might have been thinking."

Let's be clear. Aunt Peg always has an idea. About everything. When she says she doesn't, it means she's prevaricating, not confessing ignorance.

"Moving on to more important matters," she said. "What did Lara want from you?"

"Despite some beating around the bush, it seemed that what she really wanted to know was whether someone in our group had gone inside Audrey's house and taken something."

"Like what?"

"She didn't say."

Aunt Peg huffed at that. "I hope you *asked.*"

"I never had the chance," I admitted. "I was too busy professing our innocence."

"Frankly, I would rather be thought guilty and know what she was after."

When she put it that way, I would too. Too bad that hadn't occurred to me at the time.

There was a bowl of fruit in the middle of the table. Aunt Peg plucked an apple from the assortment, then swiveled around to nab a knife out of a drawer behind her. She cut off a slice and handed it to me. I'd always thought her fruit display was merely decorative. Live and learn. Maybe Aunt Peg was serious about eating carrots and kale, too.

"What else?" she asked.

"She was angry that we'd taken the dogs."

"Just like the ex-husband." She pondered that. "Do you suppose the two of them are in cahoots?"

"Like they might have gotten together to murder Audrey?" Abruptly it occurred to me that I should have started with that piece of news. Except that Aunt Peg didn't look shocked to hear it. Or even mildly surprised.

"I guess you already knew Audrey's death wasn't an accident?" I asked.

"Of course I knew. It was all over the local media this morning. 'Heiress and Dog Breeder Murdered in Ridgefield.' I assumed you saw it too."

I hadn't. I'd been occupied with making sure my children were out of bed, dressed, and fed. Then I realized what she'd said.

"Wait a minute. Audrey Kane was an heiress?"

"More or less." Aunt Peg didn't sound overly impressed. "That part was probably an exaggeration. You know how the press likes to embellish a story to make it sound more enticing. Although that property must be worth a bundle, and I think there's some old family money in the mix."

"That's interesting," I said.

"How so?" Aunt Peg passed me another slice of apple.

"Lara told me a very different story this morning. One implying that the money their family had came from her father. You know that Lara and Audrey were stepsisters, right?"

"You mentioned that yesterday," Aunt Peg said. "I wondered if there might be some kind of Cinderella story involved."

"Yes and no. Lara didn't mention any princes, but she did paint Audrey's mother, Marjorie, as the evil stepmother. She said when her father died, his entire estate went to Marjorie, and she was left out in the cold."

"Penniless? In the snow with no shoes?" Aunt Peg quirked a brow. "That's another fairy tale entirely."

"Things weren't quite that dire." I paused for a sip of

tea. "And in the intervening decades, Lara appears to have done well enough for herself."

"What did she have to say about her relationship with Audrey?"

"That it had its ups and downs. Mostly downs. They've been estranged for most of their adult lives. It began with the squabble over the will, when Audrey sided with her mother. Now, more recently, after a brief reconciliation, she and Audrey were fighting over the dog."

"The mighty Milo," Aunt Peg mused. "A Great Dane owned by one stepsister, but bearing the kennel name of the other."

It didn't take long for me to bring her up to speed on how that circumstance had come about. "Does what Lara told me make sense?" I asked at the end. "Can a dog that looks like not much when it's young turn out to be a champion when it grows up?"

"It's not the usual way of things, but it could happen. Particularly in a giant breed like Danes, which take a long time to mature and come together. Most breeders know their family of dogs. They're aware of which traits—both good and bad—are likely to pop up, even if they've remained hidden for a generation or two. They also know which flaws might be outgrown, or at least improved, with time and patience."

"Lara said Milo was sick when he was a puppy. Does that make a difference?"

"Only in that it makes me reconsider what Audrey's true motives might have been," Aunt Peg said.

"What do you mean?"

"If she gave Milo to Lara as a gesture of goodwill, with the supposed plan that they were going to show the Dane together, why wouldn't she have given Lara one of her better show prospects, or at least a healthier puppy?"

"Maybe because she knew Lara wouldn't be able to tell the difference," I guessed.

"Which is precisely my point. Audrey offered Lara one thing—a dog that was supposedly worthy of becoming a champion. Then she delivered something else entirely—a puppy who it sounds as though she'd already decided was a reject."

I nodded. As usual, Aunt Peg had ferreted out a nugget of information I hadn't previously considered.

"If Milo had turned out to be the inferior specimen Audrey expected," she continued, "it would only have been a matter of time before Lara realized she'd been duped. Perhaps she'd have found out the hard way: by repeatedly placing last in her class. How would that outcome rebuild the unhappy relationship between the two sisters?"

"It wouldn't," I said.

"And therein lies the problem." Aunt Peg frowned. "Or at least one of them. We need more information."

It was easy to agree with that assessment.

"Lara asked me to solve Audrey's murder," I mentioned.

Aunt Peg was slicing a second apple with her knife. She didn't look up. "Of course she did."

"Am I really that predictable?"

Her gaze lifted. "Would you be offended if I said yes?"

"Possibly."

"Well, get over yourself. Because it sounds as though we have work to do."

"We?" I asked.

"You know perfectly well, you're going to need my help," Aunt Peg said. "How many members of the Windsor Great Dane Club do you know?"

"Umm . . . just the two I met the other day."

"So a very limited selection. Of those two, which one is more likely to have wished Audrey harm?"

I thought back. Ralph Denby and Miranda Falk had both shown up on a moment's notice to help with Audrey's dogs. They'd also volunteered to take more than half the Great Danes home with them. As far as I could tell, those were the actions of friends, not enemies.

"Neither of them?" I guessed.

"And you would be wrong," Aunt Peg said. "It's likely that Ralph went to the Danes' aid out of the goodness of his heart. It's also equally likely that Miranda only showed up to gloat."

"I don't get it," I said. "Audrey was dead."

"Which meant that Miranda won."

"By living longer?"

Aunt Peg looked peeved. She gets annoyed when I don't keep up. "Those two women have been fierce competitors for years, decades even. Actually I'm understating the case. They've been at each other's throats."

Throats. I thought about the bruises Audrey had sustained before her death. Hopefully it was just a coincidence that Aunt Peg had used that figure of speech to illustrate her point.

"What's the matter now?" she asked. "You look as though you've seen a ghost."

"How much detail was in the news report you read?"

"Enough for me to know that Audrey had been murdered. Why?"

"According to Lara, before Audrey hit her head and died, someone had had their hands around her throat."

"I see." Aunt Peg didn't look perturbed. In fact, quite the opposite. "Then I guess we've settled the matter of who you need to talk to first."

Miranda. I pictured the woman in my mind. Like Aunt Peg, she'd towered over me. In the brief interaction we'd shared, she'd come across as brusque, and a bit overbearing. Miranda wasn't unfriendly exactly, it was more like she was indifferent to my presence. Until the time came to divvy up the Danes. I couldn't help but remember it was thanks to her forceful intervention that Daisy had ended

up coming home in my car. Even under more normal circumstances, I wouldn't have been looking forward to seeing her again.

"What if Miranda doesn't want to talk to me?" I said.

"She will." Aunt Peg was very sure of herself. "Your relationship with Lara gives you the inside scoop. I'm betting Miranda will want to hear every juicy detail."

Chapter 13

Miranda Falk lived in Weston. I set off for her home the next morning as soon as I dropped Davey off in Greenwich. As usual, Aunt Peg had been right. When I called to see if Miranda would be willing to meet with me, she'd accepted without hesitation.

I hoped that was a good sign. I suspected we'd both be pumping each other for information, and I wondered if I'd be able to hold up my end. My relationship with Lara was negligible, which meant I didn't have any real secrets to barter.

Weston was a typical Connecticut small town: not much commerce, plenty of open land, a sprinkling of historic homes, and lots of trees. Miranda lived outside of town, in a modern ranch-style house on a two-acre lot. A tall wooden privacy fence enclosed her backyard. When I parked in the driveway, I didn't hear any dogs barking to announce my arrival.

Miranda must have been waiting for me, however, because as soon as I got out of my car, she opened her front door and came outside. She was wearing jeans again, this time paired with a lightweight sweatshirt whose sleeves were pushed up. Her brown hair was streaked with gray that she'd made no attempt to cover. The half-dozen bracelets I'd seen two days earlier still jingled on her arm.

Though I'd started toward her, Miranda didn't acknowledge my presence. Instead, she walked past me, strode over to the Volvo, and leaned down to take a look inside. I had no idea what was going on. And nothing to do but wait to see what would happen next.

After a few seconds, she straightened, turned around, then finally looked at me. "Good," she said.

"Good?" I'd just arrived, and already I felt as though I was out of my depth. "What does that mean? That you like Volvos?"

"I was checking to see if you'd brought Daisy along to dump on me. That's why I agreed to meet with you today. I wanted to make sure you hadn't changed your mind about caring for her."

Wait, *what*? I stared at her. "Of course I didn't bring Daisy with me. Why would you think that?"

"I don't know, maybe because you didn't want her in the first place? It was obvious how you felt the other day. Why did you even agree to take her?"

I was still staring. Now I was baffled. I blurted out the first thing that came to mind. "Because you made me do it."

"I did?" Miranda laughed. "Oh no, that wasn't me. Your son was the one who volunteered."

"He's a teenager," I said. "What he says doesn't count."

She shook her head. "Have you tried telling him that?"

"Lots of times—"

"Does it ever work?"

"No," I admitted. "Not really. But Davey's a great kid. No, it wasn't my intention to bring a Great Dane into my home where there are already six other dogs. But you know what? I'm glad Davey spoke up. He did it because he's kind and he cares about doing the right thing, especially when it comes to animals. Even if Daisy takes up half the floor space in our kitchen, I wouldn't change a thing about what Davey did."

For several long beats after I'd finished speaking, we both looked at each other in silence. Finally Miranda said, "Six other dogs?"

I nodded. "Five Standard Poodles. And a mutt, who's more trouble than all the Poodles combined."

Miranda began walking toward her door, so I followed. "Champions?" she asked over her shoulder.

"All but one," I said, then amended my answer. "Not including the mutt."

"Of course." The thought seemed to amuse her. We walked in the house together, and she closed the door behind us. "I haven't seen you around the shows. I thought you only ended up at Audrey's house because of your connection to Peg."

"I have a husband, two children, and a job," I said. "We can't devote all our time to showing Poodles. My family does that for fun, but we don't allow it take over our whole lives."

"Then you're lucky," Miranda said.

She showed me to a living room that was lit by a row of tall windows. The furniture was a mishmash of styles and colors. Some of the seats were covered by towels or fleece throws. A battered-looking butler's table held a bouquet of pink tulips displayed in a crystal vase. One corner of the table had been gnawed to near splinters by some unknown canine's teeth.

"Dogs," she said to explain the condition of the room. "I'm sure you get it. Have a seat."

I perched on the edge of an upholstered ottoman that looked sturdy enough to hold me. Miranda, improbably, sat down on the floor and crossed her legs. "Speaking of dogs," I said. "Where are yours?"

She lifted a hand and gestured toward the rear of the house. "I took the three back rooms and converted them into a kennel. I don't like my dogs to live in pens all the time, so usually I cycle the Danes in and out of the house in pairs. Today I expected you to show up with Daisy, so I put them all away so her arrival wouldn't cause a ruckus."

"You really don't think very well of me, do you?" I said. It was odd, looking down at her like that. I was half-tempted to join her on the floor just so we could sit eye to eye.

Miranda shrugged. "Frankly, I have no frame of reference for thinking about you at all."

"I assume you heard that Audrey's death wasn't an accident?"

"Sure did. Ralph called me with the news. He was horrified. I was less so."

"How come?"

She blew out a breath. "How well did you know Audrey?"

"Not very well. We'd only just met. She seemed like a nice person."

"Yes, well, Audrey always did make a good first impression," Miranda said. "She was careful to do that."

"Meaning it wouldn't last?"

"Not usually. Not unless Audrey thought you could be useful to her. She never cared about anyone's feelings but her own. Audrey was all about what people could do for her."

"If that's how you feel, why did you go to her house to help?"

"That wasn't about Audrey," Miranda said briskly. "That was about her dogs. Despite her flaws, she always had nice Danes. It pains me to admit it, but her breeding program was pretty special."

The comment reminded me that Miranda had specifically requested bitches from Audrey's kennel. Two of them. I hadn't entered the building, so I had no idea who'd picked out the Danes Miranda had taken home with her. It was likely she'd been able to do so herself. I wondered if Miranda was hoping to incorporate a piece of Audrey's special family of Great Danes into her own breeding program.

"It sounds as though you might have some good ideas about who might have wished Audrey harm."

"No," Miranda said quickly. "I don't."

"Not even one?" My brow rose. "That seems unlikely."

"Okay, then my answer is no ideas aside from the obvious suspects. Which would include anyone who ever had to show against her."

"Why didn't you like competing against her?" I asked.

Miranda's expression hardened. "Because Audrey wasn't satisfied with just breeding very good dogs. She was always on the lookout for any other edge she could find. Audrey was an attractive woman."

I nodded. I couldn't argue with that.

"She knew how to simper and flirt, and make the judges feel like the most important people in the world."

Presumably mostly the male judges, I thought. And not even all of them. This was the dog show world, after all.

"She sent them cards on their birthdays and aged whiskey at the holidays. And she offered to keep them company in their hotel rooms when they'd had to travel so very far away from home."

It took me a moment to catch on. "Are you implying what I think you are?"

"I'm not implying anything," Miranda replied. "I'm stating a fact. One that was well known among her fellow competitors. Audrey wasn't even subtle about it. It's not that her Danes weren't deserving winners much of the time. It's that the rest of us felt like we weren't competing on a level playing field. When you lost to her, you never knew whether it was because she had the better dog on the day—or because she was just that good in bed."

I didn't mean to laugh, but I couldn't help myself. I had

to appreciate a woman who wasn't afraid to say exactly what she was thinking.

"You think that's funny?" Miranda asked accusingly.

"No," I said. "Just unexpected."

"Which part?"

"Mostly the 'good in bed' part."

Her smile had a feral quality. "I'm sorry if I shocked you."

"Really?" I said. "Because I'm pretty sure you were hoping to shock me."

The smile dimmed slightly. "Did I succeed?"

"Not really. I'm more surprised than shocked."

"Why?" Miranda asked aggressively. "Because you didn't think a woman that age could still be able to use her body to get ahead in the world?"

"No, because it seems to me that Audrey didn't need to use sex to succeed in the show ring. So maybe you're mistaken about her motive. Maybe she was just in it for the good time."

I paused, then added deliberately, "Which, as I understand it, is something women still care about at *that age*."

Miranda took a full minute to consider me from her spot on the floor. "You know," she said finally, "under other circumstances, we could probably become friends."

"What's wrong with these circumstances?"

"I'm not dumb. I know why you're here. You think I'm a suspect in Audrey's murder."

"*Should* you be a suspect?" I asked.

"Absolutely not. I didn't kill Audrey."

"Then who did?"

"I answered that question earlier," Miranda said.

"And I didn't give you a chance to expand on your answer. Maybe you would like to do that now."

"It could be anybody. Audrey wasn't a popular person."

That told me nothing, other than that Miranda was still

deflecting. At this rate, I'd never learn anything useful. That was probably her intent.

"Yes, I got that impression. But is there anyone in particular you think I should follow up with?"

Miranda scowled at me. "First you came here to accuse me, and now you're asking me to rat out my friends?"

This woman either had a very short fuse or there was something she was trying to hide. Either way, I wanted to know more.

I pulled in a deep breath, then slowly let it out. Then I slid down off the ottoman onto the floor. Now Miranda and I were on the same level. I should have done that earlier.

"First of all, I haven't accused you of anything. Nor am I asking you to rat anyone out. All I'm trying to do is gather information. You were a member of Audrey's circle. You belonged to the same breed club. You frequented the same shows. From what you've already told me, it's obvious that you know who she got along with and who she didn't."

"That part's easy," Miranda shot back. "Audrey rubbed just about everyone the wrong way."

I couldn't quite believe that. Nevertheless, I tried another tack. "Is that why only two members of your Great Dane club showed up at her house the other day?"

She shrugged. "How would I know that? People have busy lives. Frankly, the guy I was surprised to see there was Carter Ridley. Late to the party, then full of bluster about his own importance. As usual."

"You know Audrey's ex-husband?" I hadn't expected that.

"Not well, but we've crossed paths. Back when they were married, he used to come to the shows sometimes. He'd wander around, trying to look important, even though it was obvious he had no idea what was going on."

"Maybe he was trying to be a supportive husband," I said.

"Or maybe he was a husband who wanted to keep an eye on his wife's extracurricular activities," she muttered darkly.

Something was niggling at the back of my memory. Then suddenly I knew what it was. "Aunt Peg spoke with Ralph after the two of them had words in the driveway. Ralph made it sound as though he and Carter hadn't met before." Now that seemed unlikely.

Miranda confirmed my guess. "That's ridiculous. Those two knew each other all right."

"How can you be so sure?"

"How many Poodle people do you think Peg knows?"

"Dozens. Maybe hundreds. Basically, all of them."

"Correct," she said. "Because the entire dog show community isn't huge. And within the breeds themselves, it's even smaller. Everyone ends up knowing everyone else."

Of course. I'd already seen that for myself. "But you just told me that Carter was only peripherally involved in the dog show world."

"Forget Carter for a moment. Start with Ralph. He and Audrey had known each other for years. Since long before she was married to Carter. And unless I'm an idiot—which I like to think I'm not—Ralph was infatuated with Audrey the entire time."

That was news. "Did he ever act on his feelings?"

"Yes. I think so." She paused to consider. "There was a time years ago, when it looked like something might be going on between them. Then suddenly it wasn't. Like maybe she'd dumped him hard. Then a few months later, Audrey was engaged to Carter and swanning around the showgrounds showing off a diamond the size of a grape. So Ralph knew who Carter was, all right. I'd say he knew *exactly* who that man was."

"But that happened a long time ago," I said. "It's all in the past. Right?"

"Not entirely. Because I don't think the infatuation ever really ended, at least not on Ralph's side. Eventually he married his wife, Nattie, but he was still carrying a torch. It's probably a good thing Nattie doesn't spend much time at the shows. Otherwise, she would see what the rest of us do—Ralph following Audrey around the showgrounds with his tongue hanging out like a sad puppy."

It was hardly an appealing image. Nor necessarily a helpful one.

"So Ralph implied he didn't know Carter Ridley," I mused. "But since Audrey, and not Carter, is the one who's dead, I don't see why it matters. It sounds as though Ralph wouldn't have done anything to harm Audrey."

"Keep thinking," Miranda said. She put a hand on the floor and pushed herself to her feet. "I'm sure it will come to you. Ralph isn't the problem in that scenario."

I didn't agree. Maybe Miranda was more open-minded about appropriate marital behavior than I was.

"Not Carter." I stood up as well.

Miranda smirked. "Guess again. Only one person left."

"Nattie."

"It took you long enough," she said.

Chapter 14

"So . . ." Sam said that night, as we were getting ready for bed. He let the word dangle.

I assumed I was supposed to say something, but I didn't know what that might be. I'd already washed my face and brushed my teeth. Now I flipped back the covers on the bed and scooted beneath them. Faith was asleep on the small chaise near the window. Older now, she rested whenever she had the chance. The other Poodles were all in their preferred sleeping spots in other upstairs rooms. Daisy and Bud were sharing the floor in Kevin's room.

Meanwhile, it appeared that Sam was still waiting for an answer.

"I'm going to need more details," I said.

"Audrey Kane." Sam slipped in beside me. Immediately the bed grew warmer. The man gave off heat like a furnace. I was happy to snuggle closer. And cuddling might take the edge off the topic we were about to discuss. "You're looking into her murder, aren't you?"

Sam and I have been together for more than a decade. We met when Aunt Peg's champion stud dog was stolen and my Uncle Max died during the theft. Sam, who was also involved in the mystery, knew what he was getting into when he married me. But every so often he needs a reminder.

I lifted my head and looked at him. "Did I forget to mention that?"

Sam lifted a brow. "I don't know. Did you?"

I levered myself away and sat up. "It didn't occur to me that I needed your permission."

"You don't," he replied. "Of course you don't."

I was glad we had that settled.

I lay back down and rested my head on his shoulder. "This isn't something I went looking for. It was a coincidence that Kevin and I had just met Audrey. Then her Danes needed rescuing, and Davey and I happened to be there to help Aunt Peg—"

"Who finds more trouble to get you involved in than I ever would have thought possible."

"You know Aunt Peg likes useful people. Since I'm on summer break, she probably thinks it's her duty to keep me busy."

Sam wasn't buying that excuse. "I can think of plenty of other ways for you to keep busy. You could take up yoga. Or join a knitting group. Or train to run a marathon."

His choice of options made me laugh. "Do any of those things sound like me? Seriously, a *knitting group?*"

Sam chuckled too. "It was the safest thing I could come up with on short notice."

"You're worried about me," I said.

"Always."

"You know I do my best to stay safe."

"Yes, and so far, so good. But what am I going to do when your luck runs out? You end up consorting with all kinds of bad people—"

"They're not all bad," I said.

"They're not all good," Sam growled.

Point taken.

"It's possible that one day things will spiral out of your control. I just want to know . . ."

I gazed upward. "What?"

"That I won't ever have to break bad news to the boys about something that's happened to you."

"You won't," I promised. "And certainly not this time. The people Audrey was involved with are mostly just older dog breeders who've known and shown against each other for years."

"That doesn't make me feel better," Sam said. "I know how intense competition can become. And where there are old friends, there may also be old grudges. What happened to Audrey is ample proof of that."

"I'll be careful," I said.

Sam nodded. "And don't let Peg talk you into doing anything rash."

"You know I've gotten much better about that."

"Sure you have." He smirked. "That's why there's a Great Dane sleeping in Kevin's room."

"Okay, maybe you're right about that part. But Daisy's a doll, isn't she? She gets along with everyone."

"She does. And that's a good thing. It means she'll be happy in her new home, wherever it turns out to be."

I shook my head, trying to imagine where the Dane might end up. "Who could possibly be prepared to inherit ten adult Great Danes at one time?"

"Probably no one," Sam said with a frown, and we left it at that.

The next morning when I dropped Davey off at Aunt Peg's house, she invited me in for a chat. I quickly declined. Though I knew Aunt Peg hated being out of the loop, I was also well aware that once we started talking, I could lose half the morning. Besides, I hardly had any new information to share.

After spending time with Miranda, it was clear the next person I needed to talk to was Great Dane expert Ralph Denby. A bit of online stalking revealed that he and his wife, Nattie, were the proprietors of the Tokeneke Garden

Center and Nursery in Darien. The business's website was striking and colorful. Pictures showed differing views of a massive, multipaned greenhouse that was filled with a multitude of plants, shrubs, and flowers.

Ralph offered workshops on topics like wreathmaking and organic gardening. Nattie was available for private consultations in floral and landscape design. Speaking as someone who thought that using pruning shears to trim the bushes outside our front door was gardening, I was hugely impressed.

Darien wasn't far from Greenwich, and I enjoyed the drive. The day was slightly overcast, and humidity made the air feel heavy, but when I set out it had yet to rain. I had an umbrella in the car, but was hoping not to have to use it. Unfortunately, as I turned onto the street where the garden center was located, the first raindrops began to fall. Seeing the sign for the nursery up ahead, I put on my wipers and my turn signal at the same time.

Next to the greenhouse I'd seen on the website was a large, barn-like building with a gambrel roof and weathered siding. A brick walkway led to the front door, and signs directed visitors to begin their "Garden Journey" there. Midweek, there was plenty of parking available.

I glanced at the umbrella on the seat beside me. The rain was coming down steadily, but I hadn't parked far from the building's entrance. My slacks and shirt were cotton, my sneakers mostly waterproof. I figured the worst the rain could do was frizz my hair. In the time it would take me to open the umbrella, I could probably be inside the building. I decided to make a run for it.

I jumped out of the Volvo and sprinted toward the barn's double doors. My idea made sense in theory. In practice, it would have worked out better if the entrance to the building hadn't been locked. Fully expecting the wooden door to give way, I instead slammed into what felt like a hard, unyielding wall. The resounding thump I'd made must have jostled a gutter on the eave above me, because a moment later a wide stream of water came pouring down onto my head.

I shrieked in surprise and jumped back, blinking my eyes to clear them. When they refocused, I found myself looking through a window on the door's upper quadrant. Ralph Denby was standing behind a counter in the middle of a big plant-filled room, staring out at me in shock. Before I could move away—at that point retreating to my car seemed like the best option—he had already skirted around the side of the counter and was hurrying in my direction.

When Ralph got to the door, he quickly reached up, then down. I heard two latches slide open. Then he stepped back and yanked the door inward. "Sorry, we don't open until ten thirty," he said.

All the time I'd spent on the nursery's website, and I hadn't thought to check the hours of operation. Brilliant.

"My bad," I muttered.

Ralph was still staring. "Wait a minute. I know you."

Considering the state I was in, that was hardly flattering. Then again, Ralph seemed like the kind of friendly guy who would remember all his customers, and apparently any other random people who might have crossed his path recently.

"Melanie Travis," I reminded him. When I held out my hand, water dripped from my fingers. I retracted it and tried to wipe it dry on my pants. That didn't help at all. "We met at the dog show, and then again at Audrey Kane's house."

"Right. Of course." Ralph cast a glance upward at the darkening sky, then beckoned me into the building. "Please, come in! Darn forecast said maybe a little rain. They didn't mention anything about a monsoon. Let me get you a towel so you can dry off. Stay right there."

I closed the door behind me and did as I was told. Water

dripping from my hair and clothing was already forming a puddle on the concrete floor. Since the room was filled with numerous floral displays, rows of hanging plants, and a vast selection of trays offering all kinds of greenery, hopefully a bit of excess water was an everyday occurrence.

"Here we are." Ralph came striding back, holding a fluffy pink towel. He quickly handed it over. "Maybe this can undo the worst of the damage."

"No damage done," I assured him, as I used the towel to blot my hair. "Except maybe to my pride. I'd hoped you could spare a few minutes to talk to me, but I hadn't planned on making such a memorable entrance."

Ralph ducked his head and shoved his hands deep into the pockets of his khaki pants. He looked like he was biting back a grin. "Here at Tokeneke Garden Center, we pride ourselves on customer service, so you can trust me when I say that wasn't the way I expected to start my day either."

"Go ahead and laugh," I said, wringing out the bottom of my shirt. "I know how dumb I look. Believe me, I won't be offended."

"You sure about that? If there's one thing I've learned about women, it's that they're apt to say one thing and mean another. I'd hate to make you feel worse than you already do."

"Under the circumstances, I'm not sure that's possible." The towel was already soaked and I handed it back to him.

"The least I can do is offer you a cup of coffee and listen to what you have to say. If you want to follow me, we can have a sit-down in the break room for a few minutes."

"That sounds great." My shoes squished as we crossed the cavernous space together. The temperature in the room was warm, but I still felt chilly in my damp clothes. A cup of hot coffee would be very welcome.

Ralph turned down a short hallway and led me to the

room at the end. The only furniture inside was a square table surrounded by four chairs. There was a counter along one wall with a cabinet above it. It held a sink with a drying rack, a microwave, and a coffeemaker. A full-size refrigerator and a calendar near the door completed the decor.

Ralph went straight to the coffeemaker. "Have a seat," he said, motioning me to a chair. "I'll have you fixed up in a jiffy. I hope you didn't hurt yourself back there."

Now that he mentioned it, my shoulder was pretty sore. I resisted the urge to give it a rub. "Nothing to worry about," I said.

"Glad to hear that." He glanced over his shoulder. "How's Daisy working out for you?"

I smiled. "Better than I expected. Despite her size, she fit right into our household. My younger son is thrilled with her."

"Danes'll do that. They can make themselves at home almost anywhere." Ralph took out two white mugs, imprinted with the company logo, and filled them with steaming coffee. The smell alone was enough to make my mouth water.

"Milk? Sugar? Sweetener?" he asked.

"Just milk for me, please."

He added a splash of milk to both mugs, then came over and sat down. "The son you mentioned, is that Davey?"

"No, it's his little brother, Kevin."

"I'm only asking because Davey was pretty gung ho the other day about taking one of Audrey's Danes home. Now it sounds as though you must have two dog lovers in the family."

"Actually there are four, including me and my husband. Sam breeds and shows Standard Poodles."

Ralph nodded. "Seeing as how you showed up with Peg, I knew there had to be a Poodle connection somewhere."

"Pretty much everywhere," I said, and he grinned.

"That's Peg for you. She's not shy about making her feelings known." Ralph looked at me across the table. "I'm guessing you didn't stop by on a rainy day to talk about plants. So now that I've dumped water on you and made you coffee, what else can I do for you?"

"I assume you've heard that Audrey Kane's death wasn't an accident?"

"Hell, yeah. I think just about everyone's heard about that. The Dane hotline has been buzzing about it like crazy."

I got momentarily sidetracked. "You have a hotline?" Poodles didn't have a hotline. If Danes had one, we needed one too.

"That's just a figure of speech. Let's just say that the phone lines have been burning up. Everyone wants to know who did it."

"It's not surprising," I said. "Is anyone offering any guesses?"

"Lots of them." Ralph chuckled. "Most are all kinds of nutty. I've heard everyone from Jim Clark to Judge Crater."

Both of whom were long since deceased themselves.

"Any real guesses?" I qualified.

Ralph suddenly sobered. "Sad to say, I've recently discovered that it doesn't take much for members of a dog club to turn on each other. You know that group of Dane fanciers I was with last weekend?"

I nodded.

"Back then, I'd have told you we were all pretty chummy. But not now. Now, it feels like everyone's pointing fingers at everyone else."

Chapter 15

"If that's true, Audrey must have had a lot of ene-mies," I said.

"Oh, it's true all right." Ralph paused to take a gulp of his coffee. I hoped it didn't burn his throat. My drink was still scalding hot. "You'd think people would be grieving. Instead, for some of them, it's almost like a game. I actu-ally heard someone say, 'I bet it was Colonel Mustard in the library with a candlestick.'"

"That's terrible." I wrapped my fingers around the mug and drew a bit of warmth from it. "Audrey seemed like a nice person to me."

"Audrey had her moods," Ralph said. I waited for him to elaborate. Instead, he just stared at his mug.

"Moods?"

He took his time before looking up. "Sometimes Au-drey was your best friend. She could make you feel like you were the most important person in the world. And be-lieve me, that feeling was something else. Other times, she'd walk right past you like you didn't even exist."

I thought about what Miranda had told me. "Did Au-drey act like that with everyone?"

"You mean 'or just with me'?"

I nodded.

"I guess maybe you heard she and I were together at one time."

"I did."

"That was before I met Nattie," Ralph clarified.

"Nattie is your wife?" I asked. He didn't need to know that Miranda had been talking about him behind his back. And that she'd been doing some finger pointing herself— in the direction of Ralph's spouse.

"Twelve years this month," he said.

"That's a long time." I smiled at him. "I guess Nattie must have been friends with Audrey too."

"Not really. *Women.*" Ralph shook his head. "They're a mystery, all right. Who knows what makes them tick?"

Presumably, he'd overlooked the fact that he was talking to a woman.

"The two of them should have been great friends, but it never worked out that way. I'd imagine it didn't help that Nattie doesn't have much interest in the Danes. She didn't like coming to the dog shows either. While those two things were pretty much Audrey's whole life."

Considering what he'd just said about women, I hated to stereotype Ralph as a typically clueless man. *But seriously?* Did he truly have no idea why his wife might have wanted to avoid dog shows, the bailiwick of his former flame?

"Considering your mutual interest in dogs, maybe you should have stayed with Audrey," I said lightly. Just throwing the idea out there to see what might happen.

I fully expected him to take offense at the comment on his wife's behalf, but I was wrong. Ralph went in another direction entirely.

"There was a time when I believed Audrey and I were going to make a team of it. But sadly, it wasn't to be." Ralph sounded regretful. "She threw me over for someone better."

"Better?" I lifted my mug and took a sip. "I find that hard to believe."

His smirk indicated what he thought of that remark. "I'll keep that in mind the next time I'm on the market."

"You and I would never work," I told him. "I'm as committed to Poodles as you are to Danes."

"Too bad." This time he didn't sound regretful at all.

"You seem like a pretty sociable guy," I said. "I'm sure you must know everyone in your Great Dane club. Is there anyone in particular whose comments about Audrey's death seem credible enough to arouse suspicion?"

Ralph rubbed a hand along his chin. "Well, like I said, Audrey wasn't always the most popular person. You've heard of a sore loser? She was a sore winner. Audrey enjoyed lording her successes over the people she'd beaten. And that didn't sit well with any of them."

I could understand why. "Who would have been her main competitor recently?"

He thought about the question carefully before answering. "Probably a guy named Joe Wheeler. You might have seen him sitting with us at the show last week?"

"No. Sorry."

There had been at least half-a-dozen people seated around the circle. At the time, I'd been concerned with zeroing in on Lara. Except for Ralph, who'd been pointed out to me, I hadn't really noticed anyone else.

"Joe's a good guy," Ralph said. "But he and Audrey had been butting heads lately. And not just in the show ring. From what little I know, it seemed like they might have had some other kind of deal in the works. Possibly it had to do with a dog?"

The question seemed to be directed at me. I shrugged to indicate my lack of an answer. Fortunately, it was enough to keep him talking.

"Whatever the deal was, I'm guessing it must have

fallen apart. Because lately, neither one of them had anything good to say about the other."

My clothes were still damp and clammy. Now they'd begun to stick to me. Plus, I'd almost finished my coffee and I suspected it was past ten thirty. It was time for me to move along.

"Where would I find Joe Wheeler?" I asked.

"I'll answer that question after you answer one of mine." Ralph got up, walked over, and placed his empty mug in the sink.

"Fair enough." I stood up and did the same.

"What do you want to find Joe for?"

"I'd like to speak with him about Audrey's death," I said.

His eyes narrowed. "Because you think he might know something about it?"

I pinched the neckline of my shirt and plucked it away from my skin. "I can't answer that question without talking to him."

"What if he does know something?" Ralph persisted. "What then?"

"It depends what he says. If it's something important, I'll take the information to the police."

I was ready to leave, but Ralph was standing between me and the door. "I guess it's true what I've heard about you snooping around in other people's business."

"Not everyone's business," I said. "Only people who aren't here to take care of themselves."

"Dead people." He didn't make that sound like a good thing.

All at once the room felt a lot smaller than it had previously. When I made a move to go around him, Ralph reached out and put a hand on my arm. He didn't exactly stop me, but neither did he permit me to keep walking. I resisted the impulse to shake him off.

"Audrey meant something to you once," I said. "I would think you'd want her killer brought to justice."

He closed his eyes briefly. A breath hitched in his throat. "It wasn't just back then. Audrey means the world to me still. That's why I won't be part of anything that might sully her memory. But you're right about wanting justice. If it helps, Joe Wheeler works in a real estate office in Wilton. Parker/Dunn, I think it's called. You can probably find him there."

"Thank you," I said.

Ralph dropped his hand, and I scooted past him. According to a clock on the wall in the main room, it was ten forty-five. The double-doored entrance to the nursery was standing open. At least half-a-dozen customers were already browsing around the large room. A young man was behind the counter, manning the cash register. I walked past all of them and let myself out.

The rain had stopped, and the clouds overhead were beginning to break up. There were still plenty of puddles in the parking lot, however. Stepping carefully around them, I was almost to my car when a flash of light caught my eye.

The door to the greenhouse had just been opened; its panes were reflecting the newly appeared sun. A young woman with long dark braids and a bandanna wrapped around her head came outside. She was carrying a pot with a small shrub in her arms.

My gaze slid past her, then quickly returned. The woman looked familiar. It took me only a few seconds to figure out why. She was Audrey's dogsitter, Tasha Gilbert.

There was an empty alleyway between the two buildings. I waited until she'd reached it before making my approach. "Tasha?"

She paused and looked at me with no sign of recognition. "Yes. Can I help you?"

"I'm Melanie Travis. We met last week." Tasha still looked blank. "At Audrey Kane's house? My son and I took Daisy home with us?"

Mention of the Great Dane's name did the trick. "Oh, of course." She treated me to a broad smile. "How is Daisy doing?"

"Very well," I said. "We're enjoying having her with us. She sleeps beside my son's bed."

"I'm delighted to hear that. Daisy's a lovely bitch." Tasha juggled the pot from one arm to the other. Maybe it was heavier than it looked. "Is there something I can help you with?"

The question caught me by surprise. I hadn't expected Tasha to take the lead in our conversation. "Umm . . . why would you ask me that?"

Tasha looked confused. "Because I work here?"

"You do?"

"Sure. Dogsitting's a great gig when I can get it. But it's not always a reliable source of income. So I work here part-time to fill in the gaps."

"What a coincidence," I said.

"Not really. Audrey knew I was looking for more work than she could give me. She's the one who sent me to Ralph. He read the recommendation she'd written, then hired me on the spot."

"That was nice of her."

"Yeah." Tasha's gaze shifted away. "She was always nice to me. I'm really going to miss her."

"It must be hard for you now, with Audrey gone."

"I guess." She was still looking past me. Now that I knew she worked at the nursery, I hoped I wasn't keeping her from somewhere else she needed to be. "It's definitely going to be tougher for me to make ends meet. Ralph said he might be able to increase my hours, but he hasn't done it yet."

A sudden thought came to me. "You know, there are plenty of exhibitors who travel to away shows, and leave their other dogs at home. It seems like the demand for dogsitters should be pretty strong. If Audrey wasn't keeping you busy enough, I'm surprised she never passed your name along to her friends."

"Yeah. That would have helped a lot." Tasha frowned. "But I think she liked the idea of knowing I was always available whenever she needed me."

"That arrangement sounds like it was good for her, but not so good for you. If you want, I can give your contact information to my Aunt Peg. You met her last week. She knows just about everyone in the dog show world. Maybe she can drum up some business for you."

"Really?" Tasha finally looked me in the eye. "You'd do that for me? That would be great."

"Here, put your number in my phone."

I took out the device and went to give it to her, then immediately saw the problem. Tasha's hands were already full. She didn't even hesitate, however. Instead, she dumped the potted shrub into my arms and grabbed the phone at the same time. I'd been right earlier. It was heavier than it looked.

While she was busy tapping her number into my contact list, I said, "You must have been one of the first people to arrive at Audrey's house the morning her body was discovered."

"I was." Tasha swallowed. "As soon as Bill called me, I went right over. I only live ten minutes away."

"Bill." I thought back. "He's Audrey's neighbor."

"That's right."

She'd finished with my phone, and was clearly ready to exchange it for the plant. I pretended not to notice and continued to juggle the unwieldy pot. There were a couple more questions I still wanted to ask.

"Bill's the one who found her," I prompted.

"So he said." Tasha immediately looked as if she wished she hadn't spoken.

"Are you doubting his word?"

"Maybe. I don't know." Her face flamed. "All I know is that Audrey and Bill were neighbors, but they weren't very friendly with each other. Especially not in the past few months."

"Do you know why that was?"

"No. All I know is that last month, Audrey went away to a cluster of shows in the Midwest. She was going to be gone for a whole week. When she took longer trips like that one, she'd ask me to stay at her house. I liked being on-site because it made things easier for me."

I nodded.

"That time before she left, Audrey made a point of telling me that if I saw anyone on her property while she was away, I should immediately call the police. She instructed me to report the intruders, and to tell the authorities to come and make them leave."

"Intruders?" I repeated. "That seems like a strong word to use. Do you know what, specifically, she was concerned about?"

"No, Audrey didn't say. But it was the first time she'd ever said anything like that to me. And there was something else. While she was talking, she kept looking over in the direction of Bill Godfrey's property."

How very curious. "You didn't think to ask Audrey what she meant by that?"

"No, why would I? It didn't have anything to do with the Danes, so I figured it was none of my business." Tasha paused and bit her lip. "I'd actually forgotten all about it until Bill called and told me what happened to Audrey. Then my first thought was 'What is he doing inside her house?' Because I knew for sure that she wouldn't have wanted him in there."

"I hope you told the police—"

"Hello again, Melanie!" A booming voice came from behind me.

I turned to see Ralph approaching us at a rapid walk. His gaze went from me to Tasha.

"What are you still doing out here?" he asked the young woman. "I expected you inside ten minutes ago."

I stepped in before she could answer. "Tasha was just trying to interest me in buying this lovely, er . . . plant."

"Burkwood Viburnum," Tasha supplied easily. When I held up the pot as evidence, she slipped the phone into the pocket of my slacks. "I was telling Melanie it would give her garden a pop of color."

Sam and I don't have a garden. Thankfully, Ralph didn't know that.

"Yes, well . . ." He looked back and forth between us, still not convinced.

"Tasha's been a great help," I told him. "And she's a terrific saleswoman. Based on her recommendation, I think I'll take this Viburnum home with me."

Ralph's expression cleared. "That was well done, Tasha. Now you should run along, you're needed in the nursery. Melanie, if you want to step back inside with me, I'll be happy to ring that up for you."

Thank you, Tasha mouthed silently before she hurried away.

I followed Ralph to the cash register and paid nearly forty dollars for a big potted plant I didn't need. But considering the information I'd gained from talking to Tasha, I figured it was worth it.

I lugged the heavy Viburnum to my car. Maybe Aunt Peg could add it to her vegetable garden.

Chapter 16

When I arrived at Aunt Peg's house that afternoon to pick up Davey, no one was outside. No stampede of Poodles came flying down the front steps. And when I rang the doorbell, no one answered. So I opened the door and let myself in.

Immediately, I heard the sound of a loud whine. Just as quickly, I recognized its source. Someone was using Aunt Peg's big, freestanding blow-dryer. Her grooming room was at the foot of the staircase that led to the home's lower level. I went to the top of the steps and looked down.

Three black dogs—two Standard Poodles and a Great Dane—were spread out on the floor of the hallway below. I went down to join them. Aunt Peg looked surprised to see me when I appeared in the grooming room doorway.

"Goodness," she said, "is it that late already?"

I showed her my watch. She just shrugged. When Aunt Peg was involved with her Poodles, all sense of time went out the window.

The grooming room was a model of canine-care efficiency. Brightly lit and carefully designed, it wasn't a large space—but every available inch was put to good use. Mounted in the center of the room was a rubber-matted grooming table that could be raised or lowered as needed.

It also swiveled in place. An elevated bathtub—Standard Poodle size—was equipped with both a faucet and a shower-head. One wall had a row of cabinets, another was lined with shelves, ensuring that all the grooming supplies Aunt Peg might need were always within easy reach.

At the moment, however, Aunt Peg wasn't doing any grooming. Instead, she was just watching. Joker lay on his side on the tabletop, and Davey was using a pin brush and the blower to carefully straighten and dry layered sections of the puppy's long show coat.

My son glanced at me briefly, said, "Hi, Mom," then went right back to work.

"Hi, yourself." Though the top half of Joker was mostly dry, I could see from where I was standing that the puppy's underneath side was still soaking wet. Davey had at least an hour, if not more, before he'd be finished. It seemed I was going to be here awhile.

I turned to Aunt Peg and said, "I brought you a plant."

"Really?" Her brow rose. "What kind of plant?"

"A Burkwood Viburnum."

"Lovely," she replied, as if she knew what those words meant. Knowing Aunt Peg, she might have been bluffing. "What's the occasion?"

"Someone I needed to talk to was about to get into trouble for slacking on the job. So I bought a plant."

"Well, that barely makes any sense at all," she said. "Perhaps you'd better tell me more about it." She raised her voice so it would carry over the sound of the dryer. "Davey, are you able to carry on by yourself if your mother and I step away to converse somewhere we can hear ourselves think?"

"Of course," he replied.

"Good answer."

Hope, Coral, and Ebony were just as ready to be on the move as we were. When Aunt Peg and I exited the room, they were already on their feet. Joker, stuck on the table, looked unhappy at the prospect of being left behind. Come to think of it, so did Davey.

"You don't need to watch him blow dry a Poodle," I said, as we started up the stairs. "He's been doing it on his own at home for years."

"Yes, but how well?" Aunt Peg replied tartly. "Perhaps my standards are higher than yours."

It was entirely possible that her Poodle grooming standards were higher than mine. I'd occasionally been known to let a few things slide. But they certainly weren't higher than Sam's. He could turn out a Poodle for the show ring just as well as Peg could. But since he wasn't here, I decided I didn't need to be insulted on his behalf and merely huffed under my breath.

We reached the landing together. Aunt Peg propped her hand on her hips and looked around her front hall. "Where's my Viburnum?"

"I left it outside in my car."

She went marching toward the front door. "Why didn't you say so? We could have gone out through the garage."

"I was busy trying to get my thoughts in order." All at once it felt as though I had a lot to tell her.

"Start with the plant." Aunt Peg was already outside and on her way down the steps. "Who's the job slacker?"

"Tasha Gilbert."

She cast a glance back over her shoulder. "Audrey's dogsitter?"

"The very same."

"And she's now selling plants? How did that come about?"

"Apparently, it's nothing new." I hurried to catch up. "And she isn't a slacker."

"It seems to me you have a Burkwood Viburnum that says differently." Aunt Peg opened the door to the Volvo's back seat. The potted shrub was on the floor in front of it.

"It's too hot in here," she said. "The least you could have done is open some windows for the poor thing."

Had the Viburnum been a dog, of course I would have worried about temperature and ventilation. But for a plant? The thought hadn't even occurred to me. This is why I don't have a garden of my own.

Aunt Peg straightened with the shrub in hand. She lowered her head to a cluster of small white flowers and inhaled deeply. "Lovely," she said again.

It looked as though my impulse purchase had found a home.

Aunt Peg walked over to the gate that led to the yard beside her house. Deftly balancing the pot in one hand, she opened the gate with the other, then shooed both me and the three dogs through the opening. We all obeyed with alacrity.

Just in front of us was the vegetable garden Davey had been working on two days earlier. Now all the ground was turned over and the soil had been raked into three tidy rows. I didn't see anything sprouting, however. I supposed it was too soon for that.

In the shade nearby, there was a slatted wooden bench with a contoured backrest and arms. I headed that way. Aunt Peg set the potted Viburnum down near the edge of the garden, then joined me on the bench. We took seats at either end, then half turned so we were facing each other.

Hope and Coral trotted off, probably looking for a squirrel to chase. Ebony had no desire to go racing around. She came and joined us in the shade.

I nodded toward the shrub. "Are you going to plant that in the vegetable garden?"

"Heavens, no." Aunt Peg looked bemused. "Honestly, sometimes I wonder where you even get your ideas. We'll have to table that mystery for the time being, however, since I'm sure you have more interesting things to share. I believe we were on the subject of Tasha Gilbert. Aside from selling you a plant, what did she have to say for herself?"

"I ran into Tasha by accident. I had no idea she worked for Ralph Denby at his garden center."

"Both Tasha's alternative employment and Ralph's garden center are news to me," Aunt Peg said. "So perhaps you should back up and start with Ralph. I assume he was the one you were there to see?"

"Yes. But it might make more sense if I back up even further."

"Be my guest. Now who?"

"Miranda Falk."

"Even better." Aunt Peg sounded delighted about this turn of events. "Miranda's a tough broad, and I mean that in the best possible way. Did she chew you up into little pieces and spit you out?"

"Pretty much." I gave her a dirty look. "You could have warned me about her ahead of time."

"Where's the fun in that?" She settled back in her seat and folded her arms over her chest. "Besides, you'd already met Miranda at Audrey's house. I figured you knew what you were getting into."

"You were right about her being eager to talk about Audrey."

"I'm right about many things," Aunt Peg said complacently.

Sadly, she was right about that too.

"According to Miranda, Audrey wasn't satisfied with simply breeding better Great Danes than most of her competitors, she also went out of her way to charm the judges."

"Audrey was a charming woman." Aunt Peg smiled.

"You're missing the point," I told her. "Then again, Audrey's wiles would have been lost on you."

"Because I don't judge Great Danes?"

"No. Because you're a woman. Apparently, Audrey liked to entertain out-of-town judges in their hotel rooms."

Aunt Peg looked momentarily nonplussed. "You're talking about sex."

"I am."

"Miranda told you that?" Her hand dropped down beside the bench to where Ebony was lying in the grass. Aunt
Peg began to scratch behind the Dane's ears. She always
concentrated better when she had her hands on a dog.
"Do you think she was telling the truth?"

"I don't see why not. Audrey's dead. What would be the
point of lying about it now?"

"Perhaps she meant to tarnish Audrey's reputation when
it's too late for her to fight back," she proposed.

"If you're going to question the veracity of what Miranda said, why did you bother sending me to talk to
her?" I asked practically. "She also mentioned that Ralph
Denby and Audrey's ex-husband were well acquainted
with each other."

Aunt Peg frowned. "Did we think they weren't?"

"I did. When you called Ralph as we were leaving Audrey's house, he spoke about Carter Ridley as if they'd
never met before."

She thought back. "Perhaps you're right."

"I am right," I told her. "Not only that, but the reason
they knew each other is because Audrey and Ralph were
involved with each other before she dumped him and married Carter. And Ralph still hasn't gotten over her."

"Ralph has a wife, though, doesn't he?" Aunt Peg appeared to be guessing about that. I knew how much it annoyed her not to be the most well-informed person in the
room. Or on the bench, as it were.

"He does," I said. "Her name is Nattie, and she doesn't
like dog shows."

She snorted under her breath. "I suppose that explains
why we haven't met."

"Miranda said it's just as well, because if Nattie came to

shows, she'd have seen her husband drooling over Audrey."

"Drooling? Really?"

"No, not really. I'm paraphrasing," I told her. "But I'm sure you get the gist. So having talked to Miranda, I decided I should spend some time with Ralph next."

"Good idea." Now Aunt Peg was leaning sideways over the arm of the bench. Another minute and she'd be inviting Ebony up onto the seat to join us.

"It was a good idea. Because Ralph admitted to the past relationship with Audrey. He as much as said he would still be with her if Audrey hadn't ended things between them. Ralph also mentioned that no one in the Great Dane club is particularly upset about Audrey's death."

"But those people were her friends." Aunt Peg was outraged by the thought.

"They were also her fellow exhibitors," I pointed out. "And if Audrey was skewing the competition in her favor, I can understand why they might not be too unhappy about her loss. Ralph brought up someone else in connection with Audrey, a man named Joe Wheeler, who also shows Danes."

"The name sounds vaguely familiar," Aunt Peg said. "Although I can't seem to picture him."

"Ralph said he sells real estate. Does that help?"

"Nope, not a bit. Seriously, Melanie, it's been *days* since the last time we spoke. Is that all you've accomplished in the meantime?"

Aunt Peg was always impatient for results. It had been *two days*. She made it sound as though it had been a month.

"You'll be happy to know that I've saved the most interesting information for last."

"Why would I be happy about that?" she grumbled. "You should have started with the good stuff. Then we could have ignored the rest altogether."

"Where's the fun in that?" I said, echoing her earlier question.

She narrowed her eyes and gave me a flinty glare, which didn't have the effect she might have hoped. Her displeasure has been directed at me so many times that by now I'm pretty much immune.

"Remember Tasha Gilbert and the plant?" I asked.

"Of course. My lovely Viburnum is sitting right over there. I could hardly have forgotten about it."

"Good. Because this next part is about Tasha."

Aunt Peg heaved a sigh. "It's about time."

"When I was leaving Ralph's garden center—"

"Something else you neglected to explain," she said under her breath.

Really? It was a garden center. The explanation was in the name.

I humored her anyway. "Ralph and Nattie are the proprietors of the Tokeneke Nursery and Garden Center in Darien. They sell plants and flowers. And maybe small trees. Nattie does consulting about landscape design. Do you need to know more? Because if so, I can pull up the website for you."

"That's sufficient to set the stage." Aunt Peg's hand, the one that wasn't playing with Ebony's ears, reached over and patted my arm. "Now was that so hard?"

"Not at all. Would you like to hear about Tasha now?"

"I've been waiting to hear about Tasha for at least twenty minutes," she said. "It's a good thing I'm a patient person."

I figured that went double for me.

"As I was saying, when I was leaving the nursery, I ran into Tasha. She works there part-time because she can't find enough dogsitting jobs to support herself. She was hired by Ralph on Audrey's recommendation."

"Please do move things along and get to the interesting part."

Right.

"Tasha told me that Audrey and her neighbor, Bill Godfrey, were having some sort of disagreement. And that Audrey was worried about intruders coming onto her property."

"*Intruders?*" Aunt Peg repeated the word. "How very odd."

"That's what I thought. Tasha also said Audrey would have been horrified by the idea of Bill being inside her house."

She stared at me. "But he had to go into her house. He's the one who found her body."

"I know that. Bill told us he knew where Audrey kept her spare key."

"That doesn't make sense," Aunt Peg said with a frown. "If Audrey didn't want Bill to have access to her house, why did she tell him where she hid her key? Did you ask Tasha that?"

"Unfortunately, I hardly had a chance to ask her anything, because we were interrupted by Ralph, who wasn't at all happy to find the two of us together."

"Because you were keeping Tasha from doing her job? Or because he was afraid she might tell you something he didn't want you to know?"

I shrugged. I'd wondered the same thing.

"So that's when I bought a plant," I said.

"Viburnum," Aunt Peg corrected me. "Now it seems to me that you need a pretext to go and visit Bill, the neighbor."

"I'm way ahead of you," I said.

"Really?" She didn't look convinced. "That never happens."

Actually, it does. Aunt Peg just refuses to acknowledge it.

"Every time I talk to someone from Audrey's circle of friends, the first thing they want to know is how Daisy's doing. Miranda, Ralph, and Tasha all checked up on her. So I figured I should extend the same consideration to Bill. Especially since he's the only non–dog owner who took one of Audrey's Danes home."

"That's right," Aunt Peg agreed. "Bill has Betty."

"A Great Dane is a whole lot of dog for someone who isn't used to having any dogs in his house. Now that Betty's been with him for a few days, it makes sense for me to stop in and make sure all is well."

"I think that's a splendid idea," Aunt Peg said.

"I thought you would."

We smiled at each other, in perfect accord for once.

Chapter 17

"Dad and I have an important job to do," Kevin announced the following morning.

Dressed in his summer uniform of cotton shorts and a superhero T-shirt, he came racing into Sam's and my bedroom. I was making the bed before going down to breakfast. Though Sam had put all the dogs out in the backyard ten minutes earlier, Bud was bounding along behind Kevin. Before I could grab the little dog, he scooted past me, jumped up on the bed, and grabbed a pillow in his mouth. I snatched him up before he could give it a vigorous shake.

"Does your job involve teaching Bud some manners?" I asked.

I disengaged dog and pillow and debated whether I needed to change the pillowcase. It didn't look too bad, only a little damp in one corner. I put Bud on the floor, then placed the pillow back on the bed.

"Nope!" Kevin shrieked happily. "It involves tractors."

"Tractors?" I turned back to Kev. "Where are you going?"

"Power Equipment Supply in Port Chester." Sam appeared around the corner. He'd gone down to his office to look something up online. Now I knew what.

"Never heard of it," I said.

"They sell tractors," Kevin told me. In case I'd missed the news the first time.

"So far, that's the only single thing I know about the place." I looked at Sam. "Are we buying a tractor?"

Considering the size of our backyard it seemed unlikely, but I've been surprised before.

"No, but I told Kevin he can check out all the riding equipment while I get some advice. They have a help desk." Sam paused. "I need help."

I'd seen that the garage was still littered with spare parts. But since Sam hadn't said anything, I'd tactfully decided not to ask. For all I knew, Kevin or Bud might have made off with some essential cog or gizmo. But now the issue sounded like something bigger.

"The YouTube tutorial didn't fix your lawn mower problem?"

"Actually I'm pretty sure it made it worse. I need to talk to a live human being."

"That's how I always feel," I said. "Live human beings are the best."

"No, tractors are the best," Kevin corrected me. He hadn't seemed to notice that Bud was chewing on his shoelaces. Hopefully, he and Sam would get moving before the little menace shredded them and I had to find a new pair.

"If you like, Kev and I can drop Davey off at Peg's on our way to Port Chester," Sam said.

"Sure, that would be great."

That would save me a trip and free up much of my morning. With two active sons, each with a number of varied interests, I didn't often get a reprieve from mom duties. I immediately knew what I wanted to do with this one.

My relationship with Faith has been a large part of my

life for the past decade. She'd come to me as an exuberant puppy, the first pet I'd ever owned. Before meeting her, I'd had no idea that a dog could be not just a companion but also a true friend in every sense of the word. Faith made me laugh and she made me mindful. Somehow, she intuited my thoughts even before they were clear to me. I loved her unequivocally, and I knew she returned the feeling.

Faith was older now. I knew in my heart that our remaining time together was limited, and I was determined not to take a single day for granted. Years earlier, when she was an only dog, Faith and I had enjoyed taking long walks at a nearby park. Waveny Park encompassed three hundred acres of open fields and wide, tree-lined trails. We would enter the woods and explore for hours. Now, having the unexpected opportunity to do so again felt like a rare gift.

"How about a ride in the car?" I asked Faith when breakfast was finished and the rest of my family had departed.

The big Poodle immediately stood up and trotted to my side. She was ready for anything as long as we were together. I selected a leash from the rack near the back door. When they saw that, the other dogs knew something was up. They crowded around my legs, waiting to see what would happen next.

"Biscuits for everyone!" I announced to a chorus of wagging tails. While the canine crew was munching happily, Faith and I made our escape.

Two minutes later, she and I were in the Volvo, coasting down the driveway. Accustomed to driving with Davey as copilot, I came to a full stop and looked both ways when I reached the road. It was empty aside from a single car that was heading leisurely in our direction. Since my son wasn't there to advise me to wait, I pulled out in front of the slow-moving sedan, then accelerated slightly to leave it behind.

"Just like Thelma and Louise," I said to Faith, who was sitting in the back seat. "You know, except without blowing stuff up."

The Poodle pricked her ears, then tipped her head to one side. She'd never been to the movies. So it wasn't surprising she didn't understand the reference.

"They were kind of wild and crazy," I explained. "But don't worry, we're going to have way more fun than they did."

Faith was still looking at me politely. As I glanced at her in the rear view mirror, I caught sight of the car behind me. It was the same dark sedan, now travelling faster too. It seemed that driver also intended to navigate the back roads route between North Stamford and New Canaan.

Ten minutes later, Faith and I turned in the long driveway that led to the Waveny mansion. Halfway up the winding lane, we turned off into a small lot near a trailhead. I parked the car, then hopped Faith out and attached her leash.

The blue sky was above us was dappled with fluffy clouds. The air felt fresh and smelled slightly of pine. A breeze snuck between the trees and ruffled the hair in Faith's topknot. We couldn't have picked a better day for an outing.

As I paused to lock the car, Faith tugged at the end of her leash. She knew where we were going and she couldn't wait to get started. I felt the same way.

"Excuse me." A man came strolling up behind me. "You're Melanie Travis, right?"

I turned around, surprised. Another car had pulled into the lot behind us, but I hadn't paid any attention to it. Summer was Waveny Park's busiest season. People came and went all the time.

"Yes, I am." The words were out of my mouth before I

even stopped to think. Or to look at him. When I did, my eyes widened.

The man was tall, broad shouldered, and muscular for his age, which was probably his mid-fifties. His hair was short and black, and his eyes were nearly as dark. The last time I'd seen him, his full-lipped mouth had been pursed in a nasty scowl. He was Carter Ridley, Audrey Kane's ex-husband.

He and I had never met, but the brief glimpse I'd had of him had left an indelible impression. One that wasn't the least bit favorable. I thought about the dark sedan that had been visible every so often in my rear view mirror, and didn't like the conclusion that led me to.

"You're Carter Ridley," I said.

His head dipped in a curt nod. I got the impression that he'd have preferred to make the introduction himself. Maybe he was wondering why I recognized him. I hoped he was worrying what I might already know about him.

I reeled Faith in close to my side. "Did you follow me here?"

"Yes." He didn't offer an explanation, merely an acknowledgment.

"Why?" Faith could sense my unease. I looped a finger through her collar and held on tight.

"You and I need to talk."

"*Here?*"

"I would have preferred somewhere else, but"—Carter gazed around—"here we are."

There were definitely questions I wanted to ask Audrey's former spouse. However this was neither how, nor where, I'd envisioned our meeting taking place. Faith and I were supposed to be focusing on our connection, not spending our time accommodating a burly ex-husband whose attitude was too aggressive for my taste.

On the other hand, at least we were in a public place. I

wouldn't have to be concerned for Faith's or my safety. Maybe it was better to just get the conversation over with.

I unthreaded my fingers from Faith's collar and felt some of the tension ease from her body. "What do you think?" I asked her. "Should we let him come on our walk with us?"

Faith gazed up at me and swished her tail. I took that as a yes.

"You're pulling my leg." Carter was standing much too close to me. "Am I supposed to believe you're actually asking that doodle's permission to talk to me?"

Earlier, I'd been annoyed by Carter Ridley. Now I was angry. When I rounded on him, he was smart enough to take a step back.

"In the first place, Faith is a Standard Poodle, not a doodle. And in the second, I was talking to her, not you. In case you hadn't noticed, you're the one who's intruding."

"That's no Poodle," he scoffed. "It's too big. It must be crossed with something."

"For Pete's sake," I said. "Audrey showed Great Danes for decades. Didn't you ever go to a dog show with her?"

"Sure. Sometimes." He didn't sound like it was something he'd enjoyed.

"And you never saw a Standard Poodle?"

Carter waved a hand dismissively. "Not one like that."

I wondered if he could really be that ignorant, or if he was just trying to push my buttons. Actually, it didn't matter which one it was. Either way, I didn't like him.

"I'm guessing Audrey divorced you because you're obnoxious," I said.

I expected him to snap back a retort. Instead, his mouth tipped up on one side, like maybe he thought I was just being silly. It occurred to me that if he had a better personality, Carter might be a handsome man.

"I'm the one who initiated the divorce," he replied. "And the reason is none of your business."

I heartily disagreed. And now I wanted to hear more. I cast a glance at Carter's thoroughly unsuitable attire: a pressed cotton shirt, pleated slacks, and soft leather loafers. The shoes were the best part. He was going to feel every rut and pebble on the dirt path.

"Faith and I are going to walk," I told him. "Feel free to join us if you want."

I didn't wait to see whether he was coming or not. Faith and I strode across the parking lot to the entrance of a wide, pine-needle-strewn trail. The way in front of us was free of other pedestrians, so I leaned down and unsnapped Faith's leash. She leapt away from me with a joyous bound.

"Hold up," Carter said.

I glanced back. His long stride was quickly eating up the distance between us. While we were still on the level macadam surface, he was full of pep. I was betting he wouldn't feel nearly so chipper after a mile or so on the trails.

"What's the deal with the dog?" he said as he fell into step beside me. "Aren't you afraid it'll run away?"

"No." There didn't seem to be much point in trying to educate him about obedience training. Instead I simply treated him to a smile. "Faith likes me."

Carter looked as if he was trying to decide whether I was having fun at his expense. I didn't feel the need to either confirm or deny. I just kept smiling.

"Funny thing about that," he said. "Not everyone feels the same way. I hear you've been asking questions about my wife's death."

So much for chitchat. Just like that, we were on to the main event.

"Ex-wife," I corrected.

"Semantics," he said.

Not exactly, I thought. More like a legal matter.

"Who told you what I've been doing?" I asked.

"More than one person."

Sure, I'd spoken to several people about Audrey's death. But I found it hard to believe that more than one of them might have reported that activity back to Carter. Actually, even one seemed like a stretch.

"Do you have a problem with that?" I asked.

"Yes, I do."

Abruptly he stopped walking. Maybe he thought I would do the same. But Faith was out ahead of us and still moving. Since I cared a good deal more about staying with her than with Carter, I kept going.

He heaved a sigh, then called out, "Hey, dog! Come back here and I'll give you a treat."

I spun around. "Did you just lie to my dog?"

Faith was sniffing the base of a tree. She lifted her head and looked to me for guidance. I beckoned to her, and she started back.

"Um, no."

"I think you did. Show me the treat." As if I would allow this odious man to feed Faith anything.

Carter dug his hand in the pocket of his pants and made a show of fishing around. A moment later, his hand came out empty.

"So you lied," I said as Faith came up beside me.

He grinned. "What's the matter? Can't you take a joke?"

There it was, the time-honored insult men liked to hurl at women when they'd been caught doing something stupid. I couldn't imagine what Audrey Kane had ever seen in this man.

"I can when it's funny," I said, striding back to him. "Is that your deal? Did you come out here today to be funny?"

"Nothing about this situation is funny," Carter said. "Audrey is dead, and for some reason you're mucking around in the investigation. I don't find that amusing at all. But I would like to know why."

There were a number of ways I could have answered that question, but I chose the easiest one. "Because Lara Minchin asked me to."

"She did not."

I shrugged. I couldn't be bothered to argue with him. "The morning that Audrey's body was found, you went racing to her house. Why?"

"Why do you think?" he sputtered. "I wanted to find out what happened."

"You seemed concerned that we might be removing something valuable from Audrey's property."

"No," he corrected me. "I was concerned because you and your merry band of dognappers *were* removing something valuable from her property. Ralph admitted as much to me, so don't bother trying to deny it."

"The only thing we took were Audrey's Great Danes," I told him. "And we only did that to ensure that they'd be safe and well cared for. Audrey's heir, whoever that may be, can retrieve the dogs whenever they want."

I added the last part in the hope that Carter might offer up a tidbit of information. Unfortunately, he didn't rise to the bait. Maybe he didn't know the contents of Audrey's will either.

"Audrey's dogs and Audrey's will have nothing to do with you," Carter growled. "You need to leave this alone. Do you understand?"

What I understood was that Carter Ridley was upset. Despite that, he hadn't managed to convince me that his displeasure should be allowed to impact my behavior. I couldn't resist goading him one more time.

"Audrey must have really loved you," I said.

For a moment Carter's expression softened. For the first

time he appeared interested in something I had to say. "How do you figure that?"

"Because she dumped Ralph to marry you. I wonder how you convinced her to do that."

"You don't know a single thing about it," Carter snapped.

Before I had a chance to agree, he turned on his heel and walked away.

Chapter 18

After Carter left, Faith and I finally had a chance to enjoy our walk.

Even with his disruptive presence gone, however, it still felt like the mood of the morning had shifted. Despite the soothing beauty of our surroundings, I couldn't seem to settle my thoughts.

Faith sensed my uneasiness. She stayed close to my side, determined to offer whatever comfort she could.

"I'm sorry," I said. I brushed my fingers through her topknot, then rubbed the tops of her ears. "You deserve better from me. This was supposed to be our time to be together."

Faith left me and trotted to the side of the path. She picked up a pine cone and brought it back. I took it from her gently, being careful not to prick her mouth with its spikey edges. As soon as I was holding it, Faith's head snapped up. She began to dance in place. I knew an invitation to play when I saw one.

"Doodle, indeed," I muttered. "That man was an idiot."

Faith barked an assent. Either that or a request for me to hurry up and toss the pine cone. It was hard to tell which.

"Yes, but is he a murderer?" I asked her. "That's the important question."

Faith didn't bother to offer an opinion about that. She wasn't interested in contemplation. She was still hoping I would join in her game.

"Okay, you win," I said. "But we can't play with a pine cone. You could hurt yourself with that."

I swapped out the pine cone for a short, thick stick that had a satisfying heft in my hands. Poodles are retrievers at heart. Before I'd even let the stick fly, Faith was already off and running.

She and I spent the next hour covering several miles of trails, jumping a log or two, chasing the occasional chipmunk, and thoroughly enjoying ourselves. By the time the sun was high in the sky, we'd finished our loop and returned to the parking lot. I was pleased to see that Carter's car was gone. I opened the thermos of cold water I'd brought with me and poured some in a bowl for Faith to drink.

"How about a trip to Ridgefield?" I asked when she was finished.

Faith seemed amenable to the idea. That was all the encouragement I needed. I had told Aunt Peg I would pay a visit to Bill Godfrey. Now, with Davey busy at her house, and Sam and Kevin occupied with power equipment, this seemed like a good time.

I didn't have Bill's address, but since I knew he was Audrey's neighbor, I figured his place couldn't be too hard to find. When we turned on the four-lane highway I'd taken to get to Audrey's house, I slowed the car and began to look. I passed the strip mall, then Audrey's driveway. Not far beyond that, there appeared to be a second driveway. This one was paved, but unmarked.

I turned in anyway and hoped it was the right place. I also hoped that Bill was home, considering that I hadn't called ahead. Since there were two reasons for my visit, however, it seemed to me that for Betty's sake, it might be better if I stopped by unannounced.

Faith stood up on the back seat as we coasted down the narrow lane. This driveway reminded me of Audrey's. It was long and flanked by trees on either side. Because of the dense foliage, I couldn't see houses in either direction, or really much of anything at all. There was nothing for me to do but keep driving.

When Bill's house finally came into view, I found myself looking at a home that was both compact and cozy looking. Much of the area around it had been left uncleared, and since the house itself was constructed of cedar and glass, it blended into the surrounding woods as seamlessly as if it was part of them.

To my surprise, the door to the house was already open before I reached the end of the driveway. Backlit by large windows behind him, Bill was standing in the opening. He was dressed in faded jeans and barefoot, leaning against the doorframe with his arms crossed over his chest. As I parked in front of the house, Betty showed up in the doorway beside him.

"You must be lost," Bill said. His tone wasn't particularly friendly.

I opened the car door and got out. "No, I don't think so. Although I do apologize for showing up without calling first."

He squinted at me through his wire-rimmed glasses. "We've met," he said. "Your name's Melanie, right?"

I still hadn't made a move toward him, but I nodded.

"You were part of that Peg woman's contingent. All those dog people."

"Yes, I was."

"I guess that's okay then." Bill straightened, and his shoulders relaxed. "Living out here in the woods by myself, I need to be careful about security. I wasn't expecting to see anyone today, so when the buzzer went off, it gave me quite a start."

"The buzzer?"

"I have a driveway sensor. Before you were even half-way down the road, I knew someone was coming. At my age, a person can't be too careful."

"You're right," I agreed. "And again, I apologize for just showing up. I thought I'd stop by and see how you and Betty are getting along with each other. You know, make sure everything is okay."

Bill looked down at the brindle Dane fondly. "She and I are doing just fine. Betty's as big as half a horse, but she's the easiest dog I've ever lived with. There's no silly yapping or racing around the house. She has wonderful manners. I guess Audrey made sure of that."

His gaze lifted to me, still standing beside the Volvo. "So are you coming inside, or what? Now that you've taken the time to come all this way, the least I can do is offer you a cup of coffee."

"That would be great," I said. "But I have my Poodle with me in the car. In this weather, I'd rather not leave her outside. Is it all right if she comes too? I promise she won't yap or race around your house either."

Bill smiled. "I'm glad to hear that, but the answer's not up to me. This place is Betty's home now. If she doesn't mind having another dog drop by, I'm not going to stand in the way."

"Thanks. I appreciate that." It sounded as though Bill and Betty were doing better than just getting along. She'd become part of his family. I hoped he hadn't forgotten that at some point he might have to give her up. "Can Betty come outside for a minute so she and Faith can meet each other on neutral ground?"

"I don't see why not. Go on girl, shoo." Bill braced his hands on the Dane's rump, then nudged her out through the doorway. "You're about to make a new friend."

I opened the back door to the Volvo and Faith hopped out. She was both well socialized and naturally friendly. She'd also already had her eyes on Betty through the window. When the Dane came toward her, Faith advanced as well.

The two dogs met in the middle. They touched noses and took each other's measure. At the same time, both tails lifted. Then Faith stuck her muzzle under Betty's ear and blew out a breath. The brindle Dane reared up in surprise, then landed running. Faith quickly took off after her.

Bill and I stood and watched the dogs circle the driveway. Betty had a longer stride, but Faith was more agile. The two of them leapt in the air, skidded around the turns, and happily bounced off each other. It looked as though their friendship was already settled.

"That works for me," I said. "Faith's pretty easy. She gets along with everyone."

"Same for Betty, as far as I've been able to tell," Bill replied. "Now how about that coffee?"

Betty and Faith were happy to follow us into the house. While Bill closed the door behind us, I let my gaze sweep around an oversized room with a high ceiling and second story lofts on either side. The back wall of the house was almost entirely glass. And the view—looking out through the leafy trees to a pond in the distance—was spectacular.

"Wow," I said on an exhale. The single word seemed inadequate to convey my appreciation.

"Thank you." Bill nodded. "Kitchen's this way. Follow me."

"You house is amazing. Who designed it?"

"I did. Had it built to spec more than thirty years ago."

Wow again, I thought. No wonder he'd thanked me for the compliment.

"You're very talented."

"I know," he replied, then laughed. "Sorry. I shouldn't have said that. But it's true. I was an architect by trade. I bought this place as nothing but a plot of raw land, so I'm responsible for all of it."

"You've done a terrific job," I told him.

Bill's kitchen looked like a relic from the 1980s, but there was a modern coffeemaker on the counter. He brewed two cups, then poured them into a pair of clear glass mugs. I added milk to mine. Bill took his coffee black.

"There's a deck out back," he said. "It's shaded so it stays cool even in summer. I hate to waste a nice day by sitting indoors. Is that all right with you?"

"Absolutely."

Before we went outside, Bill opened a drawer and took out two big bones. He nodded toward the dogs. "Is Faith allowed? They're all natural and preservative free. It'll keep those two busy while we sit and chat."

"Sure," I agreed.

I followed him out the back door with a dog on either side of me. Faith was delighted with both the bone and her new friend. Betty looked as though she felt the same way. The dogs quickly lay down side by side and got to work.

"I'm guessing it was Peg who sent you here," Bill said after we'd taken seats in a pair of Adirondack chairs that sat facing each other on the raised deck.

"Why would you say that?"

"Because that's a take-charge woman if ever I saw one."

I'd started to take a sip of my coffee and choked on a laugh.

"If she wasn't asking questions, she was ordering people around. And everybody leapt to do her bidding. I figured she had to be the head honcho of that Great Dane club you all belong to."

It was easy to understand how he'd gotten that impression. "Actually, Aunt Peg has Standard Poodles, not Great Danes. But she's also a dog show judge, so she knew some of those people from the shows."

"I know Audrey was into all that stuff. She talked about it a lot," Bill said. "She tried a few times, but thankfully never managed to drag me to a dog show. Now that I'm retired, I'm more into fly fishing."

I glanced down at Faith. She was still happily occupied. "Even without a shared interest, it sounds as though you and she must have been good friends."

"We were. Audrey and I had known each other for a long time, since before I started building this house. Where we're sitting now was originally part of a very large tract of land owned by her family. Around the time I was looking to settle down, they'd started selling some of the property off in ten-acre parcels."

Bill sighed. "As I'm sure you probably noticed on your way here, most of those parcels have since been resold and subdivided virtually into extinction. The only two remaining ten-acre lots are her place and mine."

"That seems like a shame," I said.

"It does to me too, but I guess you can't fight progress. As a builder myself, I've seen it happen time and again. Population growth in these metro-suburban areas is gobbling up all the open land, and nobody ever stops to think about the fact that land isn't a renewable resource."

My coffee was dark and rich, and tasted delicious. Trying to make it last, I took another small sip. It was time for me to redirect the conversation. "It must have been terrible for you, finding Audrey's body like that."

"Terrible is too mild a word for what I was feeling," Bill replied. "It was like something you see on TV but think will never happen to you. I think maybe I went into shock a little bit. I'm just glad I had the presence of mind to make the phone calls I needed to, to get help."

"What did you do after you made the calls?" I asked.

He hung his head and clasped his hands in his lap, as if even thinking back to that day was painful. "I think I looked around for something, maybe a blanket, to lay over Audrey's body. Then it occurred to me that maybe I wasn't supposed to touch anything."

"It sounds as though you already suspected foul play," I said quietly.

"To tell you the truth, I'm not sure what I thought." Bill stopped and cleared this throat. "At first, I didn't believe what I was seeing. Like, surely it couldn't be true. I half-expected Audrey to pop up off the floor and yell, 'Gotcha!' The whole situation was just that surreal."

"After experiencing a shock like that, I can understand why you'd be concerned about security at your own house."

Bill took a drink, then set his mug down on the arm of his chair. "The security measures I have here predate what happened to Audrey by a long time. In fact, at one point I tried to convince her to get a similar system for her place, but she wasn't interested."

"That must have been a while ago," I mentioned. "Because recently Audrey had expressed concern about intruders coming onto her property. She'd gone so far as to advise her dogsitter to be on the alert, and to contact the police if necessary."

Bill abruptly went still. "Is that so? I had no idea about any of that."

"Maybe she didn't mention it to you because of the disagreement you'd been having?"

His eyes narrowed. "What disagreement is that?"

I shrugged, which seemed like a better idea than admitting I didn't know the answer to his question.

"You know what? It's hard when your entire neighborhood consists of just two houses. When each of you is the only person the other one has to rely on, inevitably, sometimes you might butt heads. But Audrey's and my relationship went way back and it was solid. I don't know where you heard anything about a disagreement. She and I were engaged in friendly discussion, that's all it was."

"What was it about?" I asked.

Abruptly Bill stood up. "You're asking a lot of imperti-

nent questions for someone who supposedly just stopped
by to check on Betty's welfare."

The Dane was now snoozing on the deck. "You can see
for yourself how happy she is. So you can report back to
Peg, or whoever it was that sent you, and tell them I'm
doing right by her."

"I'll be sure to do that," I said. When I snapped my fingers, Faith stood up. She left the bone behind. "I'm sorry if
our conversation upset you. That wasn't my intent."

"It wasn't the conversation that bothered me," Bill
replied. "I've been upset since Audrey died, and I doubt I'll
be getting over it any time soon. Now, if you don't mind,
it's time for me to show you out."

Chapter 19

Saturday, we had another dog show planned. That morning, we woke up to overcast skies and driving rain. Poodles, with their elaborate, hairsprayed trim, are no fun to show in wet weather, so it was lucky that Sam didn't have Plum entered. Instead, Aunt Peg would be judging the breeds in the Toy Group and we were attending as spectators.

"I don't need a raincoat," Kevin announced when we were getting ready to leave.

We were in the front hall, all trying to get our rain gear out of the closet at once. The Poodles and Bud were milling around our legs and making sure they were in our way. The dogs knew we were preparing to go out. This was their way of trying to invite themselves along.

Daisy was in the living room, observing the activity from afar. Having come to our house from a kennel situation, she often seemed baffled by the amount of commotion my family generated on a daily basis. I couldn't blame her. I often felt the same way.

"Why not?" I asked Kevin.

"I like being wet. It's like swimming standing up."

"And in your clothes." Davey laughed. He already had a slicker draped over his arm.

"How about a pair of rubbers?" Sam asked. "The grass is going to be wet. I can slip them on over your sneakers."

"No rubbers either." Kevin crossed his arms over his small chest. That, coupled with the mutinous expression on his face, made him look like a baby dictator.

"Your choice," I told him. "I was going to take you to see some Great Danes. But if you don't have any rain gear on, I guess you'll just have to stay in one place."

Kev considered his options. "Under the grooming tent with Terry?" he asked. He liked Terry.

"Good luck with that." Davey ruffled his brother's hair. "Terry's on the run all day when he's at a dog show. He won't have time to babysit you."

"Good." Kevin jutted out his lower lip. "Because I'm not a baby."

"Time's passing," Sam mentioned, tapping a finger on his watch. "How about if we set aside this discussion for now and just throw all the gear in the back of the car. We can sort out the rest when we get there."

"Good idea," I agreed. I was anxious to get on the road too.

Aunt Peg's first breed was scheduled to start at eight a.m., and I knew she'd be on time. Aunt Peg ran her ring with the precision that a Swiss clockmaker would envy.

Sam tucked Plum inside a crate to protect her hair. Davey hustled Kevin out to the SUV. Last one out the door, I handed out peanut butter biscuits to the remainder of pack, who accepted this lesser boon with good grace. Bud raced under the couch to enjoy his biscuit. The other dogs were finding spots on the furniture to await our return when I left.

The dog show was half an hour away. Rain was coming down steadily when we left home, and the weather grew worse during the trip. On a nice day, the polo field where the show was being held would have been a lovely venue. That day, the parking lot was a sea of mud, and the grass beneath the show rings wasn't much better. A brisk breeze was snapping the tops of the tents and threatening to pull their stakes from the ground.

Exhibitors are known for their perseverance, but it was clear that most of the spectators had chosen to stay home. The parking lot was only half full, and Sam was able to find a spot that was just a short walk away the handlers' tent. Even so, we were going to get soaked as soon as we got out of the SUV. Davey took a hard look out the window, then grabbed Kevin's rain gear from behind their seat and started to put it on him.

Kevin, who thought he'd already made his point, began to argue.

"It looks like a typhoon out there," Davey said. "And I'm not going to carry you around the showground."

"Me either." I looked back over my shoulder.

"Dad?" Kev asked plaintively.

"Nope. Sorry."

We were all nonplussed by the conditions. We'd planned for a rainy day, but this relentless downpour was well beyond our expectations.

"Fine." Kevin punched his arms through the sleeves of his slicker while Davey slipped the rubbers over his brother's shoes. I wished we'd thought to bring boots with us. And maybe full-body rubber suits.

"Everybody ready?" Sam asked.

The plan called for us to jump out of the car and run toward the tent at the same time. We'd probably look ridiculous, but no more so than everyone else on the grounds who'd probably done the same thing. At least we didn't have any equipment to unload.

"Davey, you hold Kevin's hand," I said. "I don't want him to blow away."

Kev's eyes widened. "Like for real?"

"It could happen," Davey told him with a grin. "You don't even weigh as much as Augie."

"I don't?"

"Not even close," Sam said. "And it would take three of you to outweigh Daisy."

That did the trick. When Davey opened his door, Kevin's small hand was firmly clasped inside his brother's bigger one. We all made a mad dash for the tent. My shoes slid on the wet grass. Water splashed up my legs. I could feel the rain pelting down through the hood of the slicker I'd pulled up over my head.

Together, we scooted beneath the roof of the tent. When I was far enough inside to reach a relatively dry spot, I stopped and shook out like a wet dog. Rivulets of water were running down the side of my face and clinging to my eyelashes. It took a moment for my vision to clear. When it did, I saw that a nearby setup had two Standard Poodles and three Minis out on tabletops. I knew that entries in the three varieties of Poodles weren't large. Those were probably Crawford's dogs.

My guess was confirmed a moment later when Terry popped out from behind a black male Standard with a massive coat. I nearly laughed at his sudden appearance. Judging by the sour expression on his face, that would have been a terrible idea.

I'd never known Terry to look anything less than impeccable. Until today. Now his blond curls were plastered to the sides of his head and the front of his shirt clung to him like a damp rag. A raincoat, dripping water, was draped over a crate behind him. His duck shoes squelched as he came around to our side of the table.

His gaze skimmed over us incredulously. "Welcome to the ninth circle of hell. I'm being paid to be here. What's your excuse?"

"Aunt Peg is judging," I said.

"Well, sure." A bead of water slid down his nose. Terry grimaced and shook it off. "But that doesn't mean you guys have to suffer."

"Suffer?" Davey said with a grin. "Are you talking about the weather or the judging?"

"Bite your tongue, young man." Terry cast a quick look behind him as if he was afraid that Aunt Peg, who was at least hundred feet away in her show ring, might overhear.

"In our defense, we didn't think it was going to be this bad," Sam told him.

"I did," Kevin piped up. "I like being wet."

Terry leaned down so he could look Kev in the eye. "Then it's a shame you can't act as Crawford's assistant for the day. Because *I* like being dry. Preferably with my feet in the sand and a mai tai in my hand."

"What's a mai tai?" Davey asked.

Terry straightened again. He mimed tossing a drink down his throat. "It's something you'll discover one night at a frat party, decide you've found the nectar of the gods, wildly over-indulge in, then spend the next day wishing you were dead. Not that I'm speaking from personal experience, mind you."

"Of course not," Davey said. He even managed to keep a straight face.

"Where's Crawford?" I asked.

"Up at the ring with a Chinese Crested. Thankfully, something small enough to tuck beneath his coat. I'd imagine he'll be back soon."

"Don't you need to get back to work?" Sam asked Terry.

The Poodles on the tabletops behind Crawford's assistant were in various stages of preparation. One of the Standards had been sprayed up, the second one hadn't. Only two of the Minis had their topknots in. All three had ears that were still wrapped.

"Sure," Terry said. "As if it will make a difference in this weather. No matter how good a job I do here, they're all going to look like drowned rats by the time the judge sees them in the ring."

"Your competitors' dogs will look equally bad," I pointed out.

"That's hardly an incentive to do better." Terry glanced upward. A small tear had opened up in the roof of the tent. Now we were standing under a new drip. "And that's just perfect."

Four of us stepped to one side. Kevin remained where he was. One way or another, he was determined to get wet.

"We came to watch Peg judge," Sam said to Terry, "but frankly, now that we're under the tent, I'm not feeling particularly motivated to brave the monsoon again to get to her ring. That being the case, how would you like an extra pair of hands?"

If the offer had come from me, Terry would have rejected it politely but firmly. But Sam? He did the kind of quality work that would make both Terry and Crawford look good.

"I can put up that other topknot and brush out ears," Davey offered.

"You're hired," Terry said, his mood brightening. "Both of you."

"What about me?" Kevin asked. "I can help too."

"No way," Davey told him. "You're with Mom."

Kevin looked so disappointed that Terry had to quickly tamp down a laugh. Even Sam looked amused, and he was supposed to be on my side.

"Thanks a lot," I said. "You don't have to make it sound like a punishment."

"Yeah, right," Kev muttered.

"And you, mister." I dropped down to his level. "You're much too young to be talking back like a teenager."

"No, I'm not," he said, totally missing the point. "I can do anything Davey can do."

"Wait a minute." Davey had started toward Crawford's setup. He stopped and turned back. "That's not right."

"Says who?" I asked him. "You're the one who started this."

Davey was a quick thinker. It was one of the things I loved best about him. He did a rapid about-face.

"Lucky you," he said to Kev. "You get to go exploring with Mom while I'm stuck here working. I bet you'll see amazing things."

"Like what?"

Davey directed his gaze to me for help.

"Great Danes," I said. "Maybe even ones that are bigger than Daisy. I'm sure we can find one or two around here. Let's take a walk and see. Then later, we'll all go over to the rings and watch the judging."

"Yay for Great Danes!" Kevin cried. He held out his hand. I took it in mine and we set out together.

Poodles weren't the only ones with a small entry. Only a few Danes were entered as well. I hoped the weather hadn't caused too many of them to cancel. Nevertheless, if there was a Great Dane on the showground, I intended to find it. And if my search turned up more of Audrey's friends for me to talk to, that would be even better.

Grooming tents are usually packed with exhibitors and dogs, but this one was ridiculous. Due to the heavy rain, no one was able to set up an ex-pen, groom an entry, or even hold a conversation outside the tent. It appeared that everyone who wasn't currently in a show ring was right here, wedged in tight, and hoping to stay dry.

"This is a lot of people," Kevin said, pressing himself to my side.

"I know. Just don't let go of my hand, okay?"

He nodded and took a firmer grip.

Sometimes I had to pick him up just so we could pass through a narrow aisle that was clogged with equipment. There were dogs everywhere I looked. They were standing on tabletops, lying down inside stacked crates, and even resting in their owners' arms.

Except for Great Danes. So far, I hadn't seen a single one.

Just when I was about to give up, I heard someone call my name. "Melanie, over here!"

"Look!" Kevin's face was suddenly flush with excitement. He rose up on his toes and pointed. "That lady knows who you are."

"That lady" was Lara Minchin. Now that she'd spotted us, she was waving her hand above her head to make sure I didn't miss her.

"We'll be right there," I called. The expanse between us was solidly packed with setups. "As soon as I figure out how to get to you."

It took a few minutes of scrambling before Kevin and I were able to make our way to Lara's location. The area she had staked out had just enough room for a large wire crate with Milo inside, Lara's lawn chair squeezed in beside it, and the tiny patch of grass on which I was standing.

I introduced Kevin, who immediately dropped to the ground in front of the Great Dane's crate. Lara reached over and opened the door so Kevin and Milo could interact without the wire barrier between them.

"Don't worry," she said to me. "Milo love kids. He wouldn't hurt a fly."

"That's not the problem. Kevin is totally obsessed with Great Danes. I'm more worried he'll want to take Milo home with us."

Lara just laughed. Maybe she thought I was kidding.

"This place is a madhouse," I said, my back up against a tower of stacked crates.

"I know. I'm hoping it'll start to clear out before too long. In this weather, I can't imagine that anyone will want to hang around after their breed judging is over."

"When do Danes go in the ring?"

"Already done," she informed me. "About an hour ago. Now we're just waiting for the group."

Unlike the dog show where Lara and I had first met, she and Milo must have won the breed today. That was a nice accomplishment.

"Congratulations," I said.

"Thank you, although it didn't take much. Two class dogs were entered and only one showed up. Then Milo was the only special." Lara shrugged. "A win is always a good thing, so of course I'm happy to have it. But in reality, it feels as though we got a free pass into the Working Group."

"And now it's your job to make the most of it," I said.

"I intend to," she replied. "I'm glad we ran into each other. I've been wondering how your investigation is progressing. I hope you have some updates for me."

I glanced down to check on Kevin. He was utterly absorbed with the fawn Great Dane. Neither of them were paying any attention to our conversation.

"It's going slowly," I admitted. "I've been talking to people who were connected to Audrey and gathering information. But I also have some questions for you."

"For me?" Lara attempted to look surprised. She couldn't quite pull it off. "I have nothing new to say. I'm quite certain I told you everything I could the last time we spoke."

Nice try, I thought. I didn't believe that lie any more than she did.

Chapter 20

Lara's choice of words was revealing. Telling me everything she *could* wasn't nearly the same as telling me everything she knew. Or even everything I needed to know in order to do the job she'd asked me to do.

Still, there was no point in getting her guard up just yet. "I understand. But there are a few more things I think we need to discuss."

"Like what?"

"Audrey's will, for one. Last time we spoke, you didn't seem to know much about it. Has that changed in the meantime? It would be helpful for me to know who Audrey's heirs are. And whether she made any bequests that might be valuable enough for to kill for."

"I don't know anything about that," Lara said firmly. "The only time Audrey and I ever discussed her will was when she said something about her jewelry. Even then, I thought she was pulling my leg. Knowing Audrey, I wouldn't be surprised if she didn't have a will at all."

That made no sense to me. From what I could tell, Audrey had possessed a substantial amount of property. I couldn't imagine she wouldn't have protected her financial interests—and seen to the safe dispersal of her beloved Danes.

"Why would you say that?"

"Because I'm sure Audrey thought she was going to live forever. She'd always gotten everything she ever wanted. Why should that change just because she was growing older?"

Sadly, the resentment Lara felt toward her stepsister hadn't diminished after Audrey's death. If anything, it seemed to be intensifying.

"What do you know about Audrey and Ralph's relationship?" I asked.

"Ralph?" Lara repeated. "Ralph Denby?"

"Yes."

"They were fellow competitors. And probably friends too, I suppose."

"I heard they were more than that," I said.

"Really? That's news to me."

I sighed. "You're the one who asked me to look into Audrey's murder. Yet every time I ask you about anything relating to your sister, you plead ignorance."

"No, I don't," Lara snapped. "I'm almost certain I told you that Audrey was an entitled bitch."

"That's not helpful."

"What's also not helpful is you giving me the impression that you're trying to pin the deed on me," she retorted.

"I'm asking questions of everyone, not just you," I said. "And now that I've learned a few things, it would be useful to hear your opinions. Especially since you probably know most of the people I've been speaking with."

Lara looked down at Kevin and Milo as if she was hoping one of them would give her an excuse to halt the conversation. Neither one cooperated. Boy and dog were still happily engaged with each other.

"Ralph's a nice guy. At least that's what he wants everyone to think," she said with a shrug. "If he has a hidden dark side, I'm not aware of it."

"What about his wife, Nattie?"

"I know nothing about Nattie beyond having seen her

at a show or two. I'm not sure we've even ever said hello to each other. The woman's fashion sense is deplorable, and she hangs on her husband's arm like she's afraid he might run away when she's not looking. There." Lara glared up at me. "Does that help?"

Actually, it did since it confirmed what Miranda had told me. As for the glare, I wasn't about to be intimidated. Now that I'd finally gotten Lara talking, I intended to learn all I could.

"What about Audrey's ex-husband? He's a man who seems like he might have a dark side."

"Carter? Why would you say that?"

"For one thing, he tried to stop us from removing Audrey's Great Danes from her house. For another, he followed me in his car, then waylaid me at a public park to yell at me for asking questions about Audrey's death."

If I had been hoping for Lara to be outraged on my behalf, I would have been disappointed. Instead she looked amused.

"That's Carter for you. Always jumping in with both feet, without stopping to consider how deep the water might be."

"I'm guessing you mean he's impetuous," I said. "But that doesn't explain why he's so ticked off at me."

Lara's fingers were picking at a loose thread on her skirt. If she kept it up for much longer, the seam was going to open up. "Carter has a short fuse—and a notable lack of patience. When something annoys him, he reacts. But his bark is worse than his bite. He didn't threaten you, did he?"

"Not exactly. But let's just say, he did plenty of barking."

"Yes, I can see that." Lara chuckled at the thought.

Kevin looked up and laughed too. He enjoyed a good joke, even when he didn't know what it was about.

"Everything okay down there?" I asked him.

"All good," he replied. If he got any closer to Milo, he

would be inside the Dane's crate. But Milo certainly looked as though he was enjoying the attention.

"Why did Audrey and Carter get divorced?" I asked.

"That's one's easy. Audrey cheated on him and Carter found out."

There was something—a fleeting look in her eyes—there so briefly that I nearly missed it. Lara looked smug. No, make that satisfied. I knew what my next question had to be.

"How did Carter find out about it?"

"How do you think? Audrey got careless." Lara smirked at me. "If you're juggling more than one man at a time, you really need to keep your stories straight."

"Good advice," I said. Too bad it had been delivered with such an air of righteousness. "What about Bill Godfrey?"

"The next-door neighbor?"

"Yes. I heard that he and Audrey were involved in some kind of dispute."

"Sorry. Can't help you there. If Audrey had a problem with him, she never mentioned it to me."

Lara's answers came shooting back so quickly they almost sounded rehearsed. I understood why there might be holes in her knowledge about Audrey's adult life. Even so, I was sure Lara knew more than she was saying.

"One last question," I said.

"Thank God," she muttered.

"Considering your lack of a relationship with Audrey—I believe 'estranged' was the word you used . . ."

Lara nodded. She looked at me warily.

"Where does your information about her life come from?"

She stood up and straightened her skirt. The loose thread was still hanging. "Just because I was angry at Audrey didn't mean I wasn't curious. The life she led . . . all those things she had? They could have been mine. I could even argue that they *should* have been mine. So yes, I kept tabs over the years."

Lara glared at me again. This time, she was daring me to object. I said nothing.

"And every time Audrey failed at something—like her marriage—I gloated a little. But after the way she and her mother treated me, I figured that was the least I deserved. You know?"

Kevin and I found Sam and Davey outside the Poodle ring watching Crawford show his Miniature Poodles. Davey had his hand cupped around the muzzle of Crawford's blue Standard dog, who'd been moved up to the variety competition after finishing his championship the week before. He'd already been awarded Best of Variety. I checked out the action in the ring. From the looks of things, Crawford was about to win the Mini BOV too.

I left Kevin with Sam and went over to stand beside Terry. "Crawford's on a roll," I said as the judge sent the Minis around the ring another time.

"Oh, please. Crawford's always on a roll."

Terry was holding both their class Minis up off the wet ground, cradling one in each arm. Something must have gone wrong earlier, because neither of the two Minis had won in the classes. Otherwise, they'd have also been in the ring for the variety judging.

"Is that so?" I said, gazing pointedly at the losing pair.

Terry huffed. "Sadly, even Crawford can't control every variable."

"What happened?"

He nodded toward the white Mini in his left arm. "Miss Dainty Toes here refused to move in the wet grass. Stacked like a star on the table, then threw a hissy fit on the ground when she was asked to gait around the ring."

"And the other dog?"

"That was just your basic confluence of crap."

Terry sounded so disgusted I couldn't help but smile. "Go on."

"The judge was examining Titus on the table and somehow his watch got caught up in the dog's ear hair. The judge didn't realize what had happened until he'd given the ear quite a yank. Titus yelped and whipped his head around. He didn't snap, mind you."

Terry was very firm about that. According to AKC regulations, a dog who tried to bite the judge was automatically dismissed from the ring.

"But with that quick move, Titus looked like he was thinking about it." Terry frowned. "Even though there was a good reason for his reaction, the damage was done. Half the ringside saw what looked like poor Titus trying to nip the judge's hand. The judge apologized for what he had to do, then excused the dog from the ring."

"That doesn't sound fair." I reached over to give Titus a scratch beneath his chin.

"No, but there's nothing we can do about it. There's fair, and then there are the rules. Sometimes it just isn't our day. So what's this I hear about you getting a Great Dane?"

"Not to keep," I said quickly. "Just to foster for a few weeks."

"So you say. But according to Davey, Kevin doesn't know that."

"He knows it," I grumbled. "He just refuses to accept it."

"So that makes how many dogs in your house now?" Terry grinned, his good mood restored. "You may feel free to count the Great Dane as two."

I poked him in the side, and he winced. "In that case, the total is eight, counting Daisy."

"Daisy. Not the name I'd have picked for a dignified Dane. Who would have guessed that Audrey Kane had a sense of humor?"

I looked over at him. "You knew her?"

"Not personally." His eyebrows waggled suggestively. "If you know what I mean."

"Pretend I don't, and explain it to me," I said.

"Crawford doesn't show any working dogs, so it's not like we'd have crossed paths with her in the ring."

I nodded. That much I knew.

"But people talk. And this is a dog show, so everyone gets in everyone else's business. Audrey had a bit of a reputation."

"Don't make me drag this out of you." I threatened to poke him again. "I know you love to gossip, so just spill it. What kind of reputation?"

"Now you're spoiling my fun."

In the ring, the judge was motioning Crawford's Mini special over to the Best of Variety marker. Since I hadn't been watching the class, I had no idea if the dog was a worthy winner, or if this was the judge's way of atoning for the unfortunate incident earlier. Either way, Crawford was about to emerge from the ring and then Terry would be moving along.

"Audrey was known for two things," he said hastily. He knew time was running out too. "Really nice Danes . . . and . . . how can I put this nicely?"

"I don't need nice. Just tell me."

Crawford was already heading our way.

"She liked to seduce men. She enjoyed having that kind of power over them. Audrey had no qualms about using people to get what she wanted, then discarding them when she was done. I'm as open-minded as the next guy, but that kind of behavior didn't win her a lot of friends in the dog fancy. Especially since she was using it to get ahead in the show ring."

What he'd told me wasn't news. Though I was surprised to learn that Audrey's exploits had been public knowledge, not just in Danes, but also across the broader dog show community.

I wondered if Aunt Peg had been aware of Audrey's reputation. Possibly not. Exhibitors tended to be on their best behavior around her, especially those who might end up showing a dog in her ring.

I didn't have a chance to ask Terry anything else, because Crawford was already upon us. He and Terry would be needed back at the grooming tent. Luckily, in the time we'd been at the rings, the rain had begun to slack off. Now it was more of an ominous drizzle than a full-out downpour.

"Enough chitchat you two," Crawford said. Although he'd won both the Miniature and Standard Best of Varieties, he didn't look happy about the day's outcome. I imagined he wasn't looking forward to explaining what had happened with his dog entry to the Mini's owner. "Hood up, Terry. Time to move along."

Since Terry had both his arms full, I lifted the hood of his slicker and slipped it over his head. "Thanks. Say hi to Peg for us."

"Will do. In this weather, I'm sure she's having a blast."

He stopped and stared at me. "What?"

"You know Aunt Peg, she's a contrarian. She thinks adversity brings out the best in people. And their dogs."

"Hunh. Maybe she should stop by the grooming tent and try telling that to Crawford."

"Terry!" Crawford called as he strode away. "Less mouth, more feet. Don't make me dock your pay."

"No sir!" Terry hurried to catch up.

Davey, who still had Crawford's Standard winner, fell in behind him. That left Sam, Kevin, and me to make our way to Aunt Peg's ring. The tent-covered aisle between the parallel rows of rings was still thronged with people and dogs. The crowding made it feel both overly warm and much too close. As he was walking, Kev shrugged out of his slicker. I grabbed it before it could hit the ground and hung it over my arm.

"There you are. Finally!" Aunt Peg called out as we approached her ring. She had just finished handing out the ribbons for Best of Breed in Affenpinschers. Now there was a momentary lull while the steward called the first class in the next toy breed into the ring. "I've been judging for hours. You missed seeing some truly lovely dogs. I hope you have a good excuse for your tardiness. And it had better not be weather related. Isn't this glorious?"

"Glorious," Sam agreed. He and Aunt Peg were usually on the same page about things, but this time his acquiescence seemed like a stretch.

"It's doable," I said.

"Don't be such a spoilsport." Aunt Peg was having none of it. "There's nothing the matter with a little rain."

"Says the woman encased in plastic from head to toe."

"I could have been a Boy Scout." She beamed happily. "I'm always prepared." She turned to her ring steward. "Where are my Pekes?"

"Coming right up," he told her.

"Glorious?" I said to Sam, when Aunt Peg had turned her attention back to the ring. "Really?"

"Really," Kevin answered for him. Now that he'd taken off his slicker, he'd somehow managed to get soaked from head to toe. Maybe he'd been rolling in the wet grass while I wasn't looking. "Today is perfect."

Chapter 21

Sunday was a relaxing beach day for the whole family. So when I dropped Davey off at Aunt Peg's house on Monday morning, I was well rested and had a hint of sunburn on my nose. I was also motivated to get back to work.

In the week that had passed since Audrey's murder, the media had been mostly silent concerning the police investigation. Though I'd worked with the police on occasion, my contacts were local and Ridgefield was beyond their jurisdiction. I knew I needed more information, enough to hone my suspicions into something tangible, before asking for an out-of-town referral. Which meant that I still had much to do.

Picturesque Wilton is another residential community in central Fairfield County. The town center wasn't large, but it offered an interesting selection of shops and small businesses, including Parker/Dunn Real Estate. According to Ralph Denby, that was where I would find Audrey's frequent competitor and sometime antagonist, Joe Wheeler.

Late morning, the downtown area was crowded with shoppers, and I had to park two blocks away. It was a pleasant stroll back to the attractive midsize building whose front windows featured multiple pictures of homes for sale in the area. Everyone in Fairfield Country is obsessed with real estate, and I was briefly tempted to stop and browse. Then I remembered I was there for a reason, averted my gaze, and went inside.

The realty company consisted of a large space that held multiple desks, most of them occupied. A pair of private offices opened off the back of the room. As soon as I walked through the door, a woman seated at a side desk looked up and smiled. Her blond hair was styled in a classic chignon and she had the whitest teeth I'd ever seen.

"Welcome to Parker/Dunn Real Estate," she said in a mellifluous voice. "May I help you?"

"Yes. I'd like to speak with Joe Wheeler, please."

Her smile dimmed slightly. "Is he expecting you?"

"No, but . . ."

A movement toward the rear of the room caught my eye. A middle-aged man came striding quickly out of one of the offices. He was tall, well-built, and surprisingly tan for this early in the season. His prominent eyebrows were lowered in annoyance, and he was pulling on a bright blue sports jacket as he approached.

"I'll take it from here, Leslie." He dismissed the other woman with a glance, then turned to me and held out hand. "I'm Joe Wheeler. How can I help you?"

"My name is Melanie Travis. I was hoping I might have a few minutes of your time?"

"Of course." Joe gestured toward the office from which he'd emerged. "I'm free at the moment. Would you like a cup of coffee?" He nodded toward an elaborate black and chrome coffeemaker that looked like it should come with its own barista. "Leslie would be happy to get one for you."

I noted the glare the woman sent his way, and said, "No, thanks, I'm fine."

Joe Wheeler's office was small, square, and windowless.

He'd brightened the space by covering one wall with framed photographs of local historic homes. The opposite wall held a detailed topographic map of Wilton, along with a dog show picture of Joe with one of his Great Danes.

Joe motioned me to one of two leather armchairs that sat facing an oversized desk. As I took a seat, he walked around behind the desk and did the same.

"Don't mind Leslie," he said. "She's always trying to drum up business for herself."

"I didn't mind her at all," I replied. "She was just trying to be helpful."

"Yes, that's what we do at Parker/Dunn. We strive to be helpful." Joe's expression wasn't nearly as cheerful as his tone. "So, let's get started. Are you buying or selling? What kind of property are you looking for? We specialize in homes and estates, of course, but we also handle commercial business and broker undeveloped land."

"I hope you won't feel I've misled you," I said. "I'm not interested in real estate at the moment. I want to talk to you about Audrey Kane's death."

Joe's face fell, then he quickly arranged his features into an expression of grief. "That was a terrible business. Audrey was a lovely woman. I can't imagine why anyone would have wanted to harm her."

"I understand she was a fierce competitor," I said.

"And a damn savvy businesswoman." His eyes flickered to the win picture on the wall. "Oh, wait, are you talking about dog shows?"

"Yes." Although now I was wondering what other kind of business he was referring to. "I have Standard Poodles myself, but I've been told that Audrey's family of Great Danes is pretty exceptional."

"It is," he agreed. "Audrey started with very good dogs, then nurtured the bloodlines for decades. Her guidance was meticulous. Kane's Danes improved with every generation. I shudder to think about where those dogs might be now."

"You don't have to worry about that," I told him. "My Aunt Peg and Ralph Denby headed up a rescue mission on the day Audrey died. Her Danes are all being fostered in good homes. I even ended up with one of them myself."

Joe looked at me with renewed interest. "That's good to know. Who is your aunt, and what was her relationship to Audrey?"

"She and Audrey were just friends, but she's also a dedicated dog lover. Her name is Peg Turnbull and—"

Joe started to laugh. "Oh, *that* Peg. I should have known. And now your Standard Poodle comment makes sense too."

"Yes, *that* Peg." I smiled at him across the desk. "I often think of her just that way."

"I can see why. Peg's an imposing woman. Is she the one who sent you here today? Do you need help finding homes for some of the Danes? Or maybe a contribution toward their care?" He opened a drawer in his desk and pulled out a checkbook. "I'd be happy to help out."

"Thank you for the offer, but we have everything under control for now. I actually wanted to ask you about something else. I heard you were involved in some kind of deal with Audrey before she passed?"

"Yeah, sure." Joe leaned forward and crossed his arm on the top of the desk. "Although by the time she died, it looked as though the proposal I thought we'd agreed upon had already fallen through."

"Do you mind if I ask what it was about?"

"Real estate. What else?" He gestured toward several commendations that were mounted on the wall behind his desk. "It's what I do. Have you ever visited Audrey's estate?"

"Yes, I have."

"Then you may have noticed that it's a good-sized piece of residential property in what is now a commercial zone?"

I nodded. That was enough to keep him talking.

"I was approached by Audrey's neighbor about six months ago. He owns a tract of land similar in size to hers. In the years since he took possession of the property, it has grown substantially in value. He had begun to think that maybe it was time to cash in."

"Are you talking about Bill Godfrey?" I asked.

"Yes." Joe looked surprised. "Do you know him?"

"I do, and I've also been to his house." I thought of Bill's charming custom-built home, nestled in the woods that surrounded it, and sighed.

Joe correctly interpreted my expression. "I felt much the same way as you do when I saw the place. But you have to remove emotion from the equation and look at things rationally. That land is worth exponentially more with a small mall, or even a factory, on it than it is with a single dwelling."

"Of course," I said.

"And selling the two lots together—Bill's along with Audrey's adjoining property—ups the ante yet again. With twenty acres, you're talking about attracting something like a hospital or a high school. Bill was pretty excited when I told him that."

"How did Audrey feel?" I asked.

Joe sat back. "To tell you the truth, initially she wasn't as positive about the idea as Bill was. Her first impulse was to throw up all sorts of roadblocks. She said she couldn't possibly consider selling, because she needed the land for her Great Danes. Then she demanded to know how I could ask her to sell property that had been in her family for generations."

"Both good points," I said.

"Here's another good point," Joe shot right back. "Audrey was nearly sixty. She wasn't married, and she didn't have children. Every little thing that needed to be taken care of on that big estate was all on her. Maintaining a property that size can be a drain on both time and money."

"I was under the impression that money wasn't a problem for Audrey."

"Maybe not right now. But things change. Stock markets tank. Elections play havoc with the financial sector. Developers who were willing to pay a premium this year, take their money and go elsewhere when it takes too long for a deal for go through. Based on the go-ahead I had from Bill, and the fact that Audrey hadn't definitely turned me down, I put out some feelers."

"That might have been a premature move on your part," I said.

"It wasn't." Joe's reply was firm. "Trust me, that's the way business is done. Nobody sits around waiting for things to happen. They make them happen. And I did. In no time at all, I'd reeled in a sizable offer. One that would have certainly been in Audrey's best interests to accept."

I had no doubt the deal would have been in Joe's best interest. He stood to make a huge commission if it went through. But Audrey's? Possibly not. It sounded as though, despite the pressure from both Joe and Bill, she still hadn't felt ready to sell.

"We were all systems go," Joe said. "And then suddenly we weren't. All because Audrey changed her mind."

"Or maybe she never made the decision to sell in the first place," I replied.

"No, that's not true. Bill and I were working together. We both made sure she understood all the benefits of selling now. Bill was the one who told me she'd agreed. That's when I jumped into action. I started making a plan to help her find a new place to live. I told her I could be of assistance in relocating her dogs."

Joe was a dedicated salesman. He seemed to believe he could make an idea become reality through sheer force of his will. I had the distinct impression that Audrey had never acquiesced to a sale. And certainly not to one that would happen in such a precipitous and peremptory fashion.

"When did Bill tell you that Audrey had agreed to sell?" I asked curiously.

"It was probably around six weeks ago, maybe a little longer. Once I had the go-ahead from Bill, I immediately set things in motion. I hired a structural engineer to check the place out, and sent a crew of surveyors to measure the land and verify the boundary lines. For a deal this size, I wanted to make sure that everything was absolutely shipshape. That's when the whole thing began to fall apart."

"What happened?" I asked curiously.

Joe shook his head. "Audrey saw the crew I'd hired and sent them packing in a hurry. She threatened to call the police if they didn't get the hell off her property."

I suddenly sat up straight. That statement had a familiar ring.

The intruders Audrey warned Tasha about must have been Joe's surveyors, whose authorization had been okayed by Bill, possibly without her knowledge. No wonder Audrey had reacted so strongly to their presence. Despite her protests, no one had been listening to her, or taking her misgivings into consideration. She'd probably begun to feel like she was under siege in her own home.

"You must have lost a good deal of money when your plan fell through," I said.

"Potential money," Joe corrected me. "I hadn't been paid anything yet."

"Nothing? Not even a finder's fee?"

"Not for an unsuccessful transaction. That's not the way it works."

"I'm sure you were upset about that."

"Of course I was." He grimaced. "In my place, anyone would have been. But there was nothing I could do."

I took a deep breath, then said, "Unless maybe it occurred to you to threaten Audrey into compliance."

Joe stiffened in his seat. His eyes narrowed. "What does that mean? Are you implying I might have had something to do with Audrey's death?"

"Not at all," I said blandly. "I'm just coming up with an idea and putting it out there. You know, much the same thing that you and Bill did to Audrey."

"Not only are you wrong, you're talking about things you don't even begin to understand," Joe growled. "The fact of Audrey's death impacts everything I was trying to accomplish—and not for the better. Maybe Audrey balked this time, but you better believe she was going to spend time thinking about what I'd said. And in six months when I approached her with a new offer, she'd already be halfway convinced it was a good idea."

"You sound very sure of that," I said.

"A woman of Audrey's age, living all by herself out in the middle of the woods? Anyone can see that's not a safe situation."

"Case in point," I muttered.

Joe ignored me. "Audrey wasn't a foolish woman. She'd have come around in time."

"Except that time turned out to be the one thing Audrey didn't have," I pointed out, even as Joe was shaking his head.

"That's not on me. As far as I was concerned, Audrey was a known quantity. Now I have no idea who I'm going to have to deal with, with regard to that property. Anyone could be inheriting the estate. Maybe they'll want to hold on to the place. Or if they do want to sell, who's to say I'll be able to convince them to let me act as their broker?"

Poor Joe Wheeler. Audrey's murder had caused him so many problems. And yet I couldn't muster a single shred of sympathy.

"It sounds as though you've got your work cut out for you," I said.

Then I stood up and let myself out.

Chapter 22

When I left Wilton, it was almost lunchtime. The talk with Joe had reminded me of my abbreviated chat with Audrey's dogsitter several days earlier. I'd been meaning to talk to Tasha again. The fact that she was relieved when I came up with a cover story for us at the nursery made me suspect that Ralph had deliberately interrupted our conversation. Now I was eager to hear what else she might have to say.

I was already heading south, so it would be easy to make a small detour to Darien if Tasha was available. Since she'd been working two jobs to make ends meet, and had recently lost one of those jobs, she might be happy to join me for a free lunch.

I pulled over to the side of the road and sent Tasha a text. Thirty seconds later, I received a reply. She named a café about a mile from the garden center, and said she'd meet me there in twenty minutes. Then I had to step on the gas to get there in time.

The lunch spot Tasha had chosen was a small, one-story building with ivy growing up the walls. A large patio offered outdoor dining. As I parked, I saw that Tasha had beaten me there. She was seated at a shaded table that had been set for two.

Tasha's hair was loose from its usual braids and hung

halfway down her back. She was wearing a polo shirt with the nursery logo, and several new friendship bracelets circled her wrist. Her head was tipped downward as she studied the menu. When she glanced up as I approached, I was surprised to see how tired she looked.

"Good. You came," she said.

I pulled out a chair and sat down. "Did you think I might not?"

"The way my life's been going lately, who knows?" Tasha frowned. "And it's not like I can afford to eat here on my own."

"Don't worry about that, I'm paying," I said, picking up my own menu. "It must be difficult for you now that Audrey's gone. Do you think Ralph might let you move to a full-time position?"

"I've asked, and he says it's a possibility. Unfortunately, he's already fully staffed for the summer, so there aren't any openings. I was hoping you might have had a chance to talk to Peg about dogsitting for some of her friends?"

"Not yet," I told her. "But I intend to."

"Thank you. I appreciate that."

The waitress stopped by, and we both ordered drinks and sandwiches. Iced tea and a Reuben for me, and root beer and a burger for Tasha. "With a mountain of fries on the side," she added.

I waited until the waitress was gone, and then said, "There's something I've been wondering about. When we first met—on the day that Audrey died?"

Tasha nodded.

"Aunt Peg proposed that rather than splitting up Audrey's Great Danes and removing them from the property, we should take up a collection and hire you to dogsit for them in their own kennel. At the time, you turned us down. You said you were too busy to take on another job."

"I know," she admitted. "I did say that."

"But apparently it's not true."

"No, it isn't."

I gazed at her across the table. "Do you have an explanation?"

"I do, but you'll think I'm stupid."

The waitress set down our drinks, then left.

"I won't," I said. "I promise."

Tasha picked up her napkin. Rather than placing it on her lap, she began to shred with her fingers. "Audrey had just died. She was still *right there*, inside the house. So maybe I got a little spooked, okay? Like if it wasn't safe for Audrey to be there by herself, in her own home, how could it possibly be safe for me?"

"That's understandable," I told her. "Why didn't you just say so?"

"I had my reasons," she mumbled.

"Did they have anything to do with the intruders that Audrey had warned you about?"

"Maybe."

"If you're interested, I found out what that comment was about. As it turns out, you wouldn't have been in any danger."

Tasha looked up. "I'm interested."

"Audrey's neighbor, Bill, was trying to convince her to offer her property for sale along with his."

"Audrey would never have done that," she said firmly. "She once told me that she intended to die in that house."

For a few seconds we were both silent, pondering the inadvertent truth of that statement. Before the conversation could resume, the waitress delivered our sandwiches. We both took the opportunity to dig in. My Reuben was delicious, salty, with just a hint of sweetness from the Russian dressing. Tasha slathered her mound of fries with ketchup, then picked one up with her fingers and popped it in her mouth.

"It appears that Audrey had at least considered the possibility of selling," I said after a minute. "Not that she would have necessarily gone ahead and done it, but Bill had put her in touch with a real estate broker. The broker told me he was working on a deal to sell the property when Audrey suddenly backed out."

"That sounds like something she would have done," Tasha said. "Audrey refused to let anyone push her around."

"He also told me that he'd sent some surveyors to map the land, and Audrey chased them away."

Her eyes widened. "They were the intruders?"

"I believe so."

"Good to know." Tasha went back to her burger as if she thought, or maybe hoped, that the conversation was over.

From my perspective, we weren't even close. As long as I could keep her at the table, I was going to continue asking questions.

"The last time we spoke, you seemed upset to hear that Bill had been inside Audrey's house," I said.

Briefly, she stopped chewing. "Of course I was. That guy wasn't supposed to have access. So how did he get in?"

"On the morning that we were all there, Bill told us he knew where Audrey kept her spare key."

"That's bullcrap," Tasha said firmly. "There was no spare key to Audrey's house. If there had been, I would have known."

I took another bite of my sandwich, then said, "Maybe whoever was in the house with Audrey when she died didn't lock the door behind them when they left."

"If that's the case, you're calling Bill a liar." Tasha didn't sound displeased by the idea.

"I'm just trying to get things straight in my mind," I said slowly. "You had to have a key, since you sometimes stayed over when you were taking care of Audrey's dogs."

"Sure." Tasha stuffed another french fry in her mouth. "But that key wasn't a spare she left lying around. It was one Audrey had given to me because I needed access. She said it made her feel better knowing that if something unforeseen happened to her, a responsible person"—she lifted a finger and pointed to herself—"could step in and take over care of the Danes on a moment's notice."

"Audrey must have really trusted you."

"She did. She knew I loved her dogs almost as much as she did."

"Since you spent so much time with her, I was wondering if she'd ever shown you an heirloom brooch she had," I said casually. "It was made of platinum and gemstones and shaped like a Great Dane."

Tasha choked on the french fry she'd been chewing. She reached hastily for her root beer and took a long swallow. I simply watched, and waited, until she was ready to speak again.

"I guess I might have seen it once or twice." Tasha's tone was just as offhand as mine had been. "Audrey didn't exactly show it to me, but occasionally I'd see her wearing it."

"Were you aware that the brooch went missing shortly before Audrey died?"

Abruptly Tasha stopped eating. "Why are you asking me that?"

"Because you just told me that you're the only person besides Audrey who had access to her house."

"So what? That doesn't mean anything. Anyone could have broken in and taken it."

"That's true," I allowed. "But when Audrey asked me to look for the brooch, she didn't mention a break-in. Only that it was missing."

"Audrey asked you to find it for her?" Tasha swallowed heavily. She was looking guiltier by the second. "I didn't know that."

"But you did know that the brooch was gone."

"I didn't say that!" she snapped, starting to rise.

"Please sit down." I raised my hands in a gesture of surrender. "Nobody's accusing you of anything and you haven't finished your lunch. We're merely enjoying a conversation. Will you stay if I promise to change the subject?"

"I guess so," Tasha muttered. As soon she was seated again, she immediately reached for her food. I was betting she would clean her plate in record time.

"Tell me about Nattie," I said.

She looked surprised. "Ralph's wife? What about her?"

"Anything. What's she like?"

Tasha considered for a moment, then said, "She's a perfectionist. It's one of the reasons she's so good at her job. You know she does landscape design, right?"

I nodded. I'd read about it on the website.

"The nursery gets tons of referrals from people who've seen gardens she designed. Her work is pretty spectacular. Not that she gets enough credit for it."

"What do you mean?"

"As far as Ralph is concerned, he's the big man in charge at the nursery. He wants everyone to think it's his flowers and little workshops that are making all the money. But that's not true. Nattie's an artist. She not only brings in the lion's share of the business, she's also the person responsible for the nursery's awesome reputation."

"How do you know that?" I asked curiously.

"Because I've heard them fight about it. That greenhouse is huge. And all those shrubs, trees, and hanging plants create plenty of nooks where people can hide out and not be seen."

"Hide out," I repeated. "You mean, from work?"

Tasha just shrugged. "Besides, Ralph and Nattie don't even try to keep their conversations private. They're as likely to get into a fight in the middle of the floor as they are in their office."

"And the business is what they fight about?"

Tasha snatched up her last french fry. "Mostly. Although sometimes it's the dogs, too."

"You mean Ralph's Great Danes?"

"Well, *yeah*." She stopped just short of rolling her eyes. "Nattie complains that Ralph spends too much time at dog shows and dog club meetings. She says the garden center could be doing even better if he would only give the place his full attention."

"Do you think she's right?" I asked.

"How the heck would I know? My job consists of watering plants and schlepping stuff around the place. It's not like I've ever seen the company's books. Or that I would even know what I was looking at if I did."

The plate in front of Tasha was empty. She lifted the frayed napkin from her lap and used it to wipe the sides of her mouth. Another few seconds and she'd be gone.

"Just out of curiosity," I said. "Have you ever heard Nattie mention Audrey Kane?"

"Audrey?" Once again, I'd surprised her. "Why?"

"I just wondered if they knew each other, that's all."

"I'm sure they did. You know, because of the Dane connection. And Ralph talks about her sometimes. But usually not when he's with Nattie."

"Oh?" I felt a sudden spike of interest. "Who does Ralph talk about Audrey to?"

"Last time, it was that lady that took a couple of Audrey's Great Danes home with her."

"Not Aunt Peg?" I blurted without thinking.

"*Duh*." She snorted. "No, the other one. The tall skinny chick. Her name was Miranda Something."

"Miranda Falk," I said. "She's a customer at the nursery too?"

"I guess she must be. I mean, if she doesn't need plants, what else would she be doing there?"

That was a good question. Miranda lived in Weston. Ralph's garden center was in Darien. Maybe Miranda liked the idea of supporting a fellow dog fancier's business. Or maybe Ralph had the best floral selection in Fairfield County. Or maybe there was another reason entirely why Miranda was willing to make a thirty-mile round trip to patronize the Denbys' nursery.

Now I needed to find out what that reason was.

Chapter 23

Tasha left shortly after that. I finished my sandwich, paid the check, then called Miranda to ask if she had time to get together with me that afternoon.

"Only if you promise not to bring Daisy with you," she said.

I swore under my breath. "Of course I'm not dropping Daisy off at your house. How many more times are you going to ask me that question?"

Miranda didn't sound the slightest bit cowed. "Probably about as often as you call out of the blue and ask to meet with me. Frankly, this whole 'you and I are buddies now and we chat frequently' thing is a mystery to me."

Wait a minute, I thought. Miranda and I were buddies? That was news to me.

"Let's meet for lunch," she said.

"I just ate lunch."

"Dessert, then."

Last time, I'd initiated our meeting and set the parameters. This time, Miranda was letting me know she'd be the one planning our get-together. Considering that she was more useful to me than I was to her, I figured that was fair.

"Fine," I said. "Dessert, it is. Pick a place."

"Denton's Diner in Norwalk." Miranda was ready with

an answer. "They have great milkshakes, and their pie is pretty good too. Give me half an hour to get there."

I hadn't been to Denton's before, but I was a huge fan of diners, and this place definitely looked promising. The lower half of the long low building was covered in aluminum siding that was shiny enough to reflect the sun. The upper half was all windows. There was a U-shaped counter inside, and a row of booths whose upholstered seats were covered in red vinyl.

I was happy even before a waiter, who looked young enough to be in high school, showed me to a booth, then handed me a laminated menu that came complete with pictures. "I'll be back to take your order when the rest of your party arrives," he said.

Ten minutes later, Miranda slid into the seat opposite me. She was wearing cropped pants with a floral silk blouse, and there was a small pink hibiscus tucked behind her right ear.

"That's pretty," I commented.

"Thanks." Miranda didn't look up. Her eyes had gone straight to the menu on the tabletop in front of her. She flipped it over to look at both sides, then said, "It's a milkshake for me. What are you having?"

"The same." I barely had a chance to reply before she had her hand in the air, signaling to the waiter. "Are you in a hurry to be somewhere?"

"No, I just don't like wasting time." Miranda sat back in her seat. "So here's hoping that we can get this business out of the way so I can move on to what's next."

"Which is?"

She was saved from answering by the speedy arrival of our waiter. I chose a mint chip milkshake. Miranda went for raspberry cream.

"Lord, they make them younger every year," she muttered under her breath when he'd written down our order and left.

I chuckled, having thought much the same thing. "Or we get older, and they just look that way to us."

She gazed at me across the tabletop. "As if you have to worry about that. I must have twenty years on you. When I was your age, I was in the prime of my life."

"Who's to say you aren't still?" I asked.

"Me, for one," Miranda replied. "And the medical industry, as well as society at large. Not to mention every single man ever born, including the ones who are even older than I am."

"Well, that's a depressing thought."

"Tell me about it."

She still hadn't answered my earlier question. "When we finish here, where are you going next?"

"Nowhere exciting. I figured since I'm in the area, I might as well do a little shopping. You know, pick up a few things."

"Sure," I said. "Like flowers?"

Miranda had been drumming her fingertips on the table. Now she abruptly stopped. "What makes you say that?"

"For one thing, the hibiscus behind your ear. For another, when I visited your house last week, there was a bouquet of fresh tulips in your living room. I thought they might need to be replaced."

Her gaze sharpened. "You don't miss much, do you?"

"I try not to."

"I'd feel better if I could see that as an admirable quality."

"And you can't, because . . . ?"

Miranda leaned closer. "Because I don't like the way you're looking at me. Like you know something about me that you think I wish you didn't."

"I don't know much," I said truthfully. "But I suspect a lot."

"I didn't kill Audrey Kane."

The waiter had just walked up to our booth with a milkshake in each of his hands. He must have heard what Miranda said, because his eyes widened. He stood frozen in place, holding the two drinks out in front of him like a shield.

"Don't worry, we're just practicing for a play," I told him. "You can put the drinks down. I promise we won't hurt you." Both milkshakes, one red, one green, were in tall clear glasses. They looked thick and creamy, and each had a swirl of whipped cream and a cherry on top.

The young man hastily delivered our order and left.

"That was quick thinking." Miranda helped herself to a spoonful of whipped cream. "Although considering the kind of things you get mixed up in, I guess you must be used to scaring people."

"Not usually innocent children," I said, and we both smiled.

The waiter had scurried to the other side of the diner. Now he was holding a hushed conversation with a woman behind the checkout counter. I hoped he wasn't planning to report us to the police.

"Back to your shopping plans," I said. "Flowers?"

"Among other things." Miranda frowned. "And you don't have to look so smug about it."

I was indeed pleased with myself, but I carefully schooled my features into a bland expression, then took a sip of my milkshake. The drink was cold enough to give me brain freeze. I didn't care, because Miranda had just confirmed an idea that had only been speculation on my part.

"Since that's supposed to be a secret, tell me how you found out," she said. "Ralph better not have told you."

Despite her words, Miranda looked almost hopeful. I wondered if she wished Ralph would leave Nattie for her. If so, bringing their relationship out in the open would be a first step in that direction. Unfortunately, I couldn't help in that regard.

"Ralph didn't say a word. And how I know isn't important." I wasn't about to throw Tasha under the bus. "But now I have to reconsider those things you told me about Ralph and Audrey. They weren't really about Audrey at all, were they? You were talking about yourself."

"Some of it," she said. "I guess."

"Which parts?"

Miranda was concentrating on her milkshake. She didn't deign to answer.

"Were you the one who had a relationship with Ralph before he married Nattie?"

That got her attention. "No, that part was Audrey, at least in the beginning. But when she dropped him for Carter . . . let's just say that I was there to step in and offer consolation."

Of all the men who had been circling in Audrey's orbit before her death, mild-mannered Ralph wasn't the one I'd have picked as a Casanova. The man must have had hidden talents. I considered what Miranda had said and took a moment to re-create the timeline in my mind.

"When Audrey and Ralph separated, his relationship with Nattie was still in the future. Right?"

"They weren't married, if that's what you're asking. But they knew each other. Nattie worked for Ralph at the nursery."

"She's a landscape designer," I said. "From what I hear, a very good one."

Miranda shook her head. "No, not back then. When Ralph was with Audrey, Nattie was just a dumpy middle-aged woman who made minimum wage for puttering around the greenhouse."

I doubted that. But if denigrating Nattie made Miranda feel better about herself, I wasn't about to interrupt.

"So you got together with Ralph," I prompted.

"Yeah, I did." She didn't look happy. "But things didn't turn out at all the way I thought they would. In the beginning, it was clear that Ralph was still pining for Audrey. He was adamant about keeping our relationship a secret, and I always figured she was the reason."

"And you were okay with that?"

"It's not like I had a choice." Miranda sighed. "When you get to be my age, the pool of women who are looking for a relationship vastly outnumbers the pool of available men. And men who are willing to share a woman with multiple dogs—especially really big dogs? That's a whole other problem. Now factor in geographical restrictions and that shrinks your possibilities down to . . ."

"Almost nothing," I finished for her.

Forget about Ralph's hidden talents. It was beginning to sound as though his biggest attractions had been that he was nearby and single. We spent a minute or two digesting that dismal thought and working on our milkshakes. Mine was delicious and worth every calorie. I hoped Miranda's was too.

"Did the two of you ever talk about getting married?" I asked.

"I would have been willing." Miranda shrugged, which hardly seemed like an endorsement. "But Ralph never even wanted to discuss it. Mostly he said he was too busy building his business."

Ouch, I thought.

"I'm guessing that's where Nattie comes in."

"Good guess. Dammit."

I almost chuckled, but caught myself in time.

"While I was trying to be an understanding partner and making do with the few hours Ralph could spare to be with me, I should have been giving more thought to the people with whom Ralph was spending the majority of his time. And *that's* where Nattie came in. Because, of course, she was with Ralph all day, virtually every day."

Miranda probably didn't want to hear this, but it needed to be said. "I imagine she was also helping him to build his business."

"What are the chances?" she grumbled. "Given an opportunity, Nattie turned out to be some kind of shrub savant. And the more jobs she booked for the nursery, the more enthralled Ralph became. Suddenly it seemed like he and I hardly had a single conversation where her name didn't come up at least once. It's not like I couldn't see the writing on that wall. So I gave Ralph an ultimatum."

"And you lost," I said quietly. "Ralph chose Nattie over you."

"No," Miranda said firmly. "It wasn't Nattie. He chose his *business* over me."

"So the two of them got married, and your affair with Ralph ended."

Miranda chewed on her lower lip. "Not exactly."

There was more? This saga had plenty of twists and turns.

"Then what exactly?"

"It turned out that domestic bliss wasn't Ralph's cup of tea."

"Poor Ralph," I said, without a single shred of sympathy. "What's the expression? Marry for money, repent in haste?"

Miranda laughed. It was nice to see her mood brighten. "I don't think that's how it goes, but I'll applaud the sentiment anyway. After a year or so, Ralph came back."

"To you," I clarified.

"Of course, to me. Who else are we talking about?" Her glass was nearly empty and she paused to lick her spoon. "I never thought of myself as the kind of person who would sleep with another woman's husband. You know?"

I nodded.

"But Ralph caught me at a weak moment. We were both

out of town at a dog show, and we happened to be staying at the same hotel. We decided to have a drink in the bar for old time's sake."

Anyone could see where this story was heading. "So the weakness was alcohol induced."

"And . . . we were in another state."

I wasn't sure why that made a difference, but I took a stab. "What happens in Vegas?"

"Precisely!" Miranda seemed pleased that we were on the same page.

"*Were* you in Vegas?"

"No, Pittsburgh."

"So . . . the perfect romantic destination, then."

She stared across the table. "Are you making fun of me?"

"I'm trying very hard not to," I said. "But seriously, Pittsburgh?"

For a moment I thought she might throw her spoon at me, but then instead, Miranda began to laugh. After a few seconds, I joined in.

"I know," she said. "Of all places!"

It took us a minute to settle down. When we did, it turned out that Miranda hadn't finished telling her story. "It only happened the one time," she said, then her voice dropped to a whisper. "And do you want to know the worst part?"

"Probably not," I said. *Definitely not*, I thought.

She kept talking anyway. "Ralph isn't even very good in bed. And it's not as if Nattie had taught him any new tricks."

"Well, you know what they say about old dogs. . . ." I said, and that set us off all over again.

We were still giggling when our very young waiter came over to stand in the vicinity of our booth. He was careful not to step too close. It probably wasn't my imagination that he looked nervous. "Is everything all right?"

"It's fine," I said. "We'll just take the check, please." He hurried away, and I turned back to Miranda.

"So those things you said about Audrey and Nattie . . ."

"Weren't entirely true," she admitted. "But they weren't entirely false either. Nattie rarely comes to the shows. Which seems like a shame for Ralph. The Danes are his passion, and Nattie couldn't care less about them."

"If she did come to a show," I said, "would she see Ralph following you around like a lost puppy?"

"Maybe." She stopped and shook her head. "No, make that probably. But that's not my problem. Ralph had his chance and he blew it. End of story."

Not entirely, I thought.

The waiter was approaching with our tab, and Miranda started to slide out of the booth. I reached out a hand to make her pause.

"Is it truly the end? Because I know you still drive all the way down here to shop at Ralph's nursery."

A smile played around the corners of Miranda's mouth. "Have you seen Nattie?"

"No, we've never met."

"She's short and round and looks like a Bavarian haus-frau."

"In other words, next to her you look like Helen Mirren. And you're making sure Ralph remembers that."

Miranda's smile widened. She waited to see if I was finished. This was my last shot, so I had to make it count.

"The first time we spoke, why did you bother to tell me that other story? The one that made it seem as though Nattie could be the person responsible for Audrey's death."

"That was your fault," Miranda said standing up. "You came into my house and started asking questions like you thought you had every right to do so. Which you did not. So I gave you the answers I figured you deserved. Besides, after the way Nattie blew up my life, I didn't mind throwing a little trouble her way."

Since she'd already started to walk away, Miranda delivered the last line over her shoulder. "Payback's a bitch, baby."

I grabbed the check and followed her to the door. When I stopped at the counter to pay, she kept going. Minutes later, when I reached the parking lot, Miranda was already gone.

Chapter 24

The busy day had given me a lot to think about. Later that afternoon, when I went to pick up Davey, I was still preoccupied. When I arrived at Aunt Peg's house, it took me a moment to realize that Davey was sitting outside on her front steps. As I turned in the driveway, he got up and walked out to meet me.

"Did you and Aunt Peg get tired of each other already?" I asked as he got in the car and fastened his seatbelt. I was only joking, but Davey looked horrified.

"Of course not."

"Then I guess you must be running out of things to do for her."

"What? No!"

"So how come you're sitting outside waiting for me and Aunt Peg is nowhere in sight?"

"She's on the phone," Davey said. "Some kind of private call with an AKC rep. We were already finished for the day and I knew you'd be here soon, so I came outside to wait."

"That's a relief." I shifted the car into reverse. "So if we leave now, Aunt Peg's isn't going to come outside in ten minutes and wonder what happened to you. Like maybe you got kidnapped or something."

"Mo-o-om!" he wailed.

"What?"

"I'm almost sixteen. Aunt Peg knows I can take care of myself."

"I know you can take care of yourself too." I paused, then added, "Mostly. But I still don't want her to worry because you disappeared when she wasn't looking."

"I'm not disappearing. I'm leaving with you." He looked pointedly behind us. The Volvo was in reverse, but we hadn't started moving yet. "You know, if that ever happens."

"You're a fresh kid." Trying not to smile, I applied my foot to the gas pedal.

"You're a fresh mom," Davey retorted with a grin. "So it probably runs in the family."

I had to give him credit. He wasn't wrong about that.

Sometimes it was hard for me to believe that Davey was already midway through his teenage years. It felt as though the time had flown by. Our lives were so much better now, with Sam and Kevin making our family complete. Even so, I occasionally felt a touch of nostalgia for the closeness we'd shared in our early years together.

Davey's father, my ex-husband, had walked out on us when Davey was ten months old. We hadn't heard from Bob again for four long years. Overnight, I'd become a single mother, with a decent job but also plenty of bills to pay. At times, it had felt like it was just the two of us against the world. I loved that we'd come so far together since then.

Without thinking, I reached over and ruffled my fingers through Davey's sandy hair.

"Hey!" he shied away. "What'd you do that for?"

"Because I love you," I said.

"Okay." My son pondered that unexpected reply. "This doesn't mean we have to have a conversation about it though, does it?"

"No." I nearly laughed at the expression on his face. "If you'd prefer, I'll change the subject."

"I'd prefer just about any other subject," Davey muttered.

We'd reached the end of Aunt Peg's small lane. I stopped the car and looked both ways, then pulled out onto the main road. Davey had taken his phone out of his pocket and was about to turn it on.

He'd asked for a change of topic. I decided to oblige.

"Tell me why you're really going to Aunt Peg's house every day," I said.

"What?" Davey set the phone aside.

I cast him a look. "You heard me."

"You know why. Aunt Peg's old, and she needs help with taking care of things at her place. Like the Poodles, and the garden."

Neither of us believed that for a minute. "And also with the mythical agility course."

"That, too," he agreed readily, as if he thought he'd scored a point.

In another few seconds, he'd realize he was wrong. I didn't bother to wait.

"Try again," I advised him. "And this time, come up with a reason that doesn't mention Aunt Peg's age."

Davey thought for a minute, then said, "If I tell you, there might be trouble."

I'd suspected as much. "For you or Aunt Peg?"

"Maybe both of us."

I sighed. "What kind of trouble are we talking about? I assume you're not doing anything illegal."

Once again, that was supposed to be a joke. But then Davey scared the crap out of me by saying, "Ummm . . ."

I turned and stared at him. "You have ten seconds to come up with a better answer. And don't even think about telling me to keep my eyes on the road. I'm a mother, I have eyes on the back of my head."

"Since you're looking sideways, they wouldn't be much help to you now," Davey pointed out reasonably enough.

Unfortunately for him, I was in no mood to be reasonable. "Speak," I said. "And this better be the truth. Otherwise, there's going to be a permanent ban on you ever going to Aunt Peg's house again."

Davey smirked. "You don't have to overreact or anything."

"Trust me. There's no such thing as an overreaction when the word 'illegal' is part of the discussion."

"It's not that bad."

"I'll be the judge of that."

Had I *really* said that? Now I sounded like my mother.

This conversation was quickly going from bad to worse. Not only that, but on the other side of the car, Davey had shrunk down in his seat like he wished he was anywhere else but here. I immediately felt a pang of guilt. Despite the gravity of the situation, I never wanted him to feel that way about being with me.

"Let's start over," I said.

Davey glanced at me warily, like maybe he suspected a trap.

"This car is going to be a safe space. Whatever you say here won't go any farther than this front seat. And we'll figure out how to deal with it together."

"Does that mean you won't tell Sam?"

Of course that would be the first thing he'd ask.

"Sam and I believe in being honest with each other," I said. "I don't have any secrets from him, because that's not how I want our relationship to work. What kind of relationship do you want to have with Sam?"

Davey sighed. "The same."

"Good." I nodded. "Then spit it out. Whatever you have to tell me cannot possibly be as bad as the things I'm imagining."

"Aunt Peg is teaching me how to drive."

My first reaction was one of relief. At least they weren't robbing banks.

My second reaction was pure outrage. What the hell did Aunt Peg think she was doing? I quickly tamped down my anger. Safe space, remember?

"Do you mean that you and she are going through the driver's manual together, or . . ."

"She lets me drive her minivan," Davey said.

I bit back a small shriek. *Safe space, safe space.* "You don't have a driver's license. Or even a learner's permit."

"I know, but I'll be sixteen in just a few months!"

"Those few months make the difference between driving legally and breaking the law," I pointed out.

"I guess," he said. "But we only go up and down her little lanc. There are hardly ever any cars on it. And I haven't even gone faster than twenty miles an hour yet."

"*Yet?*" I squeaked.

"You know what I mean."

I did. And I didn't like it one bit.

"How did this plan come about?" I asked. "And which one of you decided it was a good idea to keep it a secret from me and Sam?"

"Both of us realized that," Davey replied. "Because we knew you'd say no."

"Of course we would have said no." I glanced at him across the front of the car. "Legalities aside, Sam was looking forward to teaching you how to drive. He learned from his father, and it was a great bonding experience for them. Sam says it's a rite of passage from one generation to the next."

"Oh." Davey frowned.

"I guess you didn't think of that?"

"No. All I knew was that I wanted to drive, and you and Sam were making me wait."

"The state of Connecticut is the one making you wait," I told him. "You're not sixteen yet."

"I feel like I should be."

"Really?" I snorted. "*That's* your excuse?"

"I guess it's pretty bad," he admitted.

"It's worse than bad, it's ridiculous," I told him. "And speaking as your mother, I'm in no hurry to see you grow up."

"Why not?"

"Because then you'll leave. Until that happens, you're still my little boy."

Davey didn't like that answer. "I'm too old to be your little boy."

This time when I reached over and ruffled his hair, the move was deliberate. "Okay, then you're my big boy. Happy now?"

"Not entirely," he replied. "How much trouble am I in?"

"The driving part is bad enough. But it's the fact that you've been lying about it that really upsets me."

"I know." He sounded chastened. "I'm sorry."

I glanced over. "But you know I still love you, right?"

"I should hope so," Davey said. "I'm a lovable kid."

"Don't press your luck," I told him.

Davey made a full confession to Sam when we got home. I purposely didn't sit in on their conversation. Instead, Kevin and I went out in the backyard with the dogs, and I pushed him on the tire swing.

Our canine crew was used to that by now. Daisy, however, seemed to think that the sight of Kevin flying through the air on a big, round, rubber seat was the most amazing thing she'd ever seen. The older Dane began barking, and bouncing up and down like she was a puppy. That made Tar, Augie, and Bud come running over so they could add to the excitement.

Kevin squealed with delight as Bud leapt up and tried to nip his feet as he passed overhead. Bud was much too small to accomplish that feat; he never even came close. But what he lacked in size, he made up for with enthusiasm. After a while, all the noise we were making drew Sam and Davey outside.

Davey immediately went to join his little brother at the swing. I walked over to stand beside Sam.

"Is everything okay?" I asked.

"Aside from the fact that I'm going to have words with Peg the next time I see her," he replied, "mostly yes."

I wrapped my arm around his waist and leaned in. "Good."

"Good?" He tipped his head to gaze down at me. "You sound much calmer about this turn of events than I feel."

"Maybe I've just had more time to process it. Besides, I've always been more aware of Aunt Peg's machinations than you have. I'm probably not as surprised as you are that she'd sneak around behind our backs like this."

"What she did goes beyond sneaky," Sam growled. "It's reprehensible. What if Davey had gotten in an accident? What if one of them had been hurt? Or worse, what if he'd injured someone else? Sure, that's a quiet road. But it also gets plenty of use from joggers and bike riders—"

I reached up and placed a finger over his lips. Sam immediately went quiet.

"See?" I said with a smile. "That's why I don't have to work myself into a lather worrying about worst-case scenarios. Because I know you'll do that part for me."

"I'm supposed to take care of that part," Sam replied. "And all the other parts. You, Davey, and Kevin are my family. I'm supposed to take care of *you.*"

I tightened my arm around his firm body and snuggled closer. "You do a great job of taking care of us."

"Apparently not good enough," he grumbled.

"You can't blame yourself," I said. "Blame Aunt Peg. She's the one who set this whole thing in motion."

"Believe me, I'm already there."

I glanced up. "Do you think we should punish Davey?"

"You mean like take away his car keys?" Sam almost smiled.

I was glad he was beginning to feel better. "Something like that."

"Let's sleep on it for a day or two, and see how we feel after things have calmed down."

The plan made sense to me.

Chapter 25

A man with a name like Carter Ridley wasn't hard to find. A brief internet search revealed that he worked as a loan officer at a bank in downtown Stamford. Since he'd thought it was a fine idea to drop in on me unexpectedly, I figured he could hardly object when I did the same to him.

Sam and I had decided that Davey should take a day off from his duties at Aunt Peg's house. I left it up to Sam to report our son's absence. I also let him decide how explicit he wanted to be about the reason why. He and I had cooled down overnight, but we were in agreement that Aunt Peg was in need of a stern talking-to from both of us. Maybe that would take place later in the day. In the meantime, I was on my way downtown.

The bank where Carter worked was located on a busy corner lot near the Stamford Town Center mall. The three-story building took up a good-sized chunk of valuable real estate. It also offered parking in an underground garage for customers. When I couldn't find any on-street parking nearby, I decided I qualified. Hopefully, after I'd met with Carter, he'd still be willing validate my ticket.

A perky young receptionist was seated at a desk just inside the bank's revolving front door. When I told her I was there to see Mr. Ridley, she didn't bother to ask if I had an appointment. Instead she wrote down my name, then directed me to a pair of elevators in a side wall.

"Second floor," she said. "Turn left, and his office is the second door on the left. I'll call up and let him know you're on your way."

The directions proved to be unnecessary. As soon as the elevator doors opened at the end of the second-floor corridor, I saw Carter Ridley standing in the doorway to his office. He was dressed in a dark gray suit that was tailored to emphasize the breadth of his shoulders. His loafers were shiny enough to reflect the overhead lights. With his jacket unbuttoned and knot of his blue tie loosened, he didn't look as though he was expecting visitors.

Carter's expression was impassive, but the set of his shoulders was stiff, and his arms were folded tightly across his chest. I hadn't been particularly welcoming when he followed me and Faith to Waveny Park. Maybe now we were even.

Carter waited until I was almost right in front of him before he spoke. "I'm assuming you're not here to apply for a loan."

"No," I said. "Sorry."

"Don't be sorry. I'm swamped with work. It's not like I need more to do."

He stepped aside, and I walked past him to enter a spacious office whose wall of tinted windows overlooked the Town Center. The back of the room held a desk and chair with a tall bookcase behind it. Instead of heading that way, Carter pointed me toward the space near the windows where two minimalist leather chairs were angled to face each other. There was a low chrome and glass coffee table between them.

"Sit," he said. "I'd offer you something to drink, but I'm also assuming you didn't drop by to be sociable."

"You're right, I didn't." When I took a seat, the chair's design tilted me backward. I righted myself, and said, "I'm still trying to learn more about the events that led to Audrey's death."

"Then you came to the wrong place." Carter sat down opposite me.

I was perched on the edge of my seat. Carter made himself comfortable. Leaning back, with his arms relaxed and legs slightly apart, he looked like a man who had nothing to hide. I wasn't impressed.

"I disagree. You were married to Audrey. You probably knew her better than just about anyone."

"She and I were also divorced," he pointed out. "Five years ago. Audrey moved on, and so did I."

"From what I hear, Audrey was the one who moved on first."

I hoped that might get a rise out of Carter. Instead, he looked amused. "You've been talking to Lara again."

"I have. She told me you divorced Audrey because she cheated on you. That must have hurt."

Carter remained unfazed. "If you're trying to make that circumstance look like a motive for murder, you're five years too late."

Score a point for Carter. I needed to try harder.

"When was the last time you saw Audrey?"

"I don't see how that makes the slightest bit of difference."

"Then what's the harm in answering?" I asked. "Unless there's something you're trying to hide."

"Not me." Carter lifted his arms and spread them. "I'm an open book."

"Great. Then I'm sure you won't mind answering my questions. Did you and Audrey remain in touch after the divorce?"

"We saw each other occasionally. I had taken over Audrey's finances when we were married, and she continued to rely on me for advice afterward."

"That's seems unusual," I said.

"What can I say? I'm good at what I do." Carter smirked. "Audrey was a smart woman. She knew I wouldn't steer her wrong. Recently she'd received an offer to sell her property. She came to ask me if I thought it was a good idea."

"And did you?"

"No. From what I could see there were too many moving parts to the deal she'd been offered. And too many people involved. Her property is worth a great deal of money on its own. Tying it to the sale of the property next door—as this deal did—could only benefit the neighbor and hurt her."

Interesting. That was the opposite of what Joe Wheeler had told me.

"In what way?" I asked.

"Though the two parcels are of equal size, the neighboring lot contains nearly two acres of wetlands, which makes that part of the property unusable, and the lot worth considerably less than Audrey's. Bill Godfrey was hoping to enhance the value of his land at the expense of hers, and I told her so."

"And that's what caused the agreement to fall through?" I said.

Carter shrugged, as though the outcome made no difference to him. I suspected he wasn't being entirely truthful about that.

"You made several people very unhappy when you advised Audrey not to sell."

"I'm aware. But frankly, that's not my problem."

"I hope it didn't turn into Audrey's problem," I told him.

"It didn't."

"Under the circumstances, how can you be so sure?"

"Because Audrey's death didn't change anything about the transaction."

Carter sounded very sure of himself. As if he was privy to information I didn't have. I wondered what would happen to Audrey's property now that she was gone. It couldn't hurt to ask.

"Since Audrey was still consulting you about financial matters, did you ever give her advice about her will?"

Carter didn't answer right away. For a minute I didn't think he was going to answer at all. "Yes," he said finally. "Some. Not a lot. It was her money, after all. But Audrey insisted that I be involved. She said there was no one else she could trust to do the job."

"The job?"

"I'm Audrey's executer," Carter told me.

I stared at him, shocked. "The last time we spoke, you made it sound as though you didn't know anything about Audrey's will."

"No, I did not. What I said was that her affairs were none of your business. Which is still true, by the way."

"And yet here you are, talking to me," I said. In fact, compared to our previous conversation, Carter was being positively voluble. "What's changed in the meantime?"

"For one thing, you don't have the damn doodle with you."

I glared at him. "Really?"

"No." Then he smiled at me, and his face was transformed. Perhaps it wasn't so hard to see why Carter had such a high opinion of himself. "Actually, it was Lara."

"What about her?"

"You told me she asked you to look into Audrey's death."

"Yes," I said. "And you didn't believe me."

"Now I do."

"Why?"

"Because I asked Lara about you. And she verified your story."

"I don't have a 'story,' " I said.

"No, just an endless stream of questions." Carter still didn't sound happy about that. "But Lara told me to bear with you."

Carter and Lara. I pondered that. "Do you and she speak often?"

"Every day." A smile played around his lips. "I guess she didn't tell you."

"Tell me what?"

"Lara and I have been seeing each other for the past six months."

No, Lara hadn't mentioned that. *Dammit.* That would have been useful to know.

"So . . . you and your ex-wife's sister," I said, trying not to sound as though I'd just been gobsmacked. "How's that working out for you?"

"Quite well. Lara's a lovely woman. She's fun to be around. Audrey could be a little . . . intense. The two of them were so different, it was hard to tell they were even sisters."

"Stepsisters," I said.

Carter waved away my objection as if it didn't matter. But it did. A lot. Both Audrey's and Lara's lives had been greatly impacted by that relationship. Under normal circumstances, a woman dating her former brother-in-law would seem like a questionable choice. Under these circumstances, it felt truly bizarre.

I wondered how Lara and Carter's relationship had come about. Had the attraction between them always been there—even when Audrey and Carter were married? When had they first acted on it? Carter said their relationship was fairly new. I wasn't sure whether or not to believe him.

Even if Carter was telling the truth, Audrey would still have been alive when he and Lara got together. I wondered what she'd thought of that. It was, perhaps, the most interesting question of all.

"How did Audrey feel about your relationship with Lara?"

"To be honest, I'm not sure she was aware of it."

"You're not sure?" I repeated. That seemed unlikely.

"That's right. Audrey and I had been divorced for years. I wasn't privy to the details of her love life, and there was no need for her to know anything about mine."

"Even though the two of you were still close enough that she felt comfortable having you handle her finances?"

"I don't see what difference that makes," Carter said with a smile. "Don't forget, I'm a banker. Which means I certainly know better than to mix sex and money."

Carter was pretty damn smooth. He seemed to have an answer for everything.

Then something else occurred to me. "Audrey and Lara would have been estranged during the time you and Audrey were married," I said. "So how did you and Lara meet?"

"You're right, they weren't particularly friendly with each other. But they weren't entirely out of touch either. Occasionally, family events brought them together. The death of Audrey's mother and Lara's stepmother, for one. So yes, Lara and I became acquainted during my marriage."

"Merely acquainted?" I asked.

"That, and nothing more," Carter said firmly. He rose to his feet. "I think you've taken enough of my time. May I show you out?"

"Of course. Thank you for seeing me." I stood up, but didn't move. "Before I go, what can you tell me about Audrey's will?"

"Not a thing." Carter was already walking toward the door. "That information is confidential. And since you're not one of the beneficiaries, no part of it will be shared with you."

He paused in the doorway to his office and pointed toward the elevator at the end of the hall. "That's the way out. Goodbye, Ms. Travis."

I hadn't learned everything I wanted to know, but the news about Lara and Carter was interesting. As was the fact that neither one of them had mentioned it before now.

Why were they were keeping their relationship under wraps—and was it possible the reason had something to do with Audrey's murder? Not only that, but now that I knew Lara and Carter were involved with each other, it called into question much of what she'd previously told me about him.

For one thing, Lara had downplayed the aggression I'd felt from Carter during our first encounter. She'd also implied she was the one who'd supplied the information that led to Carter and Audrey's divorce. Had Lara done that out of spite, or because she was attracted to Carter herself? And if the latter, why had it taken the two of them so long to get together?

Not for the first time I found myself in the frustrating situation of finishing a conversation with more questions than answers. I still didn't find either Carter or Lara to be particularly trustworthy. It was bad enough when I'd thought they were only looking out for themselves. Now I knew it was possible that both of them were shading the truth about Audrey's murder in order to protect each other.

Less than a minute later, the elevator deposited me on the ground floor. It was then that I remembered the parking stub I'd stashed in my pocket. I pulled it out and handed it to the receptionist by the front door. She was happy to validate it for me.

"Have a nice day!" she said cheerfully, and I wished her the same.

Chapter 26

As I drove away from the bank, I paused to consider my options, then went up the ramp onto the Connecticut Turnpike. From downtown Stamford it was only a short distance to downtown Greenwich, where Detective Raymond Young was a member of the police force. He and I had pooled our resources to solve several previous mysteries, and we'd developed a respect for each other's abilities. The detective also made an excellent sounding board.

The Greenwich Police Department was located in the town's Public Safety Complex. The connected buildings covered almost a whole block, and everything about the complex looked intimidating. I'd been there enough times before to know my way around. I parked the Volvo in a visitor's spot, then walked inside through the two-story, glass-walled entrance.

Luckily, I didn't have to wait long before a uniformed officer came to escort me to the other side of the building, where Detective Young met me at the door to his office. He was a tall Black man with a lean body and a great smile which, in my opinion, I didn't get to see nearly often enough.

His dark hair was short, and beginning to gray around the temples. When he reached out and took my hand, his grip was firm. Young was smart, capable, and fair-minded. It wasn't hard to understand why he had risen quickly through the ranks at the department.

"I'll take it from here," he told my escort. As the man spun on his heel and left, Detective Young turned to me. "I hope this is a social call."

I stared at him. "Do we do those?"

"Not yet, but you never know. Someday it could happen. Otherwise, the likely alternative is that you've found yourself in trouble again."

My silence in response to that remark probably spoke volumes.

Young sighed. "You'd better come in and sit down."

We entered the office together. The space was well lit, and the air-conditioning was cranked up high. Detective Young's large desk was near the windows. The slatted chair behind it faced out into the room. A second chair for visitors, wooden with a padded seat, was on my side of the desk. As I headed toward it, Young reached over to close the laptop on his desk before stepping around to take his seat.

"I don't suppose we're talking about a parking ticket?" He sounded surprisingly hopeful for a man who knew me pretty well.

I wasted no time before disillusioning him. "No, unfortunately, it's a murder."

The detective had barely had a chance to sit down. Now he suddenly stiffened. "Where?"

"It happened in Ridgefield."

He relaxed fractionally, now that he knew this wasn't his problem. "And you became involved how?"

"It started with a dog," I said.

"Of course it did." Detective Young wasn't surprised. He had often seen Faith by my side.

"My son wanted to meet a Great Dane, and my Aunt

Peg happened to have a friend who bred them. She arranged for us to pay a visit to a woman named Audrey Kane."

The detective couldn't help himself. Even though the case had nothing to do with him, he was already reaching for a pen and a pad of paper to begin jotting down notes.

"Great Danes," he said. "Wonderful dogs."

"They are," I agreed. "Do you have one?"

"No, not at present. Please continue."

"That was the first time—and only time—Audrey and I met. Several days later, she was murdered inside her home."

Young looked up from his pad. "You are bad luck, aren't you?"

"That's not funny," I said.

"Perhaps that depends on which side of the desk you're sitting."

"Also not funny." But I was smiling when I said it.

"Knowing you, you began to talk to people," he said. "You're some kind of talker. It's like your superpower. People who won't even open their mouths for the police, somehow manage to tell you all sorts of things."

"It's because I'm not threatening," I told him. "Especially compared to big men in uniforms who demand answers, rather than asking for them."

Detective Young frowned. He didn't write that down.

"And also because I'm chatty. One minute, we'll just be talking about dogs, and then the next thing people know . . ."

"You slip in something about murder," he muttered. "Rather like the way this conversation seems to be proceeding."

The clouds in the sky outside had shifted slightly. Now the sun was shining through the window directly into my eyes. I squinted for a moment, then half stood and inched my chair around to a different angle.

Detective Young noticed the movement. "If you were a suspect, I'd tell you to sit still, under the theory that a little discomfort might be good for you."

"If I were a suspect," I retorted, "I'd have my attorney with me, and I probably wouldn't be talking to you at all."

"What? You don't trust me?"

"Not entirely." I hoped he wouldn't be offended.

Instead, Young nodded. "Good. Keep it that way. The way you're going, I wouldn't be surprised if the day comes when you and I aren't on the same side. When it does, I won't hesitate to do what I have to do."

"Noted," I said.

"Back to the topic at hand: I assume the Ridgefield PD is investigating?"

"I'm sure they are," I told him. "But there haven't been any updates about their investigation in the media."

Young looked at me across the desktop. "That's because they're not obligated to keep the public informed. And because in some cases, releasing information prematurely can hinder an investigation."

I tried to look contrite as he delivered his little lecture. I probably failed.

"How large is the pool of suspects?"

"Big enough," I said. "Audrey had a stepsister from whom she'd been estranged for many years and recently reconciled. Also, an ex-husband who's currently involved with that sister. There's a dogsitter with easy access to the house, who may have been stealing from her. And a neighbor and a real estate dealer, both Audrey's friends, who had been pressuring her to sell her property. They thought they had a deal worked out, but it recently fell through. There are also various other dog show competitors of Audrey's who have what seem to me to be lesser motives."

"You've been busy," Detective Young said.

"It's summer," I said with a shrug. That was easier than

trying to explain why I seemed to have a knack for getting mixed up in other people's problems. Frankly, I didn't really understand it myself.

The detective bit back a smile. "I hadn't realized this was what you did to keep busy when school was out."

"And sometimes during the school year too," I admitted. He already knew that. "So what do I do now?"

This time, he did crack a smile. "I suppose it wouldn't make any difference if I told you to go home, play with your Poodles, and put this problem out of your mind?"

"Probably not," I replied. "My question was more about the fact that I don't know anyone at the Ridgefield PD. So I have all this information and nothing to do with it."

Young sat back in his chair. "You do realize that their investigative team has probably compiled much of the same information, right?"

I nodded.

"So maybe you should just relax and let them do their jobs."

That wasn't the answer I'd been looking for. "Did I mention that Audrey's stepsister is the one who asked me to get involved?"

"No."

"Does it make a difference?"

"Also no."

"Usually you're more helpful," I told him.

"There is no *usually* here," Detective Young said firmly. "On those *rare* occasions when we've been able to help each other, it's because you've had something useful to share that's pertinent to one of my cases. But that's not what's happening here."

No, it wasn't. Even so, I'd harbored hopes that meeting with Detective Young would give me a way to move forward. I took one last shot.

"Do you have a contact in Ridgefield you could put me in touch with?"

He didn't answer. I took that to mean that he didn't want to lie. Also, that he didn't want to help me. When the detective stood up, I did too. It wasn't as if I had a choice.

"I appreciate your taking the time to see me," I said.

"No problem," he replied. "It's always interesting. Do you know your way out?"

I assured him I did, and left. So far, my day hadn't been stellar. It didn't improve from there.

Aunt Peg called as I was leaving the building. Rather than bothering with a conventional greeting, she simply said, "Where are you?"

"Just leaving the Greenwich Police Department."

"Were you arrested?" Being Aunt Peg, she sounded hopeful.

"No, just visiting."

"Too bad. In that case, you may come and visit me too. As you might be able to tell, I'm not pleased."

She wasn't the only one. Sam and I weren't happy either.

"I'll expect you in twenty minutes," she said, then disconnected the call.

As it happened, the St. Moritz Bakery was a block away from where I was standing. Aunt Peg's sweet tooth wasn't merely prodigious, it was near legendary. If I hurried, I could pick up a cake and still make it to Aunt Peg's backcountry house in the allotted time. She could hardly start yelling upon my arrival if I showed up carrying a bakery box.

When I parked in front of Aunt Peg's house, I saw that Ebony had joined the Poodle posse that came streaming down the front stairs to greet me. In little more than a week's time, the black Great Dane had become an integral part of Aunt Peg's household, just as Daisy had done in Sam's and mine. I got out and said hello to the dogs, then reached back into the Volvo for the cake.

Aunt Peg was standing in the doorway. "What's that?" she asked.

As if anyone would believe she didn't recognize the box. "You know perfectly well what it is."

"You're trying to butter me up with cake." Now her hands were propped on her hips.

"Actually, I'm trying to start this visit on a sweet rather than sour note. Because from my vantage point, it could go either way."

Aunt Peg's eyes narrowed. Apparently it hadn't occurred to her that I might also have good reason to be every bit as annoyed as she was. "It had better be mocha cake."

We both knew that was her favorite. "It is."

"Then I suppose you can come in."

Never mind that I was already climbing the stairs. She eyed the box then leaned down and took a delicate sniff. At close range, the cake smelled just as delicious as it was going to taste.

"I should hope you'd invite me inside," I said, stepping around her. "Considering you're the one who called me."

"What else was I supposed to do when Davey failed to show up this morning?"

"I don't know. Maybe talk to Sam when he called to tell you why?"

"Pish. Sam was in a hurry. I didn't want to trouble him for a long explanation."

I shook my head in disbelief. More likely, she'd decided that if she had to do battle with one of us, she'd rather it was me.

Leaving her behind, I headed down the hallway to the kitchen. I put the box on the counter, then got out plates and silverware, while Aunt Peg called the four black dogs into the house. Five sets of feet made quite a bit of noise upon approach. With the three Standard Poodles, her kitchen had never felt crowded before. Now it suddenly did. Ebony took up a lot of space.

"I hope you have something useful to tell me," Aunt Peg said, as she removed the cake from its box and set it down in the middle of the table. "According to Davey, you've been talking to all sorts of people."

"I have, and I do. But before we get to that, you and I need to talk about what you and Davey have been up to."

"*Up to.*" She snorted under her breath as we took seats on either side of the table. "You make it sound as though my giving Davey a little driving experience was something nefarious."

"Actually, that's a very good word for what you did," I told her. "You and Davey both knew Sam and I wouldn't approve. Otherwise, you wouldn't have kept it a secret."

"Here." Aunt Peg cut off a generous wedge of cake, slid it on a plate, and handed it to me. "Maybe this will improve your mood."

"My mood is appropriate to the topic at hand," I said firmly, then helped myself to a big bite of cake. "I assume you're aware that Davey doesn't have a learner's permit."

"He told me he's getting one in September."

I didn't see how that had any bearing on the topic at hand.

"After what you and he conspired to do, maybe not," I said. "Sam and I will have to see how we feel when the time comes. Besides, it's June now and Davey hasn't turned sixteen yet. No matter how you feel about it, *legally*, he's not old enough to drive."

"Which is why we never left this little lane." Aunt Peg was being deliberately obtuse. She'd also already managed to devour half her piece of cake. "Davey was very careful behind the wheel. With more experience, he's going to be a fine driver. I have no idea why you're so upset."

"You lied to us," I said.

She considered that. "Not really. Only by omission."

"And you encouraged him to do the same."

Aunt Peg shook her head. "Trust me, Davey didn't need any encouragement from me to keep quiet."

"Because he knew he would be in trouble if he told us what he was doing." This was like arguing with a brick wall.

"Don't be so prissy," she sniffed. "Some rules are made to be broken."

"Said no parent ever," I growled.

"Seriously, Melanie, you need to lighten up. Davey's in high school now. It's time for him to spread his wings."

"That's not up to you to decide. Why can't you understand that?"

Suddenly the mocha cake tasted like ashes in my mouth. I had said what I needed to say, and it made no difference at all. I hadn't expected an apology. But I'd thought Aunt Peg might offer an acknowledgment that she'd overstepped. Instead, she had doubled down on her conviction that she was right. As always.

I pushed back the bench and stood up. Aunt Peg was reaching for another piece of cake. "Do you need something to drink?" she asked.

"No, I'm leaving."

She looked surprised. "But you haven't told me what you've found out about Audrey's murder."

"That's because you're not listening to me. So I guess there's no point in my continuing to speak. Enjoy the cake. I'll let myself out."

I was tempted to look back as I left the kitchen, if only to see the expression on her face. But then it occurred to me that I probably wouldn't like what I saw. So instead I just kept walking.

Chapter 27

"It didn't go well at all," I told Sam.

I'd only been home for five minutes before offering my confession. The boys and most of the dogs were out back doing something that involved a lot of shrieking from Kevin. Only Faith and Plum had remained inside.

The puppy was sitting next to Sam's chair in the living room, and Faith was lying across my lap on the couch. I rested my hand on her warm back. It was nice to know that I had someone's unconditional support.

"You lost your temper, didn't you?" Sam said.

I skirted the question. "I brought Aunt Peg a mocha cake from St. Moritz."

"I'm sure she appreciated the gesture." He sounded amused. "Until you laid into her."

"Since you and I were in agreement, I thought we were going to talk to her together," I said.

"So did I, but then apparently you went rogue."

We both smiled. It wasn't the first time.

"Aunt Peg called and demanded my presence. So I went. The worst part was, she wasn't the least bit penitent."

Sam's brow lifted. "Did you expect her to be?"

"Yes! Well . . . maybe not. But I *wanted* her to be."

"Good luck with that."

"Instead of apologizing, she told me to lighten up," I grumbled.

"That sounds like Peg. Going on the offensive rather than admitting that she did something wrong."

"Do you think I need to lighten up?" The comment had definitely gotten under my skin. I wanted my sons to feel like I set reasonable boundaries on their behavior. Now, thanks to Aunt Peg, I was beginning to wonder if I'd over-reacted.

"Not in this case," Sam replied. "It's up to us to steer Davey and Kevin away from making bad decisions. Parenting isn't a lightweight job, no matter what Peg says."

I heard the back door fly open. I was pretty sure it hit the wall and bounced off. That sharp smack was just the beginning of the commotion. A trio of Standard Poodles, one Great Dane, a small mutt, and two energetic boys were all racing in our direction. It sounded like we were being invaded by Mongol hordes.

"Brace yourself," Sam said, and I did so happily. I had been away a lot lately. A little family time was just what I needed.

The Poodles came running into the room first. Everyone else was right behind them. Plum jumped up and began to bark. Bud skidded sideways on the wooden floor before regaining his footing. Kevin saw me and made a beeline for the couch.

"Mom's home!" He threw himself into my arms, narrowly missing Faith who'd had the good sense to move away when she saw him coming. "Now we can go get ice cream!"

"We can?" That wasn't what I'd expected to hear. I'd just been eating cake. "What about lunch?"

"It's summer vacation. We're having ice cream for lunch," Kevin informed me. "Dad promised."

I looked at Sam. He shrugged. Something must have

happened that I wasn't aware of yet. Okay. I was nothing if not flexible. I could get on board with this plan.

"Where are we going?" I asked Kevin.

"The Creamery. Right now!" He wriggled away from me and began to slide off my lap. I loosened my arms and let him go. "I call shotgun!"

"No way," I told him. "I'm not riding in the back seat."

"Then you'd better hurry," Davey said with a grin.

Kev and Sam were way ahead of us. They'd already left the room. Davey was waiting for me.

"I heard you yelled at Aunt Peg," he said.

"News travels fast." I looked at him as I stood up. I hated the idea of Davey and Aunt Peg conspiring behind my back. "She texted you, didn't she?"

He nodded.

"Did she tell you she yelled at me too?"

"She implied it. I told her she was wrong. And that I was wrong too."

I stopped walking. "You did?"

Davey held out his phone. "Do you want to see?"

"No, of course not. I believe you. I'm just surprised, that's all."

"Why?"

"Because yesterday you didn't seem convinced of that."

Davey shrugged. "I've had some time to think about what you said. Yesterday, all I could think about was that I wasn't going to be able to drive anymore. Today, I kind of get it. I shouldn't have lied to you and Sam. And I shouldn't have been driving. I mean, even when I was doing it, I knew it was wrong. But Aunt Peg offered, and I just wanted so badly to . . ."

"To be sixteen?" I said.

"Yeah, I guess."

"It's only three more months."

"That's easy for you to say, you're old." Davey caught my eye and began to laugh. After a moment, I joined in.

"I apologized to Sam earlier. I told him I hoped he'd forgive me and still be willing to teach me to drive when the time comes. Because I hardly learned anything from Aunt Peg. She was a terrible driving instructor."

I could see that. "She's impatient."

Davey nodded.

"And she thinks there's only one way to do things, and it's her way."

"Yup," he agreed.

"Sam will do a much better job."

"I know. I told him that too."

"I'm glad the two of you have made up," I said.

"Me too." He blew out a breath.

I started walking toward the hallway. It sounded as though Sam and Kevin were already in the garage. "Is this why we're having ice cream?"

"Yes." Davey fell into step beside me. "And because when Kevin fell off the tire swing, Sam told him he was fine, and that an ice cream cone would make his arm feel all better."

Wait. *What?*

I whirled around to face him. "Kevin fell off the swing?"

Davey looked abashed. He probably wasn't supposed to mention that.

"Tell me," I said.

"It's not a big deal. Kevin didn't get hurt. Sam said he's fine."

"Sam's not a doctor."

"Mom. Let it go." Davey stopped walking and placed a hand on my shoulder. "Really. Kevin is okay."

I sighed. I had just seen Kevin, and he'd appeared to be uninjured. I hadn't noticed anything wrong with his arm. Davey was probably right. I should just go and enjoy my ice cream.

Motherhood. There were days when I wondered how anyone ever survived it.

* * *

When we returned from the ice cream parlor, I called Lara Minchin.

She said she was happy to hear from me, but her tone didn't match her words. When I invited myself over for a visit, at least she didn't turn me down. Since Lara was the one who'd initiated my involvement, I figured the least she could do was listen to what I had to say. And maybe provide me with more information.

Lara lived in a newly constructed town house community on the Norwalk border, just over the line from Darien. Four rows of handsome red brick buildings surrounded an inner courtyard whose landscaping looked like it was still a work in progress. An area that was covered with freshly laid sod sported a NO DOGS ALLOWED sign.

I hoped it was only in reference to the courtyard and not the development as a whole. Because Lara's Great Dane, Milo, was hard to miss.

I had to knock twice before Lara's front door opened. At my house a delay like that would have been accompanied by a lot of barking. If Milo was inside the town house, however, he wasn't saying a word.

Lara finally pulled the door open, then stood there staring at me. She was wearing a pair of Bermuda shorts with a silky V-neck top that dipped low in the front. Her feet were bare, and her toenails were painted a bright shade of pink.

"May I come in?" I asked.

Lara stepped back out of the way. "You know, when you first told me you were looking for Audrey's brooch, I didn't realize this was going to become a whole thing."

"What does that mean?"

"In the past two weeks, I've seen more of you than I have of people I like. It seems like every time I turn around, there you are."

"You're the one who asked me to look into Audrey's murder. You wanted answers. This is how it works."

"Yes, but wouldn't it work better if I wasn't involved?"

"No," I told her firmly. "Not even close."

Apparently Lara wasn't going to offer me a seat, so I walked past her into a living room that looked as though a decorator had been given instructions to re-create a set from *Downton Abbey*. I perched on the edge of a spindly velvet-covered settee that thankfully was stronger than it appeared, and waited for her to join me.

"Where's Milo?" I asked.

Lara waved a hand. "He's around here somewhere. Probably asleep upstairs."

"He must not be much of a watchdog."

"Milo's pretty chill," she said. "Which is a good thing, because I have to keep him mostly out of sight. Each unit here is allowed to have one pet, but it has to weigh under fifty pounds."

I snorted out a laugh. Milo wasn't even close.

"Yeah, I know." Lara finally took a seat on a straight-backed chair. She brought one leg up and curled it underneath herself, then wiggled around until she was comfortable. "So far, I've been able to work around it. I walk him very early in the morning and then again late at night, so usually no one's around. During the day, Milo exercises on a treadmill. Other than that, he mostly sleeps."

None of that sounded normal. Especially not for a big healthy dog who was in the prime of his life. But Lara was already moving on.

"I know you didn't come here to talk about my dog," she said. "How much longer is it going to take before you can tell me who killed Audrey?"

"I'm working on it."

"Maybe you could work faster."

"Maybe you could help," I said. "Let's talk about Audrey. She surrounded herself with interesting people."

Lara shrugged. "That's not surprising. Despite her flaws, Audrey was an interesting woman."

"Were you aware that she was thinking about selling her property?"

"I suppose I heard something about it." Her lips flattened in an unhappy line. "The place wasn't just her home, you know. After our parents got married, it was mine too."

I hadn't thought about that before. Maybe I should have.

"I was told the house had been in Audrey's family for generations."

"It was. That's why Marjorie insisted that my father and I join her there. She wouldn't consider living anywhere else. That's the home where Audrey and I first became family. Of course, my sentimental attachment to the place meant nothing. I had no say in what happened to any of it."

"I'm sorry," I said. "If it's any consolation, Audrey also felt conflicted about letting the house go. The idea was initiated by her neighbor, Bill Godfrey. He and Joe Wheeler put together a deal to sell the two properties together."

Since Joe had been sitting in the circle of Great Dane fanciers at the dog show where Lara and I first met, I assumed they knew each other. When she nodded in recognition, I added, "However, Audrey pulled out before the transaction could go through."

"She did the right thing. That deal wasn't in her best interests."

"Did Audrey tell you that?"

"Not exactly," Lara hedged.

"Then it must have been Carter Ridley who was keeping you apprised of Audrey's business dealings," I said.

Lara's expression darkened. She didn't reply.

"Why didn't you tell me that you and he were a couple?"

"Obviously because it wasn't something you needed to

know. My private life has no bearing on what happened to Audrey."

"Even when the man you're currently involved with is Audrey's ex-husband?"

"Even then," Lara insisted.

She either was very naïve or else thought that I was very stupid. But for now, I was willing to humor her by changing the subject. "Carter is the executor of Audrey's will. Has it been read yet?"

"Yes, a couple of days ago. At least Audrey didn't lie about leaving me her jewelry, so I guess that's something."

"Who inherited Audrey's property?" I asked.

"Some distant cousin whose last name is Kane," Lara replied bitterly. "Like the only thing that mattered was making sure the land stayed in the family for another generation. Whoever the guy is, Carter said the bequest came as a shock to him. I wouldn't be surprised if he unloads the place at the first opportunity."

So the dispersal of Audrey's assets had turned out to have no bearing on her death. That was one question answered.

"What about her Great Danes?" I asked.

Lara chuckled, but she didn't sound amused. "Dog people are bizarre. Audrey's will devoted more attention to her Danes than to anything else. Ralph Denby inherited them, which I guess is only fitting. He was concerned about those dogs from the beginning. I'm sure he'll do right by them now."

I nodded in agreement. That choice made perfect sense.

"Are we finished?" Lara started to rise.

I remained seated. "Almost, but not quite."

She sank back down, looking resigned. "Go ahead."

"The first time we spoke about Audrey's murder, you were concerned with the whereabouts of something in her house. You brought it up the day we were there picking up the Great Danes, and all but accused us of rifling through Audrey's private things. What were you afraid we might find?"

"It was nothing," Lara said quickly. "You're mistaken."

"No, I'm not. So I need you to rethink your answer. And before you do, remember that was the morning when Audrey's body had just been discovered. Were you in the house with her the night before? Did you leave something incriminating behind?"

"What a ridiculous question," Lara snapped. "I didn't kill Audrey."

"That's not what I asked you."

"My answer remains the same."

"Tell me what you're worried about, Lara. Because I've been giving that morning some thought. And I realized there were only two people who were less upset about what happened to Audrey than they were about what might be found inside the house: you and Carter Ridley. Now that I know the two of you are a couple, I have to wonder whether you plotted something together."

"That doesn't make sense," Lara said quickly. "What would either of us have to gain from Audrey's death?"

"I don't know. Why don't you tell me?"

"Okay, look." She blew out a breath. "Maybe I was at her house earlier in the evening. But it's not what you think."

"Keep going." I leaned forward in my seat.

"Audrey and I had been arguing. That was nothing new." Lara made a face. "It was about the house. Her family's house. But also my home too."

"Was it about the sale?"

"Only indirectly, in that when Joe and Bill had been throwing around numbers that were big enough to make Audrey's head spin, she'd decided that she needed to update her will."

So Lara had been lying when she'd initially told me she didn't think Audrey had a will. I wasn't about to stop the flow of words to point that out.

"Audrey planned to leave the property to her closest Kane family relative. I tried to convince her that it should come to me. She refused outright." Lara paused to glare at me. "I'll admit her attitude ticked me off royally. And justifiably. So I plotted a little revenge."

She held up a hand. "And no, before you open your mouth again, I did *not* kill her."

I nodded and remained silent.

"I told you why Carter and Audrey got divorced. Even though it was Audrey's fault, she refused to accept the blame. According to Audrey, she never stopped loving Carter. She once told me she still had all the love notes he'd ever written to her. She was convinced that one day he'd come back to her."

"But that wasn't going to happen," I said.

"Of course not. Everyone knew that, except for Audrey. Look, you wanted honesty, so here it is. The fact that Audrey still had feelings for Carter is one of the reasons I went after him. Of all the things she and I ever fought over, he was just about the only one I could have and she couldn't. I liked knowing that I'd finally managed to best her in something."

I never thought I would feel sorry for Carter Ridley. But now I did. Just a tiny bit.

"The day before Audrey died, she and I argued about her will again. I got mad and blurted out that having a stupid piece of land was nothing compared to knowing that I was the sister Carter truly loved."

"Before that, Audrey hadn't known that the two of you were together?"

"No, of course not." Lara smirked. "That was our little secret."

Judging by her expression, she had kept the relationship

secret for this very purpose—so it could be revealed at a moment when it would cause maximum damage.

"I thought Audrey would be devastated," Lara said. "But instead, she laughed and said she didn't believe me. That there was no way Carter would ever be interested in someone as ordinary as me."

I sucked in a breath. That was harsh. When this lifelong feud had finally come to a head, both sisters had known not only where to stick the knife but also just how to twist it once it was in.

"Our whole lives, Audrey had had the upper hand, but now I couldn't wait to prove her wrong. I returned the next evening with something I knew she would immediately recognize: a packet of love letters Carter had written to me."

And the cruelty continued, I thought. "What did she say when she saw them?"

"When I got to Audrey's house, she said she didn't have time to talk to me. She was expecting someone else to arrive shortly. But I didn't care. I was *done* with letting Audrey dictate everything. I followed her into the house, and when she refused to even acknowledge me, I untied the ribbon holding the notes together and threw them at her."

Lara recounted the scene with relish. "You can't imagine how satisfying that was. All those little white papers floating through the air like tiny angels of doom. Audrey picked one up and read it. Then she raised her eyes. You know the saying 'if looks could kill'? That was the expression on her face. I swear I felt a shiver go down my spine."

If Lara was hoping I'd feel sympathetic, she needed to be telling a very different story. Especially since Audrey was the sister who had ended up dead, while Lara was still here to enjoy her revenge.

"What happened next?" I asked.

"Audrey started screaming, 'Get out! Get out of my house! I never want to see you again!' She snatched up a jade statue and came charging at me. I never intended to leave Carter's notes behind, but Audrey gave me no choice. She all but chased me out the door."

"So those love letters were what you didn't want anyone to find in Audrey's house?"

"Of course," Lara said, as if the answer was obvious.

"Did you tell this to the police?"

"No way. I'm not stupid. Since Audrey was expecting company, I figured she probably gathered up the notes after I left. Maybe she threw them out. But they were still there somewhere, inside the house, and that was bad enough. If I'd also admitted to being there shortly before she was killed, the police would decide I was suspect number one."

Not without reason, I thought.

"Audrey told you she was expecting someone. Do you know who that person was?"

"No, and I didn't ask. I had more important things on my mind, like showing Audrey proof that Carter loved me and not her. The stupid thing was, even then I could hardly get her to pay attention to me. Audrey was totally distracted, she was just ranting about crazy stuff."

"That's interesting," I said. "What was she saying?"

"All sorts of things." The memory made Lara look annoyed all over again. "She even said something about that damn brooch. Why was she still going on about that? I told her I didn't know where it was. Surely it was time to put that stupid accusation to rest."

"The brooch." My breath caught in my throat.

"Yes." Lara frowned. "The one *you* still haven't found."

"I think I'm getting closer," I said.

Chapter 28

The following morning, Davey once again stayed home, and I went to Aunt Peg's house by myself.

She was outside when I arrived. The gate to her field was open to allow the passage of a hose that was attached to the spigot beside the garage. Aunt Peg stood with her back to the driveway, watering the small garden she and Davey had planted the week before. Her blue jeans were rolled up to just beneath her knees, and her sneakers were covered in mud.

Her three Poodles and Ebony all came running to give me a boisterous greeting when I got out of the car, so Aunt Peg had to have been aware that she had a visitor. Even so, she didn't bother to turn around. Maybe she'd already sneaked a peek and knew it was me.

I guessed that told me where we stood.

I patted the tops of Hope's and Coral's heads, then scratched beneath Joker's chin. Ebony, who could have easily pushed all of the Poodles aside, politely waited her turn. I rewarded her by running my hands along the sides of her muzzle, then rubbing my thumbs gently beneath her eyes. The Dane's long black tail wagged slowly back and forth in response.

Then, finally, I headed in Aunt Peg's direction. Since she still hadn't acknowledged my presence, I figured there was a fifty-fifty chance that she would spray me with the hose. As I passed through the gate into the field, I saw she'd all but flooded the small garden plot.

"If you drown those seeds, they won't grow," I commented.

Aunt Peg abruptly cut off the flow of water. "They don't appear to be growing anyway."

She was always impatient. That was nothing new.

"You planted them a week ago," I said. "I think it's too soon."

Finally Aunt Peg turned to look at me. "Is that why you came—to lecture me again?"

If she was still on the offensive, I wasn't about to back down either. When she was indignant, Aunt Peg behaved like an irate bull. Reveal the slightest bit of apprehension, and she would lower her head and charge.

"No," I replied. "But I also won't deny that you deserved the lecture you already had."

She tossed the nozzle on the ground. "Maybe."

Even a partial capitulation was a first for Aunt Peg. For a moment I was so surprised, I couldn't think of anything to say.

"Now what?" she demanded. "Are you waiting for an apology?"

"No, I—"

"Then here it is. I'm sorry. Upon reflection, I overstepped. I'd say it won't happen again, but it probably will. So consider yourself forewarned, and let's move on."

I'd heard better apologies. But coming from Aunt Peg, I was willing to take what I could get. I was also ready to reciprocate.

"I'm sorry too," I said. "I shouldn't have lost my temper. I turned what should have been a rational discussion into a bit of a brawl."

Aunt Peg shrugged, but I could tell she was mollified.

"At least you brought cake. That removed some of the sting."

She turned away from me to call the dogs. "You lot! Stop sniffing around the driveway and come in here so I can close the gate."

Like her family, Aunt Peg's canines were well trained. The Poodles leapt to comply and Ebony wasn't far behind. Aunt Peg ushered the four dogs through the opening, then latched the gate behind them. No sooner were they in the field than the dogs saw something interesting at the other end, and went racing away.

"Look at her." Aunt Peg gazed after the Great Dane fondly. "I would swear Ebony's begun to think she's a Standard Poodle. I never for a moment pictured myself living with a Dane, and yet she's such a dear dog. I hope she'll be happy in her next home, wherever it turns out to be."

"Ralph Denby," I said. The cedar bench was in the shade nearby. I walked over and took a seat.

"What about him?"

"Audrey left all her dogs to him in her will."

"Is that so?" Aunt Peg considered the information. "Good choice on her part. How did you find that out?"

"I've learned all sorts of things in the past few days." I patted the seat beside me. She came over and sat down too. "I thought we might discuss them yesterday, but then we got sidetracked."

"That was hardly my fault," Aunt Peg stated.

"Don't start," I warned her.

"That same goes for you," she shot back.

At the same time, we both stopped talking. First, I smiled. Then she finally did too.

"Truce," I said.

"If you insist." So help me, she almost looked disappointed.

I ignored that and said, "I need your help."

"So what else is new?" Aunt Peg settled in against the slatted backrest. "I suppose you'd better start at the beginning."

"You already know the beginning. And the middle. I'll start with Carter Ridley because he's the executor of Audrey's will."

"Really? Even though he and Audrey are divorced?"

I nodded. "Carter's a banker, and after the divorce he continued to act as her financial advisor. But you might be right to be suspicious about whether he was acting in her best interests, because it turns out that he and Lara, Audrey's stepsister, are involved with each other."

I'd already managed to surprise her twice in quick succession. Aunt Peg looked quite pleased by the way the conversation was proceeding.

"Was Audrey aware of that?" she asked.

"Not until the night she died. Had she known earlier, I suspect she would have found a new advisor. Lara admitted to me that the main reason she was attracted to Carter was because she knew Audrey wanted him back."

"Sibling rivalry," Aunt Peg muttered.

"Precisely. It was bad when they were children, and only got worse when they became adults. And here's something else. Remember the story Miranda told me about Ralph having the hots for Audrey and his wife, Nattie, being upset about it? It turns out that was only half true."

"Well, that's interesting. Which half?"

"The half which makes Nattie no longer a suspect in Audrey's death," I told her. "Nattie would have had no reason to despise Audrey, because the person Ralph actually had an affair with is Miranda."

"No!"

"Yes. She told me they first got together after Audrey dumped Ralph and before he married Nattie. Miranda had had her eye on Ralph for a while. She hoped their re-lationship would turn into something permanent."

Aunt Peg considered that. "So if I'm understanding cor-rectly, Ralph could have married Miranda if he'd wanted to . . . but then Nattie came along and he chose her in-stead."

"You're correct," I said. "That's the way it worked out."

"But why?"

"You're not going to like the answer," I said.

"I often dislike your answers, but that never seems to stop you."

A sad commentary on our relationship, but true never-theless.

"Nattie and Ralph met when she came to work for him at the nursery. And then she turned out be very good for business. She's some kind of genius when it comes to land-scape design."

"You're right. I don't like that," Aunt Peg decided. "He chose money over love. And I'm guessing he now regrets that decision?"

"More like he now wants to have his cake and eat it too." I knew she would enjoy the cake reference, but Aunt Peg didn't smile. Instead, she was frowning on Miranda's behalf.

"I hope Miranda told Ralph to take a flying leap," she said.

"For the most part, yes." I wasn't about to mention Pittsburgh. Otherwise, we'd be here all morning, and I still had several other topics to get to. "Remember the intrud-ers Audrey warned Tasha about?"

"How could I forget?" Aunt Peg abruptly sat up straight. "Speaking as another older woman who lives alone in a somewhat secluded house, what she said made me think twice about my own security."

"Then this will make you feel better. The intruders

turned out to be a team of property surveyors, sent by a real estate agent who was working with Audrey's neighbor, Bill Godfrey. The two men were hoping to list Audrey's property for sale in a package deal that also included Bill's place."

"That's ridiculous." Aunt Peg snorted. She was outraged all over again. "They started the process without Audrey's knowledge or permission? Bill must have been delusional."

"From what I was told, Audrey initially agreed to explore the possibility of a sale, but then she changed her mind—"

"As she had every right to do," Aunt Peg snapped.

"Yes, absolutely. But Bill and Joe Wheeler, the real estate guy, were reluctant to take no for an answer. Plus, they'd already begun to move forward with some aspects of the deal."

Aunt Peg huffed out a breath. "More controlling men. It sounds as though Audrey was surrounded by them."

"I agree. Which makes what I have to tell you next even more surprising. It's about Tasha."

"Tasha." Her expression brightened. "She of the lovely Viburnum. I've replanted it in a sunny spot on the other side of the house. I shall have to thank her the next time I see her."

"I'm hoping that will happen shortly," I said.

"Oh?" Aunt Peg turned to me with interest. "Why is that?"

"Because I'm almost certain Tasha is the person responsible for Audrey's death."

Chapter 29

"What?" Aunt Peg swiveled in her seat to stare at me. "You might have led with that information."

"I intended to. I came here today to talk to you about Tasha. But then you told me to start at the beginning, so I backtracked a bit."

"Oh pish!" she said. "Since when have you ever done a single thing I told you to?"

Only like . . . *always.*

"Tasha Gilbert." Aunt Peg closed her eyes and thought. "I'm trying to remember what I know about her, which beyond the fact that she was Audrey's dogsitter, is only slightly more than nothing."

"The dogsitter part is important," I told her. "Because that's what gave Tasha easy access to Audrey's house. In fact, she had her own key. It also meant that Betty, Audrey's house Dane, was comfortable having her around. And since Betty wouldn't have been wary of Tasha, it explains how Tasha was able to get close enough to Audrey to harm her."

Aunt Peg nodded. She could see that. "I seem to recall there was something peculiar about the timing of when Betty was loose in the house and when she was subsequently locked away in the pantry. Am I remembering that correctly?"

"You are, and it's something I've continued to puzzle over. The problem was that Betty was nowhere to be seen when Bill discovered Audrey's body. Which means the Dane must have been confined somewhere. Yet later, when the police arrived, Betty was loose in the house. As Davey pointed out that morning, for both those things to be true, someone had to have been inside Audrey's house between the two times."

"Quite right," Aunt Peg agreed. "That was exactly the problem."

"Someone *was* inside the house that morning, and just about the only person it could have been is Tasha. Bill told us that he'd called her right away, remember? He even commented on how quickly she arrived. I think that's because she was already there."

"Let's just say you have me slightly convinced," Aunt Peg said. "If what you're saying is correct, you've cleared up a minor mystery while leaving a much larger one untouched. What could Tasha possibly have had to gain by Audrey's death?"

The Poodles and Ebony came trotting back. All four dogs were out of breath and panting, their tongues hanging out of their mouths. Aunt Peg took one look at them and stood up.

"Let's move this discussion inside, shall we? Those four look like they could use a drink of water and a cool place to lie down."

"You're just angling to get to your kitchen," I teased. "I'm guessing that means there's leftover cake."

"I should hope so," she huffed. "You only brought it by yesterday. I suppose it wouldn't hurt to share a piece or two while we continue our conversation."

Ten minutes later, the dogs had drunk two bowls of cold water and sacked out on the kitchen floor. I'd helped myself to a cup of coffee. Aunt Peg had her usual Eary Grey tea. The mocha cake was sitting on the table between us. I cut off two slices and put one on each of our plates.

Aunt Peg picked up her fork and said, "Now that we're settled again, tell me about Tasha, and how she might have profited by Audrey's death."

"Actually, it seems to me that the answer is less about what Tasha had to gain than what she stood to lose."

"Intriguing." She pondered that briefly, then motioned for me to continue.

"Once again, think back to that day when we picked up Audrey's Danes." I used a small pause to slip a piece of cake in my mouth. "Do you remember proposing that rather than taking all the Danes away, we should hire Tasha to care for them in place?"

"Of course I remember that. It was a sensible idea. It's a shame it didn't work out."

"Right. And the reason it didn't work is because Tasha said she was too busy to take on the care of so many dogs on short notice. Except that she wasn't."

Aunt Peg's fork had been on its way to her mouth. Her hand stilled, and she peered at me with interest. "How do you know that?"

"Later, when I talked to her at the nursery, she said she'd taken a part-time job there because she needed to supplement her income."

"Maybe the nursery job was what Tasha was referring to when she said her time was already engaged."

I shook my head. "It couldn't have been, because Tasha made it clear that she was still looking for additional work. She was hoping Ralph would increase her hours, but he hadn't done so yet. So money was still an issue for her. Then, a few days later, she came up with another bogus reason to justify turning down your offer. Tasha said she couldn't do it because she was too spooked to go back inside Audrey's house."

"That's just silly," Aunt Peg sniffed. "There was no need for Tasha to go inside Audrey's house. Just put Betty in the kennel with the other Danes, and the problem is solved."

"Indeed." I sipped my coffee, then quickly helped myself to another bite of cake. Aunt Peg watched, impatient for me to move along. "Now that I've laid some of the groundwork, I need to circle back to the event that set everything in motion."

She cocked a brow. "Kevin and his love for Great Danes?"

"Not exactly." I smiled though, because she was partly correct. "I was thinking of Audrey's missing platinum brooch."

"Oh, yes. The harlequin Dane with the sapphire eye. With everything that's happened since, I'd forgotten all about it. Have you finally found it?"

"Not yet. But I'm pretty sure I know where it is."

"It's about time." Aunt Peg helped herself to another piece of cake. "Do tell."

"If my suspicions are correct, Tasha took Audrey's brooch, and she still has it. Not only that, but the theft is directly related to the reason that Audrey ended up dead."

"Surely the brooch wasn't worth killing someone over," Aunt Peg said thoughtfully. "I'm going to require additional explanation."

"Okay, let's start with this. Audrey's house is a veritable treasure trove of collectibles. Small, valuable items that Tasha could easily sell or pawn to make some quick cash. I suspect Tasha has been making ends meet for a while by stealing from Audrey. And that when she nabbed the brooch, it was just bad luck she took something Audrey would immediately notice was gone."

Aunt Peg had been to Audrey's home, too. She was already nodding before I'd finished speaking. "I can see how a missing crystal bowl might have gone unnoticed, but a platinum and diamond brooch? What was Tasha thinking? She must not be very bright if she thought she could get away with that."

Aunt Peg and I both set our cake plates aside so we could concentrate. I had uncovered clues and put them in order. Now I was hoping the conclusion I'd reached was correct. If Aunt Peg agreed with my assessment, I would feel more confident that I was on the right track.

"There's something else," I said. "Lara told me she was with Audrey early in the evening on the day she was murdered. Lara knew Audrey had been thinking about selling the property, which led to a dispute about Audrey's will. That night, Lara told Audrey she was seeing Carter. Audrey denied it was true, then kicked Lara out of the house. She said she was expecting someone else to arrive shortly."

"Tasha?" Aunt Peg said.

"I'm guessing yes. Because Audrey mentioned her missing brooch as Lara was leaving. The brooch that I asked Tasha about a few days ago. She wasn't even slightly convincing when she denied knowing anything about it."

Aunt Peg gazed at me across the table, considering everything she'd heard. "That's quite a lot to take in at once. And a fair amount of supposition on your part. How sure are you that you're right?"

"Maybe ninety percent," I admitted. "But that's still pretty good. Even better, I think I have a plan that will enable us to find out. But I'm going to need your help to make it happen."

"I believe you mentioned that earlier." Aunt Peg looked pleased to be included. Especially now that I was finally getting to the point. "What do I need to do?"

"This part's easy. All you have to do is offer Tasha a job."

"Excuse me?" she sputtered.

"Last week, when Tasha said she was looking for more

work, I told her that dog show judges travel a lot and are often in need of a reliable dogsitter. Since she was eager to book extra jobs, I volunteered to recommend her to you."

"And yet you've just made an excellent case for her lack of reliability," Aunt Peg pointed out.

"Yes, but that won't matter, because you're not actually going to hire her. You're only going to make her think it's a possibility. You'll invite her to come here for an interview and to meet your Poodles, just as you would if you were actually considering her services."

"And then what?" She eyed me suspiciously.

"Then we'll confront her with everything we know. If we're lucky, we'll be able to convince Tasha to tell us what happened that night when she went to Audrey's house."

"That's a terrible plan," Aunt Peg grumbled. "What if Tasha tells us we're out of our minds and leaves?"

I shrugged. "In that case, we'll have no choice but to take what we know to the authorities."

She frowned. Like me, she'd had her own run-ins with the police. "They may not believe us."

There was nothing I could do about that. And I certainly wasn't going to tell her about the conversation I'd already had with Detective Young.

"I don't see that we have a choice," I said. "Unless you think that despite having come this far, we should just give up now."

Aunt Peg was never one to back down from a challenge. The comment stiffened her spine, just as I'd known it would. She nodded decisively. "Right. Then let's get on with it, shall we?"

Ebony was sound asleep on the floor next to the table, but the Poodles were beginning to stir. Aunt Peg looked down at Hope who was beside her chair. The bitch lifted her head questioningly.

"What do you think?" Aunt Peg asked her. "Are you

ready to entertain a visitor?" Hope rolled up off her side, then sat up. She was always happy to meet new people.

"That's what I thought." Aunt Peg turned to me. "Text me Tasha's phone number. I'll call her right now and see when she's available."

Aunt Peg stepped out of the kitchen to make the call. Hope went with her. While they were gone, I gathered up our silverware, plates, and mugs, and put them in the dishwasher. I returned the remaining piece of cake to its box and put it back in the refrigerator. Then I checked the water level in the dogs' bowls.

Coral and Joker watched this sudden flurry of activity with curiosity. Even Ebony eventually sat up. "You're going to play a role too," I told them. "If there's any hope of Tasha telling us what she knows, we all have to be totally convincing."

"Speak for yourself," Aunt Peg said, coming back into the kitchen. "I'm always convincing."

I couldn't argue with that. I didn't even try.

"What did Tasha say?" I asked. "Is she willing to meet with you for an interview?"

"Not just willing," Aunt Peg replied. "Eager. She thanked me for the opportunity and said she'd clear her schedule. She'll be here in half an hour."

Hearing that, I couldn't help but sigh.

"Now what's the matter?"

"This would easier if I didn't like Tasha," I said unhappily.

"And I would like Tasha more if you didn't suspect she was a murderer," Aunt Peg retorted. "So it looks as though we're both out of luck."

Chapter 30

With half an hour to kill, Aunt Peg and I took the dogs for a walk on the riding trails behind her house. It turned out that we didn't need to hurry back.

Forty-five minutes passed before Tasha pulled into Aunt Peg's driveway.

If I had been the one trying to make a good impression, I would have been on time. Or maybe even early.

"Strike one," Aunt Peg said, obviously agreeing with me.

As the Poodles ran to the front door, she and I were looking out her kitchen window. Tasha had pulled her car up beside my Volvo, but she still hadn't gotten out. I wondered if she recognized the other car as mine and, if so, that was why she was hesitating.

"This isn't a real interview," I said to Aunt Peg. "After today, you'll never have to worry about Tasha's lack of punctuality."

"Tardiness is a character flaw. Maybe it's indicative of other flaws." She didn't sound displeased by the idea. "Let's go see what else we can turn up."

When Aunt Peg went to open the front door, I walked past her to wait in the living room. The Poodles raced through the opening and down the steps, but Ebony remained in the doorway at Aunt Peg's side. The big black Dane stood like a statue. It almost looked as though she'd appointed herself as Aunt Peg's guardian. Then Ebony realized who our visitor was, and her tail began to wag.

Tasha slowly got out of her car. She was dressed as though she'd come directly from her job at the nursery. Her hair was pulled back in a long French braid, and I could see the Tokeneke logo on her shirt. When she saw the trio of Standard Poodles coming toward her, her face broke out in a huge smile. She opened her arms and bent down to say hello. A show of enthusiasm like that was going to soften Aunt Peg's attitude considerably.

After a minute, Tasha straightened and started up the steps. She paused at the top to greet Ebony with a hug, then turned to Aunt Peg and said, "Your Standard Poodles are gorgeous. Do you show them yourself?"

"Whenever I can," Aunt Peg replied. She moved back out of the doorway, taking Ebony with her so that Tasha could enter. "Unfortunately, I seldom have time to do so now."

"Aunt Peg judges all over the country." I stepped forward as Aunt Peg ushered the Poodles inside. "She travels frequently. Hi, Tasha. Thank you for coming."

The young woman's smile faltered briefly. "I didn't expect to see you here."

"Is that a problem?" I asked.

"No, of course not." Tasha didn't sound at all sure of that.

"Melanie and I do many things together," Aunt Peg said easily. "Let's sit down and have a chat, shall we?"

Her living room was spacious and filled with comfortable furniture. There was an antique captain's desk against one wall, and several armchairs were scattered about. Near the fireplace, two chintz-covered love seats faced each other across a low coffee table.

Aunt Peg headed that way, and Tasha and I followed. When we were settled, the Poodles and Ebony found places on the floor around us.

"I admire anyone who can show their own Poodles," Tasha said. "I didn't know anything about dog shows before I met Audrey, but now I've been to several. Poodles are a lot of work!"

"They are," Aunt Peg agreed. "But it's also a labor of love. Anyone who's lucky enough to have a Poodle will tell you that the time and effort spent on grooming is well worth it."

"Aunt Peg has her own grooming room downstairs," I said. "It looks like a professional salon. We'll show it to you later, if you like."

"Yes, please." Tasha leaned forward in her seat. "I'm always eager to add to my roster of clients. Go ahead and ask me anything you like. I have plenty of experience with puppies, adult dogs, and multiples." She paused to glance around at the group on the floor. "And I happen to have some openings at the moment, in case you might need someone to sit for you soon."

"What about references?" Aunt Peg asked. "Before we move forward, I would need to speak to several of your other current clients."

"I understand completely." Tasha nodded. "Leaving your dog with a sitter is almost the same as leaving your child with one. There's a huge element of trust involved."

"I couldn't agree more," Aunt Peg replied. "Trust is important in many endeavors. I hope you won't mind if I grill you about your capabilities."

"Of course not." Tasha bit her lip, then offered a small smile. "Fire away."

"I mentioned references a moment ago. As we're both well aware, your most recent client, perhaps your biggest client, is no longer able to vouch for the quality of your services."

"Sadly, no."

"How long had you been caring for Audrey's Great Danes?" I asked.

"Almost two years," Tasha said, then turned back to Aunt Peg. "Audrey often had me come and stay when she was going out of town. She liked having me on-site, because it meant there would be less upheaval in the dogs' routine."

"That makes sense," Aunt Peg agreed. "Did you get along well with Audrey's Danes?"

"Yes, very well. They're wonderful dogs. I'm sure you've been able to find out for yourselves." As if to punctuate the comment, Ebony let out a loud snore, and we all laughed.

"The last time we spoke," I said to Tasha, "you told me you were the only person who had a key to Audrey's house."

"That's right," she replied carefully.

"I also mentioned an heirloom brooch that had recently gone missing from her home. I believe you said you were familiar with the piece."

"Yes." The word was barely louder than a whisper.

I waited in case Tasha wanted to elaborate. She didn't.

"I got the impression that you knew where it was."

Her eyes widened. "I never said that!"

"Not in so many words," I allowed. "But it was obvious that you were the only person who'd been inside Audrey's house when she wasn't there."

Tasha's gaze skittered back and forth between Aunt Peg and me. "Audrey used to wear the brooch when she showed her dogs. It could have fallen off at a dog show. Maybe that's how she lost it."

"That's not what happened," I said mildly. "According to Audrey, the brooch wasn't lost. It was stolen."

"I don't know what you're talking about!"

Abruptly Tasha stood up. She banged her knee on the coffee table and Joker, whose body was near her feet, lifted his head to see what was going on. Before Tasha had a chance to move, Aunt Peg rose, too.

"Perhaps we should all take a step back," she said. "Melanie appears to be a bit overwrought. Tasha, would you like to take a tour of the house with me?"

"Yes, please!"

The two of them left the living room together. I stared after them unhappily, then got up and followed. What was Aunt Peg doing? I had been *this close* to backing Tasha into a corner. It was time to rachet up the pressure, not cool it down.

Instead, we were now heading toward the kitchen so that Aunt Peg could show Tasha where she stored her dog food. As if that was something Tasha would ever need to know. If Aunt Peg offered her cake next, I was going to get in my car and go home.

I watched as Tasha and Aunt Peg checked out the pantry. Then Aunt Peg refilled the dogs' water bowls. The entire time I was humming with impatience.

Finally, after Aunt Peg replaced the bowls on the floor, she turned to Tasha and said in the blandest of tones, "The thing is, dear girl, we know for a fact that you have Audrey's missing brooch. We also know you took it from her house, and that perhaps you were even thinking of returning it."

My mouth fell open. *Who knew that?* Certainly not me—at least not all of it. Aunt Peg had taken the story I'd told her earlier and built it into something that was more substantial, but also lacking in proof. Apparently she thought she could bluff her way to a confirmation.

Even more annoying, the tactic appeared to be working. Tasha had replied to my pointed questions with bluster of her own. But Aunt Peg's calm recitation of the supposed "facts" elicited a completely different response.

"How do you know that?" she asked.

"That's not important, now, is it?" Aunt Peg placed a hand on Tasha's back and guided her out of the kitchen. "Why don't we keep walking? I always find it easier to walk and talk, don't you?"

I didn't. But nobody asked me. Or even seemed to care that I was there.

"My grooming room is state-of-the-art, if I do say so myself," Aunt Peg said. "Let's go have a look. You never know when you might need to clip a nail or replace a wrap."

Joker, Hope, and Coral were waiting for us in the hallway. The Poodles stood in a row at the top of the staircase and watched as we descended to the lower floor.

"Audrey's house was certainly tempting, wasn't it?" Aunt Peg was still talking. "All those trinkets and knick-knacks just lying around. A study in excess, it seemed to me. That's what happens when a family of collectors lives in a house forever, and no one ever throws anything out."

Tasha's head dipped in a slight nod.

"I would have hated having to dust all those little odds and ends. Good for you for saving Audrey the trouble." Aunt Peg smiled cheerfully. "I imagine it was just that easy to slip something into your pocket every now and again, wasn't it? After all, it's not as if Audrey *needed* so many things. Or spent any time appreciating them. Or would even miss half of them if they were gone. Am I right?"

Aunt Peg glanced at Tasha. The young woman was still silent, but now she was wringing her hands in front of her.

"And you *did* need those things, didn't you?" Aunt Peg's voice was nonchalant. "I'd imagine most of those baubles were more valuable than they looked. Valuable enough to be turned into real money. Who wouldn't want to take advantage of that? It wasn't your fault you couldn't make a proper living, even when you were working two jobs."

"No," Tasha replied, speaking for the first time in several minutes. "It wasn't my fault."

Aunt Peg had reached the foot of the steps. Instead of responding, she merely turned the corner and walked into her grooming room. Her finger flipped the switch, and the overhead lights sprang to life.

Tasha stared around the room in wonder, taking in everything from the matted table in the center, to the raised bathtub, to the wall of shelves that were fully stocked with brushes, combs, rubber bands, wraps, and half a dozen different kinds of scissors.

"Wow," she said. "This place is amazing. You could open a grooming business in here."

"Thankfully, I'm old enough to be retired," Aunt Peg replied.

The statement was entirely untrue, since she wasn't retired at all. Tasha would have realized that if she'd thought about it for even a moment. But it turned out Aunt Peg wasn't about to give Tasha time to consider anything other than what she wanted to talk about.

By this point, I'd pretty much given up on joining the conversation. Aunt Peg was doing a far better job of drawing Tasha out than I had. The only thing left for me to do was watch and learn.

"The other thing Melanie and I know," Aunt Peg said calmly, "is that you were at Audrey's house the night she died. Audrey told someone she was expecting you."

Tasha opened her mouth. Aunt Peg held up a hand for silence.

"Don't bother to deny it, it's too late for that. The only question now is whether we reveal the information to the police, or you tell us what happened while you were there." Aunt Peg leaned back against the counter, like she had all the time in the world to listen. "It's entirely up to you."

Tasha glanced toward the doorway, as if she was thinking about making an escape. I had that route blocked. She was effectively trapped in the small room with us.

Aunt Peg and I didn't look at each other, or say a word. We simply waited for Tasha to speak next. After a minute, she gave in.

"You were right about what you said before." She pulled in a shuddering breath. "None of it was my fault."

"Of course not," Aunt Peg agreed easily.

"And you're right about the brooch, too. I had taken it. I didn't realize . . ." Tasha's gaze lifted. She stared briefly at the ceiling. "I had no idea how much it was worth. I mean, who leaves something with real diamonds just lying around where anyone could pick it up? Audrey had never noticed anything else was missing, but she knew the brooch was gone right away."

"She must have asked you about it," I said.

"She did. I told her I hadn't seen it, and she believed me. That made me feel worse than ever."

"I can understand that," Aunt Peg said.

Tasha walked over to the wall that was lined with shelves. She picked up a pin brush and twirled it between her fingers. Maybe she found it easier to talk when she wasn't looking at us.

"I knew I had to give the brooch back. I'd made a mistake. I had to own up to it, and try to fix it. I mean, it's not like I'm a thief or anything."

Hearing that, I bit my tongue hard enough to hurt. When I gave a small squeak, Aunt Peg glared at me to keep still. That made two things I was keeping quiet about. Because despite what Tasha had just told us, I was quite certain Audrey hadn't believed her denial either.

"So, you went to Audrey's house that night and you brought the brooch with you," Aunt Peg prompted.

Tasha nodded. She put down the brush and picked up a greyhound comb, testing its weight in her hand, then running the pad of her thumb along the row of stiff tines. The shelves held a cornucopia of things to keep her hands busy while she spoke. I hoped she didn't decide to start shooting rubber bands around the room.

"Like I said, I knew I had to make things right. When I

got there, Audrey and I went into her office to talk. I told her I'd found the brooch on the floor in the kennel. I figured she'd be so grateful to get it back that she wouldn't ask any questions." Tasha looked to Aunt Peg for reassurance. "I mean, that was the important thing, right?"

"Yes," Aunt Peg replied without hesitation. She probably had her fingers crossed behind her back. "That was the important thing."

"I'm glad you understand that, and I wish you had been there to tell Audrey, because she didn't think so." Tasha was clearly indignant about the way things had turned out. "Audrey took the brooch out of my hand and put it in her desk drawer. Then she came around to stand in front of the desk, looked me in the eye, and fired me."

Chapter 31

"That must have come as quite a shock," I said.

"Of course it did," Tasha snapped. "Audrey had no right to do that. After all the time I'd put in taking care of her Great Danes? She owed me more consideration than that."

"Time for which you had been well compensated," Aunt Peg said mildly.

"That's a matter of opinion. I was barely making more than minimum wage." Tasha slapped the comb back down on the shelf, and I saw Aunt Peg wince. Her grooming tools were important to her.

"Perhaps you should have asked Audrey for a raise," I said. "Rather than deciding to steal from her."

Tasha whirled around to face me. "Whose side are you on?"

I hoped that wasn't a serious question. Because telling her that I was on the side of justice would make me sound pretty pompous. It also wouldn't further our cause.

"Let's not choose sides at all," Aunt Peg said reasonably. "Instead, why don't you tell us what happened after Audrey fired you?"

"She told me to leave," Tasha grumbled. "She wouldn't even let me take a minute to say goodbye to Betty. Or to the other Danes in the kennel, who wouldn't know that I was never coming back."

Boo-hoo, I thought uncharitably. It was a good thing I was still attempting to stay in silent mode.

"Audrey was my only regular client," Tasha continued. "The others were just one-offs here and there. And Ralph wouldn't give me more hours at the nursery, no matter how many times I asked. I couldn't afford to lose Audrey's business."

Aunt Peg caught my eye, and I knew we were both thinking the same thing. Tasha's subsequent actions *had* cost her Audrey's business. It was a shame the young woman hadn't stopped to consider all the possible ramifications before she'd acted.

"I tried to make Audrey see reason. I even groveled," Tasha said. "I would have done anything to get my job back. But Audrey wouldn't listen. She just kept telling me to get out of her house. She pointed at the door, like I was a child who was just supposed to obey."

Tasha did sound almost childlike as she tried to justify what she'd done. She still couldn't seem to understand that she was the one to blame for everything that had gone wrong. She alone was responsible for the loss of her job—and for the tragic outcome of the confrontation she'd set in motion.

"You're quite right about Audrey." Aunt Peg goaded Tasha on. "She could be unreasonable when she wanted to be."

"Right?" Tasha shot back, happy for the support. "Audrey had already come out from behind her desk to try to intimidate me. Then she put her hands on me. She actually tried to push me out of the room. That was all on her. I didn't have a choice about what happened next."

"The two of you must have struggled," Aunt Peg said. "Maybe you even put your hands around her neck."

"I don't know." Tasha shook her head. "I don't remem-

ber that part, it's all a blur now. I just know that I was trying to get away from her. I was acting in self-defense. Then
Audrey went stumbling backward. Maybe she tripped."

Tripped, indeed. I was highly skeptical of Tasha's sani-
tized version of the event. Especially since her hands had
left marks around Audrey's neck. Considering she was
claiming not to have a clear memory of what took place,
Tasha sounded very certain Audrey's death had been an
accident.

"It was the fall that killed her," I said, unable to remain
quiet any longer. "Audrey hit her head on the corner of the
desk. And you were there when it happened."

"I wasn't!" Tasha's voice rose. "As soon as Audrey let
go of me, I ran out of the room."

"A moment earlier, you hadn't wanted to leave," I said.
"Now Audrey was on the floor, and you couldn't even
take the time to check and make sure she was all right?"

"I was only doing what she wanted," Tasha whined.
Her hand was resting on the edge of a nearby shelf, as if
she needed it for support. "She told me to go. So I did. I
figured Audrey would wake up in a few minutes. I knew
she was going to be okay."

"But you didn't stay around to find out," I said.

"Of course not. Why would I want to be there when
Audrey woke up? I was sure she'd only start yelling at me
again."

"Such a dilemma." Aunt Peg tsked as she pulled her
phone out of her pocket. "And such a poor decision to go
with it. If you're very lucky, when you recount this story to
the police, they'll be more forgiving of your shortcomings
than we are."

"Wait a minute." Tasha's gaze went to the device. She
looked shocked. "What are you doing?"

"I'm about to make a call." Aunt Peg was scrolling
through her contacts.

In contrast to Aunt Peg's calm demeanor, the expression

on Tasha's face was suddenly frantic. "No, wait! You don't understand. If you tell the police what I said, they'll arrest me. What happened to Audrey was her own fault. I can't take the blame for something I didn't do."

Tasha had to be delusional if she thought Aunt Peg and I were going to keep what we'd learned to ourselves. I would have said as much, but Tasha wasn't paying any attention to me. Instead, she was staring at the phone in Aunt Peg's hand.

"I'm warning you," she said grimly. "Put the phone down."

Tasha's hand slipped quickly along the shelf and settled on a soft suede pouch. She must have recognized it and known what would be inside. In an instant, she'd grasped the handle of Aunt Peg's Japanese shears, pulled them out, and shaken off their protective cover. She spun around to face us, holding the long, pointed tool out in front of her.

I stifled a small gasp. With their carefully honed blades and sharp tip, the shears made a surprisingly effective weapon.

With all of us, plus the grooming table in the room, it was crowded. Tasha was no more than a few feet away from either Aunt Peg or me. A quick lunge with the knife-like implement would put her nearly on top of us. Standing very still and staring at the furious expression on Tasha's face, I was grateful the dogs had remained upstairs out of harm's way.

When Aunt Peg had taken out her phone, she'd moved closer to the door. Now she was the one blocking Tasha's exit. I hoped she wouldn't be tempted to try something heroic. I just wanted everyone to remain calm. With luck, we could still manage to talk our way out of this situation.

"So now what happens?" I asked Tasha.

Her gaze whipped back and forth between me and Aunt Peg as if she wasn't sure. That wasn't a good sign. Desperate, but without a plan to implement, Tasha might be even more dangerous.

"I need to leave," she said.

I probably wasn't the only one who heard echoes of our earlier conversation in Tasha's plea. Remembering how the scene with Audrey had ended made a chill slip down my spine.

"Where will you go?" Aunt Peg asked.

I thought it was a reasonable question, but Tasha swung the tip of the Japanese scissors in her direction. Now their sharp point was angled upward toward Aunt Peg's chest.

"Don't ask me that," she snapped. "Don't ask me anything. You've already caused enough trouble."

"That wasn't us," I said. "You made your own trouble."

"Shut up, okay?" Tasha glared at me, and I noted that the hand holding the shears had begun to shake. "I need to think. You"—she motioned toward Aunt Peg—"move out of the doorway."

I expected Aunt Peg to balk at the peremptory command. Instead, she acceded readily. Her phone was still cradled in her hand, but she'd made no further attempt to put through a call.

Maybe she was thinking the same thing I was. This claustrophobic setup wasn't helping matters. Instead, the pressure was escalating. The safest thing for us to do was stand aside, and let Tasha make her escape. Once she was gone, Aunt Peg and I could contact the authorities.

A sudden rumble penetrated my thoughts. It took me a moment to realize that what I'd heard was a low and very deliberate growl. The sound was deep and fierce. It raised the hackles on the back of my neck. While Tasha, Aunt Peg, and I had been concentrating on each other, Ebony must have come padding down the stairs.

Now the Great Dane was standing in the spot Aunt Peg had just vacated. Her large body filled the doorway. It looked as though Ebony had sensed the tension in the room, assessed the threat, and decided who was responsible. Her dark eyes were fastened on Tasha. The Dane's intent expression was enough to make me want to take a step back, even though I was on the other side of the room.

Tasha's eyes widened. Other than that, she didn't move a muscle. Her voice was soft and quiet as she spoke to the Dane. "Hey, Ebony girl, what's the matter? You know me. Sure, you do. You and I are friends. There's no need to be upset, everything's fine. You just need to stand down, okay? Do you think you can do that for me?"

The big black dog listened to Tasha's crooning patter, but didn't alter her aggressive stance. Ebony knew Tasha as an occasional caretaker. But the Dane had been living in Aunt Peg house for the past ten days. She had probably been sleeping on Aunt Peg's bed. If Ebony had to choose sides, it was clear where her loyalties lay. She stared at Tasha and curled her lip, revealing several very large teeth. It was a small move, but it was enough to make her point.

Ebony meant business. Her gaze was implacable, her stance unwavering. The Dane wasn't going to back down. And she made sure each of us stuck inside the small room knew it.

"Tasha," Aunt Peg said in a level tone. "I need you to listen to me and do exactly as I say. And I need you to do it right now. Lower your arm and put the shears on the grooming table."

Several seconds passed. I realized I was holding my breath. At first, nothing happened. Then, slowly and carefully, Tasha put the shears down. Also moving with great care, Aunt Peg inched her hand over and picked them up. She slowly brought her hand around and placed the shears on the counter behind her, out of Tasha's reach.

"Now what?" I asked.

"Now we relax," Aunt Peg said.

I shot her a look. "You're kidding."

"When we relax, Ebony will too."

At least the black Dane hadn't growled again. But she was still standing stiff-legged and blocking our way out of the room.

"Let's just give her a minute," Aunt Peg said. "We'll let Ebony take a deep breath and reassess. She's a smart dog. Hopefully she'll realize that the danger has passed." She glanced at the Great Dane, and her voice softened. "Good girl, Ebony. You knew just what to do. What a good dog you are."

Aunt Peg waited for the Dane to process the soothing words. Then she gently held out her hand, her palm facing upward and fingers extended. Ebony took a halting step forward. Then she finally dropped her head to give Aunt Peg's fingertips a delicate sniff.

"There you go, good girl," Aunt Peg murmured. "Ebony is such a good dog. Everything's going to be just fine now."

"That's easy for you to say," Tasha muttered.

Aunt Peg slid her hand along the side of the Dane's muzzle until she could reach the dog's ears. When her fingers began to fondle them, Ebony's shoulders finally loosened. I saw the tension begin to leave her body. She closed her eyes and leaned into the caress.

I drew in a huge breath and slowly let it out. Still jittery, I leaned against the wall behind me for support. It felt as though I'd aged ten years in the past ten minutes.

Aunt Peg was occupied with Ebony, so I was the one who made the call. My hand was shaking slightly as I got out my phone. By the time I was connected to Detective Young, however, I knew exactly what I needed to say.

Chapter 32

The last time I talked to Detective Young, he'd made it clear he was humoring me. We were both aware that Audrey Kane's murder wasn't his problem. Now, however, the person responsible for Audrey's death had threatened both Aunt Peg and me with a lethal weapon on the detective's home turf. I figured that was reason enough for him to become involved. Fortunately, this time he agreed with me.

When Detective Young arrived at Aunt Peg's house, he'd already been in touch with the Ridgefield PD. That department now had two of its own detectives on their way to Greenwich. Young listened and took notes as Aunt Peg and I added more details to those I'd already given him over the phone. Tasha sat sullenly nearby, glaring at me and disputing everything we said. None of us paid attention to her.

When the interview was finished, Detective Young took Tasha into custody and placed her in the back seat of his sedan. He assured us that he and the Ridgefield police would finish sorting things out downtown. He advised us to remain available, in case they had additional questions.

For several days, Aunt Peg and I didn't hear a thing. Then a local news station reported that dogsitter, Tasha Gilbert, had confessed to playing a part the death of Ridgefield heiress and dog breeder, Audrey Kane. Speaking on Tasha's behalf, her lawyer claimed that she was the injured party and that Ms. Gilbert had acted in self-defense. It would now be up to the courts to decide who was telling the truth.

Aunt Peg said she was hoping to be called as a witness for the prosecution. Heaven help Tasha's defense attorney if that happened.

I got a call from Ralph Denby later in the week. He was the new owner of Audrey's ten Great Danes, a group that included both our houseguest, Daisy, and Aunt Peg's bitch, Ebony.

In the days since he'd received the news, Ralph had worked quickly. Having taken immediate steps to reclaim the harlequin dog, Rufus, from Tasha, he now had half the Danes in his possession. When I asked about the two bitches Miranda was fostering, Ralph just chuckled. I wasn't surprised to hear that she would be keeping the pair and adding them to her own breeding program. Betty would also be remaining in her foster home with Bill Godfrey.

Ralph and Nattie were planning to host a small get-together for Audrey's friends at their home in Wilton that weekend. He invited us to come and to bring Daisy with us. Aunt Peg was also attending, and she would return Ebony at the same time. I accepted the invitation readily. It was a relief to know that when Daisy left us, she would be going to someone who would adore her as much as Audrey had.

Now, however, I had to break the news to Kevin.

I sat him down in a kitchen chair and gave him an Oreo. I figured we might as well begin the conversation on a happy note. To my surprise, it turned out that Kevin was excited about attending a party for Great Dane lovers and their dogs. Even when I explained it meant that Daisy would be leaving us.

"But she'll be happy in her new home, right?" he asked.

"Of course. Ralph knows everything about Great Danes. He'll take wonderful care of her. And she'll be reunited with Audrey's other Danes, whom she's lived with for years."

"Good," Kevin said with a nod. "I want Daisy to be happy."

"So do I. We all do. That's the goal." I looked at him curiously. "Is there a reason you think she hasn't been happy living here with us?"

"Not Daisy. She's been great." He hesitated.

"But?"

Kevin had already scarfed down the cookie. Now he squirmed uncomfortably in his seat. "Bud's the one who's unhappy about Daisy being here. I think it's my fault. Maybe I haven't been paying enough attention to him."

"I wouldn't worry about that," I said. "Bud knows he's your favorite dog. He even sleeps on your bed."

"Not lately."

"No?" *Damn.* I should have noticed that. "Where has he been sleeping?"

"*Under* the bed," Kevin grumbled. "Where I can't touch him at night. Or even see him. I don't think Bud likes me anymore."

I bit back a smile. Trust that wily little dog to figure out a way to make his feelings known.

"I know that's not true," I said. "If Bud didn't like you, he wouldn't be jealous of the attention you've been paying to Daisy. Once Daisy goes to her new home, you and Bud are going to be best friends again."

Kevin looked up at me. "Are you sure?"

"I'm positive. Bud never stopped loving you. He's just been sulking a bit while he waits for you to come to your senses."

"I'm sensible right now," Kev announced. "I want Bud to play with me, and start sleeping on my bed again."

"I'm sure he'll be happy to that. Should we go ask him?"

"Yes!" Kevin quickly slid down off his chair.

Daisy and the three female Poodles were with Sam in his office. Bud, Augie, and Tar were outside in the backyard. When we stepped out onto the deck, we saw that the three dogs were playing keep-away with a giant rubber ball. Tar, the dog with the longest legs, was easily winning the game.

For a moment, Kevin stood and watched. Then I reached down and placed a hand on his small shoulder.

"Give Bud a call," I said. "I know he wants to hear from you."

Kevin cupped his hands around his mouth and shouted, "Bu-u-ud! Come here!"

The little spotted dog abruptly skidded to a halt. The ball went flying past him, but he didn't even notice. Instead, he whipped around on his hind legs and looked for Kevin. Bud's stubby tail began to wag. He took off running in our direction.

"Bud's coming as fast as he can," I said, giving Kevin a small nudge. "Why don't you go out in the yard and meet him halfway?"

Before I'd finished speaking, Kevin was already running. He hopped off the low deck and took off across the lawn. Heading straight toward him, Bud never even broke stride. He simply made a flying leap and landed in Kevin's arms. The two of them toppled over together and rolled around in the grass.

Kevin's arms were tightly wrapped around Bud's wriggling body. The little dog was reaching up to lick Kevin's face. The sound of his delighted laughter floated in the air.

In that moment, it felt as though everything in my world was just as it was meant to be. I thought about how lucky I was, then walked out to join them in the sun-dappled yard.